CW00829152

ISBN 978-1-331-98633-1
PIBN 10139735

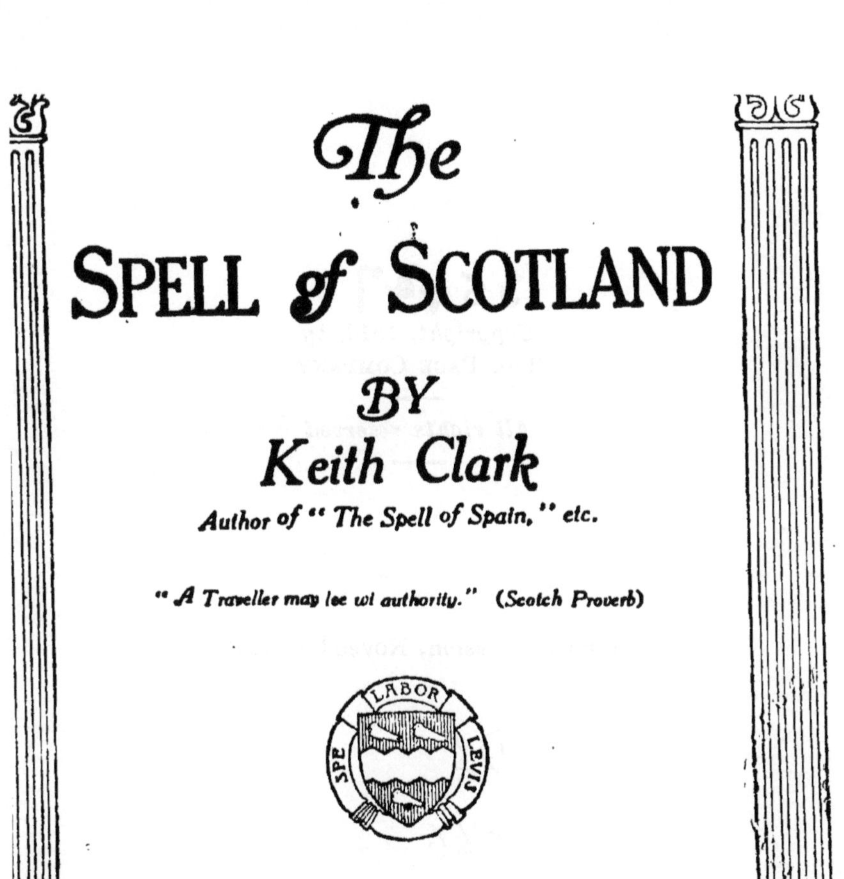

The SPELL of SCOTLAND

BY

Keith Clark

Author of "The Spell of Spain," etc.

"A Traveller may lee wi authority." (*Scotch Proverb*)

SPE LABOR LEVIS

ILLUSTRATED

BOSTON
THE PAGE COMPANY
MDCCCCXVI

First Impression, November, 1916

THE COLONIAL PRESS
C. H. SIMONDS COMPANY, BOSTON, U. S. A.

TO

THE LORD MARISCHAL

CONTENTS

LIST OF ILLUSTRATIONS

List of Illustrations

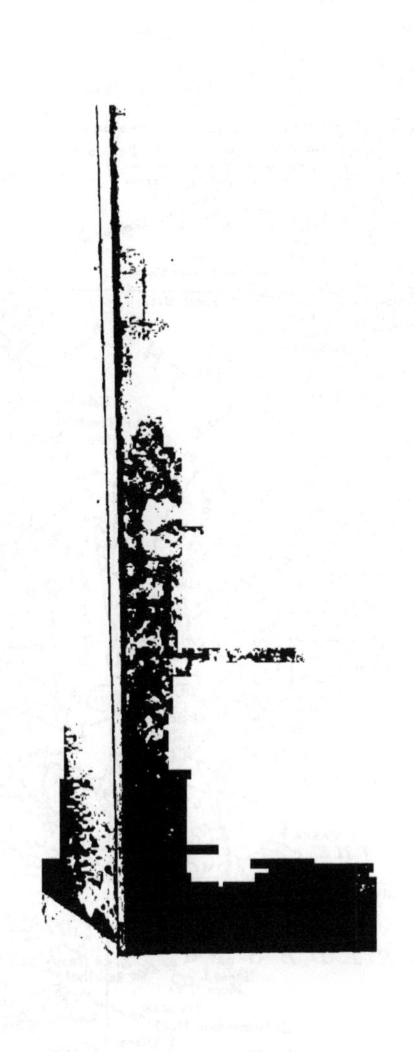

ISLANDS
Swainbost
Cellar Head
Fivepenny
Borve
Barvas
Tolsta
Tolsta Head
Carloway
Great Bernera
Gallon Head
Stornoway
Sandwick
Broad Bay
Tiumpan Head
Eye Peninsula
Garrabost
Bayble
Knock
Mhangursta
Ross Shire
Leurbost
Stornoway Harbour
Mealasbhal
Scarp
Kebock Head
Hushinish Pt.
N. Harris
Ben Mhor
Srianach Head
Taransay I.
Tarbert
Toe Head
Shiant Is.
Scalpa
Suillay
Pabbay
Berneray
Boveray
Renish Pt.
Vallay I.
Griminish Pt.
Sollas
North Uist
Weavers Pt.
L. Eport
Paible
Baleshare
Monach Is.
Ronay
Benbecula
Inverness Shire
Ardivachar Pt.
Howmore
Usinish Pt.
South
Mt. Hecla
Rudha Ardvula
L. Eynort
Uist
L. Boisdale
Dalburgh
Boisdale
Kilbride
Sound of Barra
Scurrival Pt.
Eriskay
Barra
Bruernish Pt.
Borve
Castlebay
Watersay
Flodday
Muldoanich I.
Sandray
Pabbay
Mingalay
Barra Head
Berneray
Passage of Barra
Hebrides or Western
Little Minch
The Minch
Gulf of the
Hebrides
Harris
Vaternish Pt.
Dunvegan Hd.
Duirinish
Portree
Bracadale
Idrigill Pt.
L. Bracadale
Talisker
Drynoch
Sligichan
Cuillin Hills
L. Eynort
L. Brittle
Dunan
Soay I.
Canna I.
Sanday I.
Hysker Is.
Harris
Papadil
Eigg
Sound of Rum
Sound of Eigg
Horse I.
Muck I.
Raasay
Scalpay
Sound of Raasay
Applecross Sound
Broadford
Armadale
Sleat Sound
L. Hourn
Rona I.
L. Torridon
Diabaig
Gairloch
Melvaig
Loch Ewe
Ben Clachair
Applecross
Lochcarron
Kyleakin
Glenelg
Arnisdale
Inverie
L. Nevis
Loch Morar
Arisaig
Kinlochailort
L. na Nuagh
Ardnamurchan Pt.
Kilchoan
L. Sunart
Salen
Strontian
Coll
Gunna I.
Tiree
Scarinish
Hynish
Passage of Coll
Tobermory
Mull
Staffa I.
Fingals Cove
Iona
Ross of Mull
Firth of Lorne
Oban
Skerryvore
Passage of Skerryvore
Atlan
The Burra Is.
Kettla Ness
Cunningsburgh
Channerwick
Sandwick
St. Ninian's I. and B.
Fitful Head
Sumburgh Head
Siggar Ness
Quendale Bay
Horse I.
Fair Isle
60°
58°
57°

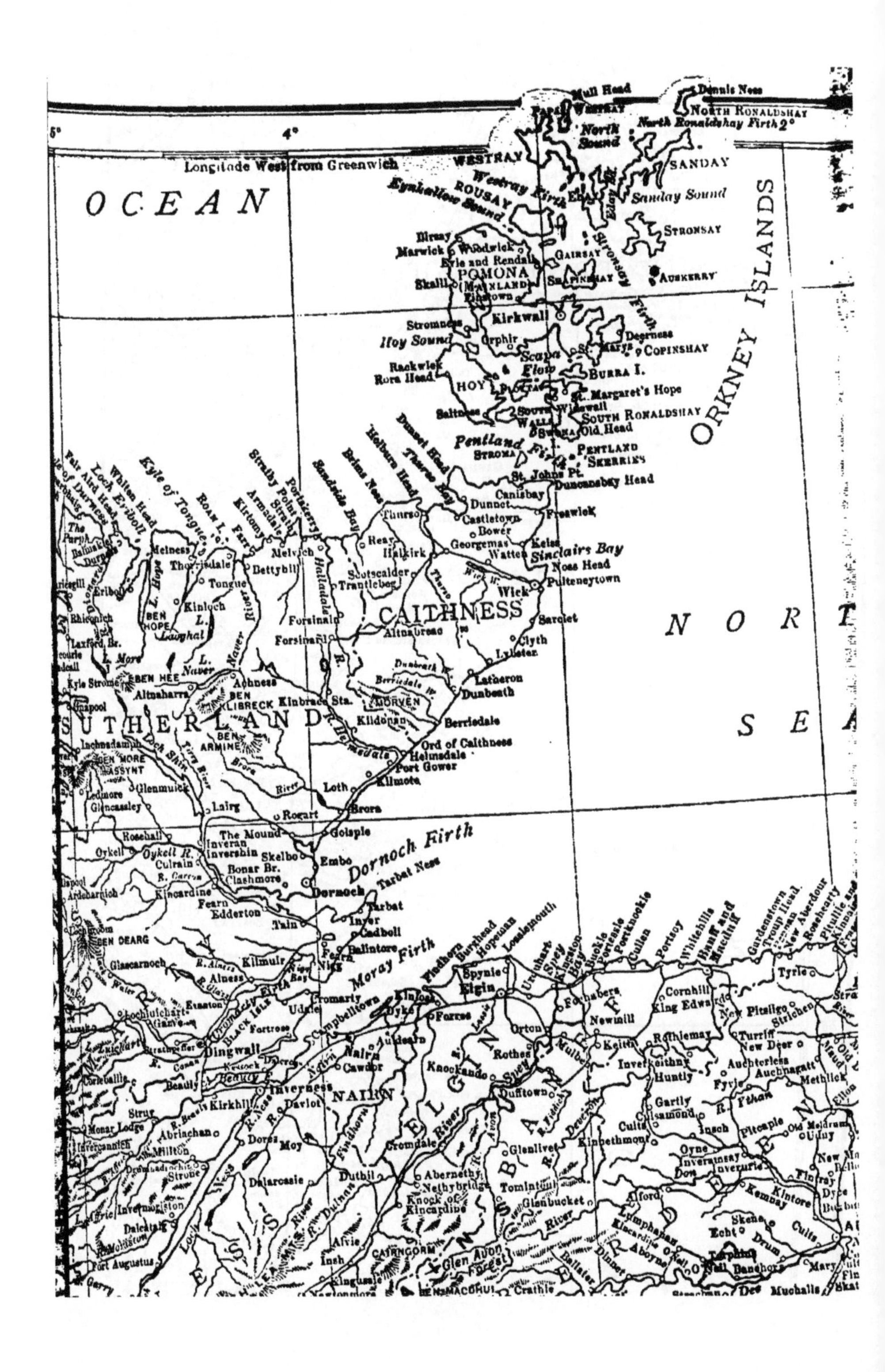

OCEAN
Longitude West from Greenwich
ORKNEY ISLANDS
Mull Head
Dennis Ness
North Ronaldshay
North Ronaldshay Firth
North Sound
Westray
Westray Firth
Rousay
Eynhallow Sound
Sanday
Sanday Sound
Stronsay
Auskerry
Gairsay
Pomona
Mainland
Birsay
Marwick
Woodwick
Kyle and Rendall
Skaill
Kirkwall
Stromness
Hoy Sound
Orphir
Scapa Flow
Deerness
St. Marys
Copinshay
Burra I.
Rackwick
Rora Head
Hoy
St. Margaret's Hope
South Ronaldshay
Old Head
Pentland Firth
Stroma
Pentland Skerries
Duncansbay Head
Dunnet Head
Thurso Bay
Holburn Head
Brims Ness
Sandside Bay
Portskerry
Strathy Point
Kyle of Tongue
Whiten Head
Loch Eriboll
Canisbay
Dunnet
Castletown
Bower
Freswick
Thurso
Reay
Halkirk
Georgemas
Watten
Keiss
Sinclairs Bay
Noss Head
Wick
Pulteneytown
Melvich
Bettyhill
Scotscalder
Trantlebeg
Tongue
Melness
Kinloch
Ben Hope
CAITHNESS
Altnabreac
Forsinain
Forsinard
Sarclet
Clyth
Lybster
Latheron
Dunbeath
Berriedale
Ord of Caithness
Helmsdale
Port Gower
Kilmote
Loth
Brora
Rogart
Golspie
The Mound
Skelbo
Embo
Dornoch Firth
Tarbet Ness
Dornoch
Kinbrace Sta.
Kildonan
Morven
Ben Klibreck
Ben Armine
Ben Hee
Altnaharra
Achness
SUTHERLAND
Loch Shin
Ben More Assynt
Inchnadamph
Ledmore
Glencassley
Lairg
Rosehall
Invershin
Culrain
Bonar Br.
Clashmore
Kincardine
Fearn
Edderton
Tain
Tarbet
Inver
Cadboll
Balintore
Nigg
Cromarty
Moray Firth
Ben Dearg
Glascarnoch
Kilmuir
Alness
Evanton
Udale
Fortrose
Dingwall
Strathpeffer
Black Isle
Cromarty Firth
Campbelltown
Nairn
Cawdor
Auldearn
Kinloss
Dyke
Forres
Findhorn
Burghead
Hopeman
Lossiemouth
Spynie
Elgin
Rothes
Knockando
Dufftown
Orton
Fochabers
Buckie
Portsoy
Cullen
Portknockie
Whitehills
Banff and Macduff
Newmill
Keith
Cornhill
King Edward
Rothiemay
Huntly
Inverkeithny
Turriff
New Deer
New Pitsligo
Strichen
Auchterless
Auchnagatt
Methlick
Fyvie
Gartly
Insch
Old Meldrum
Udny
Inverness
Beauly
Kirkhill
Daviot
Moy
Dores
NAIRN
Duthil
Abernethy
Nethybridge
Grantown
Tomintoul
Glenlivet
Glenbucket
Alford
Kintore
Kemnay
Skene
Echt
Drum
Cults
Lumphanan
Aboyne
Banchory
Muchalls
Dinnet
Ballater
Crathie
Cairngorm
Kingussie
Newtonmore
Alvie
Insh
Dalarossie
Strathglass
Invermoriston
Fort Augustus
Abriachan
Milton
Strone
Monar Lodge
Struy
Dalcataig
Corriemulie

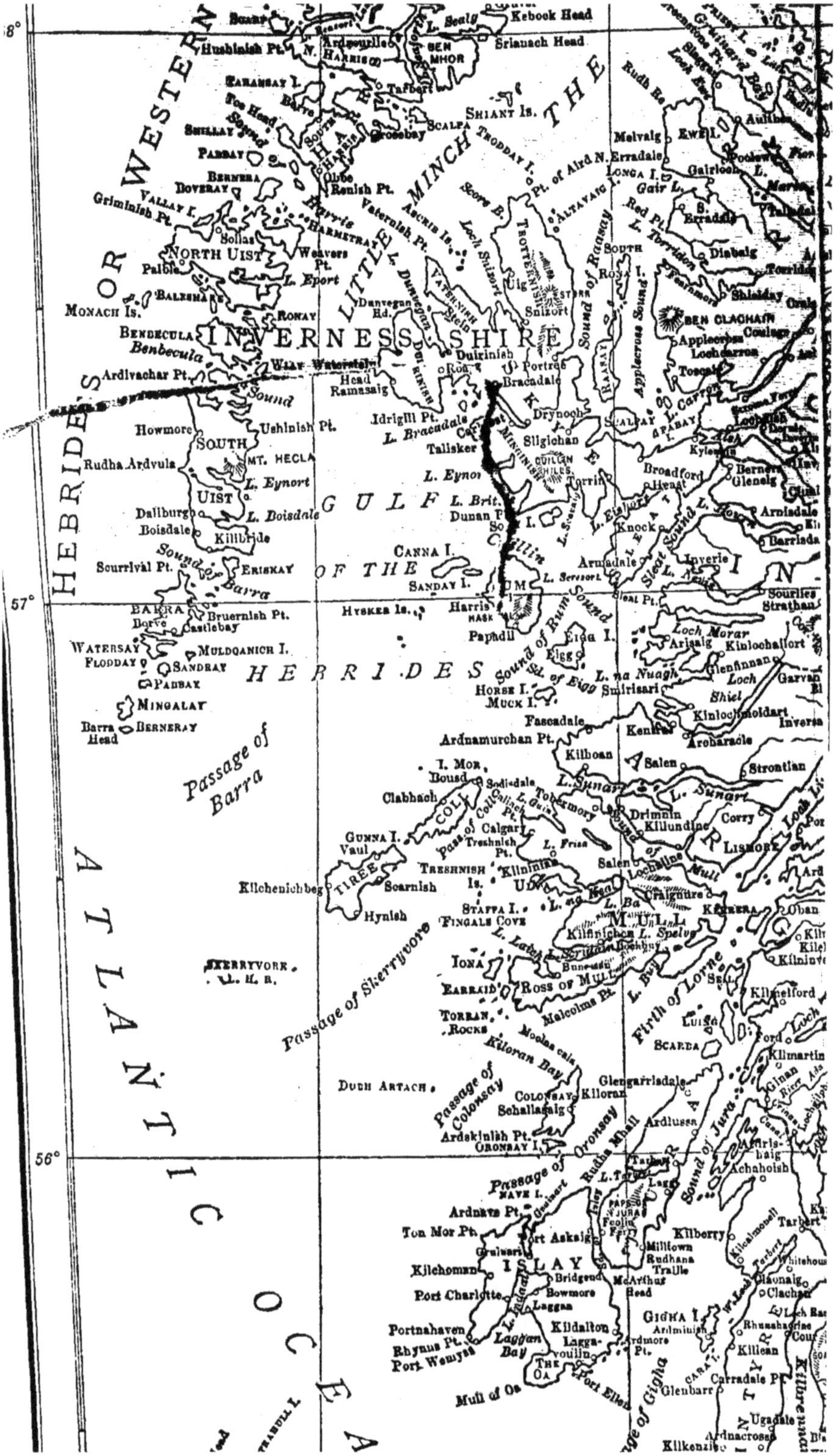

58°
Kebock Head
Hushinish Pt.
Ardgowillc
N. Harris
Ben Mhor
Srianach Head
Tarbert
Shiant Is.
Toe Head
Sound of Harris
Pabbay
Berneray
Boveray
Renish Pt.
Vallay I.
Griminish Pt.
Sollas
North Uist
Weavers Pt.
L. Eport
Harmetray
Vaternish Pt.
Ascrib Is.
Pt. of Aird N.
Erradale
Longa I.
Gair L.
Gairloch
Melvaig
Ewe I.
Rudh Re
Red Pt.
L. Torridon
Diabaig
Torridon
Shieldaig
Ben Clachain
Applecross
Lochcarron
Toscaig
Monach Is.
Baleshare
Ronay
Benbecula
Inverness Shire
Dunvegan Hd.
Duirinish
Portree
Bracadale
Snizort
Uig
Trotternish
South Rona I.
Raasay
Applecross Sound
Sound of Raasay
Ardivachar Pt.
Little Minch
The Minch
Loch Snizort
Head
Ramasaig
Idrigill Pt.
L. Bracadale
Talisker
Drynoch
Sligichan
Scalpay
Pabay
L. Carron
Kyleakin
Howmore
Ushinish Pt.
South Uist
Mt. Hecla
L. Eynort
Rudha Ardvula
Dalliburg
Boisdale
L. Boisdale
Kilbride
Gulf
L. Eynort
L. Brit.
Dunan Pt.
Cuillin Hills
Torrin
Broadford
Glenelg
Bernera
L. Eishort
Knock
Sleat Sound
Arnisdale
Barrisdale
Canna I.
Sanday I.
Sourrival Pt.
Eriskay
Sound of Barra
Of the
Armadale
L. Scresort
Inverie
L. Nevis
Sleat Pt.
57°
Barra
Borve
Bruernish Pt.
Castlebay
Hyskeir Is.
Harris
Papadil
Sound of Rum
Eigg I.
Loch Morar
Arisaig
Kinlochailort
Glenfinnan
Sourlies
Strathan
Watersay
Floddy
Muldoanich I.
Sandray
Pabbay
Mingalay
Barra Head
Berneray
Hebrides
Sound of Eigg
Sd. of Eigg
L. na Nuagh
Smirisari
Horse I.
Muck I.
Loch Shiel
Kinlochmoidart
Fascadale
Ardnamurchan Pt.
Kentra
Acharacle
Kilchoan
Salen
Strontian
L. Sunart
Passage of Barra
I. Mor
Bousd
Clabhach
Coll
Sorisdale
Tobermory
Calgary
Drimnin
Killundine
Corry
Lismore
Gunna I.
Vaul
Tiree
Treshnish Pt.
Treshnish Is.
Salen
Lochaline
Sound of Mull
Kilchenichbeg
Scarnish
Hynish
Staffa I.
Fingals Cove
Craignure
Kerrera
Oban
Mull
L. Spelve
Atlantic Ocean
Skerryvore
Iona
Erraid
Ross of Mull
Passage of Skerryvore
Firth of Lorne
Kilmelford
Torran Rocks
Malcolms Pt.
Luing
Scarba
Ford
Kilmartin
Dubh Artach
Kiloran Bay
Passage of Colonsay
Colonsay
Kiloran
Scalasaig
Glengarrisdale
Ardlussa
Ardskinish Pt.
Oronsay I.
Sound of Jura
Achahoish
56°
Passage of Oronsay
Nave I.
Rudha Mhail
L. Tarbert
Lagg
Paps of Jura
Ardnave Pt.
Ton Mor Pt.
Port Askaig
Kilberry
Tarbert
Islay
Kilchoman
Milltown
Bridgend
McArthur Head
Port Charlotte
Bowmore
Laggan
Clachan
Portnahaven
Rhynns Pt.
Port Wemyss
Laggan Bay
Kildalton
Lagavoulin
Gigha I.
Ardminish
Ardmore Pt.
Killean
The Oa
Mull of Oa
Port Ellen
Cara I.
Glenbarr
Carradale Pt.
Ugadale
Ardnacross
Kilkenzie

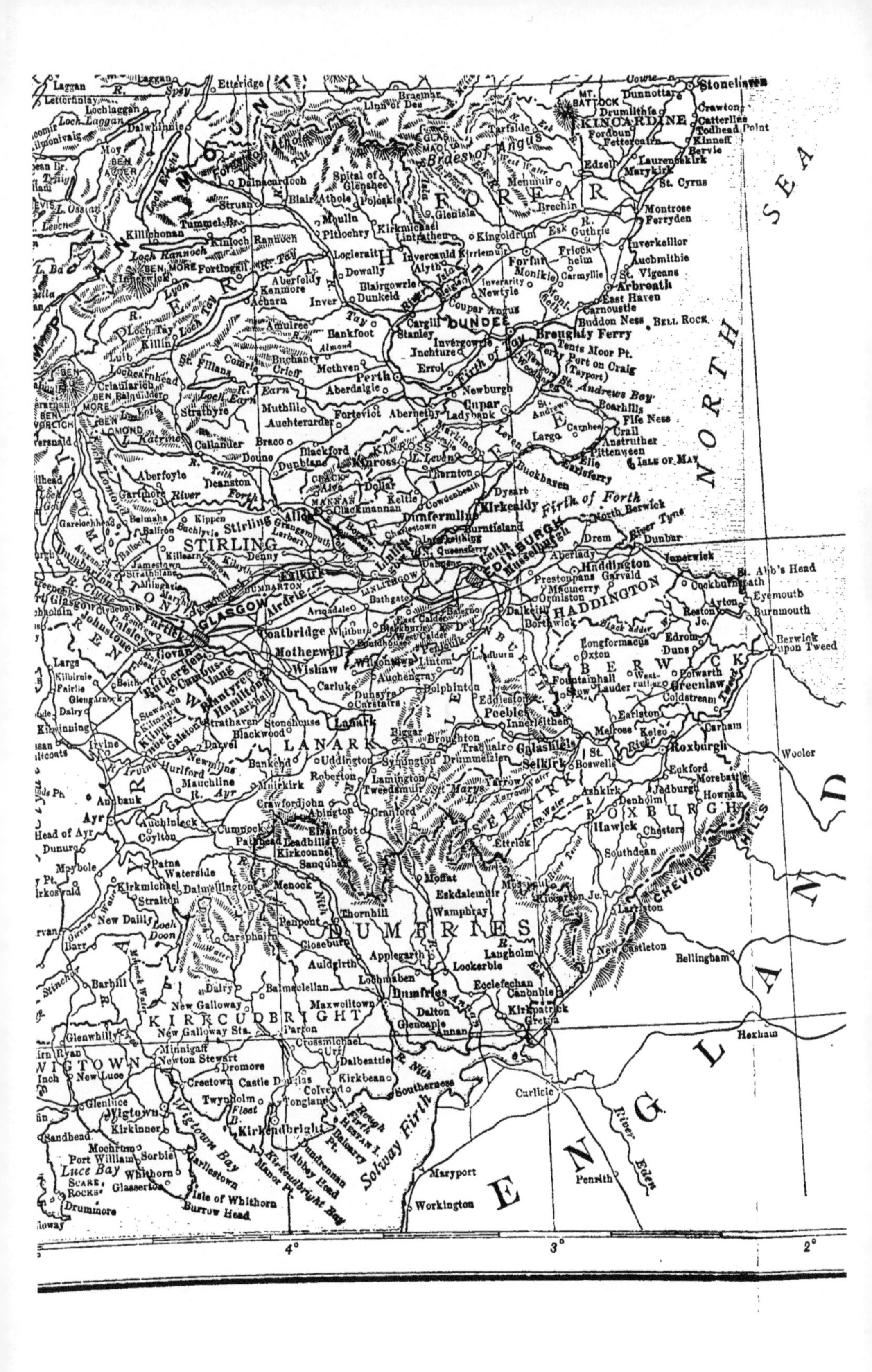

KINCARDINE
FORFAR
FIFE
KINROSS
STIRLING
DUMBARTON
LANARK
DUMFRIES
KIRKCUDBRIGHT
WIGTOWN
HADDINGTON
BERWICK
ROXBURGH
SELKIRK
PEEBLES
NORTH SEA
ENGLAND
CHEVIOT HILLS
Stonehaven
Dunnottar
Drumlithie
Crawton
Catterline
Todhead Point
Kinneff
Bervie
Fordoun
Fettercairn
Laurencekirk
Marykirk
St. Cyrus
Edzell
Montrose
Ferryden
Brechin
Menmuir
Tarfside
MT. BATTOCK
Braemar
Linn of Dee
Etteridge
Laggan
Loch Laggan
Dalwhinnie
BEN ALDER
Loch Ericht
Dalnacardoch
Struan
Blair Athole
Spital of Glenshee
Glenisla
Kingoldrum
Kirriemuir
Forfar
Guthrie
Friockheim
Inverkeillor
Auchmithie
St. Vigeans
Arbroath
East Haven
Carnoustie
Buddon Ness
Bell Rock
Monikie
Carmyllie
Newtyle
Coupar Angus
Alyth
Blairgowrie
Dunkeld
Pitlochry
Moulin
Logierait
Dowally
Kirkmichael
Tummel Br.
Killichonan
Kinloch Rannoch
Loch Rannoch
BEN MORE
Fortingall
R. Tay
Aberfeldy
Kenmore
Acharn
Loch Tay
Killin
Luib
Amulree
Bankfoot
Almond
Inver
Cargill
Stanley
DUNDEE
Broughty Ferry
Tents Moor Pt.
Ferry Port on Craig (Tayport)
Invergowrie
Inchture
Errol
Firth of Tay
Perth
Methven
Buchanty
Crieff
Comrie
St. Fillans
Lochearnhead
Crianlarich
Balquidder
Loch Earn
Strathyre
Aberdalgie
Forteviot
Abernethy
Newburgh
Cupar
Ladybank
St. Andrews Bay
St. Andrews
Boarhills
Fife Ness
Crail
Anstruther
Pittenweem
Isle of May
Carnbee
Largo
Leven
Elie
Earlsferry
Buckhaven
Markinch
Thornton
Dysart
Kirkcaldy
Burntisland
Firth of Forth
North Berwick
Muthill
Auchterarder
Braco
Blackford
Kinross
L. Leven
Dollar
Alva
Kettle
Clackmannan
Dunfermline
Cowdenbeath
Charlestown
Callander
L. Katrine
Doune
Dunblane
Teith
Deanston
Aberfoyle
Gartmore
River Forth
Kippen
Buchlyvie
Balfron
Balmaha
Stirling
Alloa
Grangemouth
Larbert
Denny
Killearn
Kilsyth
Strathblane
Jamestown
Balloch
Garelochhead
Dumbarton
R. Clyde
Greenock
Glasgow
Clydebank
Renfrew
Paisley
Johnstone
Partick
Govan
Rutherglen
Cambuslang
Blantyre
Hamilton
Larkhall
Airdrie
Coatbridge
Motherwell
Wishaw
Carluke
Falkirk
Linlithgow
Bathgate
Armadale
Whitburn
Queensferry
Dalmeny
Leith
EDINBURGH
Musselburgh
Aberlady
Prestonpans
Haddington
Garvald
Drem
Dunbar
River Tyne
Innerwick
Cockburnspath
St. Abb's Head
Eyemouth
Ayton
Burnmouth
Reston Jc.
Berwick upon Tweed
Edrom
Duns
Longformacus
Oxton
Lauder
Westruther
Polwarth
Greenlaw
Coldstream
Earlston
Melrose
Kelso
Carham
Roxburgh
Wooler
Dalkeith
Borthwick
Ormiston
Macmerry
Penicuik
Leadburn
Linton
Auchengray
Dolphinton
Dunsyre
Carstairs
Lanark
Eddleston
Peebles
Innerleithen
Galashiels
Selkirk
Traquair
Drummelzier
Broughton
Biggar
Symington
Lamington
Tweedsmuir
Yarrow
St. Boswells
Ashkirk
Denholm
Jedburgh
Eckford
Morebattle
Hownam
Hawick
Chesters
Southdean
Ettrick
Moffat
Eskdalemuir
Wamphray
Langholm
Riccarton Jc.
Larriston
New Castleton
Bellingham
Lockerbie
Ecclefechan
Canonbie
Kirkpatrick
Gretna
Annan
Dalton
Dumfries
Lochmaben
Applegarth
Closeburn
Thornhill
Penpont
Auldgirth
Sanquhar
Kirkconnel
Leadhills
Elvanfoot
Abington
Crawfordjohn
Crawford
Douglas
Muirkirk
Roberton
Uddington
Lesmahagow
Stonehouse
Strathaven
Blackwood
Darvel
Newmilns
Galston
Kilmarnock
Stewarton
Kilmaurs
Hurlford
Mauchline
R. Ayr
Irvine
Dreghorn
Ardrossan
Saltcoats
Kilwinning
Dalry
Kilbirnie
Beith
Largs
Fairlie
Annbank
Ayr
Head of Ayr
Dunure
Maybole
Kirkoswald
Kirkmichael
Straiton
Dalmellington
Patna
Waterside
Cumnock
Auchinleck
Coylton
Menock
New Dailly
Girvan
Barr
Loch Doon
Carsphairn
Stinchar
Barhill
Dalry
Balmaclellan
New Galloway
New Galloway Sta.
Parton
Crossmichael
Urr
Dalbeattie
Maxwelltown
Glencaple
Kirkbean
Southerness
Colvend
Tongland
Kirkcudbright
Twynholm
Fleet B.
Creetown
Castle Douglas
Dundrennan
Balcarry Pt.
Hestan I.
Rough Firth
Abbey Head
Kirkcudbright Bay
Solway Firth
Minnigaff
Newton Stewart
Dromore
Glenwhilly
New Luce
Glenluce
Wigtown
Kirkinner
Sorbie
Mochrum
Port William
Sandhead
Luce Bay
Scare Rocks
Whithorn
Glasserton
Garlieston
Wigtown Bay
Isle of Whithorn
Burrow Head
Drummore
Carlisle
River Eden
Penrith
Maryport
Workington
Hexham
4°
3°
2°

THE SPELL OF SCOTLAND

CHAPTER I

HAME, HAME, HAME!

"It's hame, and it's hame, hame fain wad I be,
And it's hame, hame, hame, to my ain countree!"

TIME was when half a hundred ports ringing round the semi-island of Scotland invited your boat to make harbour; you could "return" at almost any point of entry you chose, or chance chose for you.

To-day, if you have been gone for two hundred and fifty years, or if you never were "of Scotia dear," except as a mere reading person with an inclination toward romance, you can make harbour after a transatlantic voyage at but one sea-city, and that many miles up a broad in-reaching river. Or, you can come up the English roads by Carlisle or by Newcastle, and cross the Border in the conquering way, which never yet was all-conquering. There is shipping, of course, out of the half hundred old harbours. But it is largely the shipping that goes and comes, fishing boats and coast pliers and the pleasure boats of the western isles.

You cannot come back from the far corners of the earth—to which Scotland has sent such majorities of her sons, since the old days when she squandered them in battle on the Border or on the Continent, to the new days when she squanders them in colonization so that half a dozen of her counties show decline in population—but you must come to Glasgow. The steamers are second-class compared with those which make port farther south. They are slower. But their very lack of modern splendour and their slow speed give time in which to reconstruct your Scotland, out of which perhaps you have been banished since the Covenant, or the Fifteen, or the Forty Five; or perhaps out of which you have never taken the strain which makes you romantic and Cavalier, or Presbyterian and canny. We who have it think that you who have it not lose something very precious for which there is no substitute. We pity you.

More clannish than most national tribesmen, we cannot understand how you can endure existence without a drop of Scotch.

Always when I go to Scotland I feel myself returning "home." Notwithstanding that it is two centuries and a bittock since my clerical ancestor left his home, driven out no doubt by the fluctuant fortunes of Covenanter and Cavalier, or, it may be, because he believed he carried the only true faith in his chalice—only he did not carry a chalice—and, either he would keep it undefiled in the New World, or he would share it with the benighted in the New World; I know not.

All that I know is that in spite of the fact that the Scotch in me has not been replenished since those two centuries and odd, I still feel that it is a search after ancestors when I go back to Scotland. And, if a decree of banishment was passed by the unspeakable Hanoverians after the first Rising, and lands and treasure were forfeited, still I look on entire Scotland as my demesne. I surrender not one least portion of it. Not any castle, ruined or restored, is alien to me. Highlander and Lowlander are my undivisive kin. However empty may seem the moorlands and the woodlands except of grouse and deer, there is not a square foot of the twenty-nine thousand seven hundred eighty-five square miles but is filled for me with a longer procession, if not all of them royal, than moved ghostly across the vision of Macbeth.

Nothing happens any longer in Scotland. Everything has happened. Quite true, Scotland may some time reassert itself, demand its independence, cease from its romantic reliance on the fact that it did furnish to England, to the British Empire, the royal line, the Stewarts. Even Queen Victoria, who was so little a Stewart, much more a Hanoverian and a Puritan, was most proud of her Stewart blood, and regarded her summers in the Highlands as the most ancestral thing in her experience.

Scotland may at sometime dissolve the Union, which has been a union of equality, accept the lower estate of a province, an American "state," among the possible four of "Great Britain and Ireland," and enter on a more vigorous provincial life, live her own life, instead of exporting vigour to the colonies—and her exportation is almost done. She may fill this great silence which lies over the land, and is fairly audible in the deserted Highlands, with something of the human note instead of the call of the plover.

But, for us, for the traveler of to-day, and

at least for another generation, Scotland is a land where nothing happens, where everything has happened. It has happened abundantly, multitudinously, splendidly. No one can regret—except he is a reformer and a socialist—the absence of the doings of to-day; they would be so realistic, so actual, so small, so of the province and the parish. Whereas in the Golden Age, which is the true age of Scotland, men did everything—loving and fighting, murdering and marauding, with a splendour which makes it seem fairly not of our kind, of another time and of another world.

You must know your Scottish history, you must be filled with Scottish romance, above all, you must know your poetry and ballads, if you would rebuild and refill the country as you go. Not only over fair Melrose lies the moonlight of romance, making the ruin more lovely and more complete than the abbey could ever have been in its most established days, but over the entire land there lies the silver pall of moonlight, making, I doubt not, all things lovelier than in reality.

We truly felt that we should have arranged for "a hundred pipers an' a' an' a'." But we left King's Cross station in something of disguise. The cockneys did not know that we were returning to Scotland. Our landing was to be made as quietly, without pibroch, as when the Old Pretender landed at Peterhead on the far northeastern corner, or when the Young Pretender landed at Moidart on the far western rim of the islands. And neither they nor we pretenders.

The East Coast route is a pleasant way, and I am certain the hundred pipers, or whoever were the merry musicmakers who led the English troops up that way when Edward First was king, and all the Edwards who followed him, and the Richards and the Henrys—they all measured ambition with Scotland and failed—I am certain they made vastly more noise than this excellently managed railway which moves across the English landscape with due English decorum.

We were to stop at Peterborough, and walk out to where, "on that ensanguined block at Fotheringay," the queenliest queen of them all laid her head and died that her son, James Sixth of Scotland, might become First of England. We stopped at York for the minster, and because Alexander III was here married to Margaret, daughter of Henry III; and their daughter being married to Eric of Norway in those old days when Scotland and Norway were

JAMES VI.

kin, became mother to the Maid of Norway, one of the most pathetic and outstanding figures in Scottish history, simply because she died—and from her death came divisions to the kingdom.

We paused at Durham, where in that gorgeous tomb St. Cuthbert lies buried after a brave and Scottish life. We only looked across the purpling sea where already the day was fading, where the slant rays of the sun shone on Lindisfarne, which the spirit of St. Cuthbert must prefer to Durham.

All unconsciously an old song came to sing itself as I looked across that wide water—

"My love's in Germanic,
Send him hame, send him hame,
My love's in Germanic,
Fighting for royalty,
He's as brave as brave can be,
Send him hame, send him hame!"

Full many a lass has looked across this sea and sung this lay—and shall again.

The way is filled with ghosts, long, long processions, moving up and down the land. A boundary is always a lodestone, a lodeline. Why do men establish it except that other men dispute it? In the old days England called it treason for a Borderer, man or woman, to intermarry with Scotch Borderer. The lure, you see, went far. Even so that kings and ladies, David and Matilda, in the opposing edges of the Border, married each other. And always there was Gretna Green.

Agricola came this way, and the Emperor Severus. There is that interesting, far-journeying Æneas Sylvius Piccolomini, the "Gil Blas of the Middle Ages," who later became Pius II. He came to this country by boat, but becoming afraid of the sea, returned by land, even opposite to the way we are going. Froissart came, but reports little. Perhaps Chaucer, but not certainly. George Fox came and called the Scots "a dark carnal people."

With the Act of Union the stream grows steady and full. There is Ben Jonson, trudging along the green roadway out yonder; for on foot, and all the way from London, he came northward to visit William Drummond of Hawthornden. Who would not journey to such a name? But, alas, a fire destroyed "my journey into Scotland sung with all the adventures." All that I know of Ben is that he was impressed with Lomond—two hundred years before Scott.

And there trails Taylor, "water poet," hoping to rival Rare Ben, on his "Pennyless Pilgrimage," when he actually went into Scotland without a penny, and succeeded in getting gold to further him on his way—"Marr, Murraye, Elgin, Bughan, and the Lord of Erskine, all of these I thank them, gave me gold to defray my charges in my journey."

James Howell, carries a thin portfolio as he travels the highway. But we must remember that he wrote his "Perfect Description of the People and Country of Scotland" in the Fleet.

Here is Doctor Johnson, in a post chaise. Of course, Sir! "Mr. Boswell, an active lively fellow is to conduct me round the country." And he's still a lively conductor. Surely you can see the Doctor, in his high boots, and his very wide brown cloth great coat with pockets which might be carrying two volumes of his folio dictionary, and in his hand a large oak staff. One tries to forget that years before this journey he had said to Boswell, "Sir, the noblest prospect that a Scotchman ever sees is the highroad that leads him to London." And, was there any malice in Boswell's final record—"My illustrious friend, being now desirous to be again in the great theater of life and animated existence"?

The poet Gray preceded him a little, and even John Wesley moves along the highroad seeking to save Scottish souls as well as English. A few years afterward James Hogg comes down this way to visit his countryman, Tammas Carlyle in London; who saw Hogg as "a little red-skinned stiff rock of a body with quite the common air of an Ettrick shepherd."

There is Scott, many times, from the age of five when he went to Bath, till that last journey back from Italy—to Dryburgh! And Shadowy Jeanie Deans comes downward, walking her "twenty-five miles and a bittock a day," to save her sister from death.

Disraeli comes up this way when he was young and the world was his oyster. Stevenson passes up and down, sending his merry men up and down. And one of the most native is William Winter—"With a quick sense of freedom and of home, I dashed across the Border and was in Scotland."

There is a barricade of the Cheviots stretching across between the two countries, but the Romans built a Wall to make the division more apparent. In the dawn of the centuries the Romans came hither, and attempting to come to Ultima Thule, Picts and Scots—whatever they were, at least they were brave—met the Romans on the Border, as yet unreported in the world's history and undefined in the world's geography, and sent them back into what is England. The Romans in single journeys, and in certain imperial attempts, did penetrate as far as Inverness. But they never conquered Scotland. Only Scotland of all the world held them back. And in order to define their defeat and to place limits to the unlimited Roman Empire, the Great Wall was built, built by Hadrian, that men might know where civilization, that splendid thing called Roman civilization, and barbarism did meet. Scotland was barbarism. And I think, not in apology but in all pride, she has remained something of this ever since. Never conquered, never subdued.

The Wall was, in truth, a very palpable thing, stretching from the Solway to the North Sea at the Tyne, with ample width for the constant patrol, with lookout towers at regular and frequent intervals, with soldiers gathered from every corner of the Empire, often the spawn of it, and with much traffic and with even permanent villas built the secure side of the barrier. If you meet Puck on Pook's hill, he will tell you all about it.

Our fast express moves swiftly northward, through the littoral of Northumberland, as the ship bearing Sister Clare moved through the sea—

> "And now the vessel skirts the strand
> Of mountainous Northumberland;

> Towns, towers, and hills successive rise,
> And catch the nun's delighted eyes."

Berwick

The voyager enters Berwick with a curious feeling. It is because of the voyagers who have preceded him that this town is singular among all the towns of the Empire. It is of the Empire, it is of Britain; but battled round about, and battled for as it has been since ambitious time began, it is of neither England nor Scotland. "Our town of Berwick-upon-Tweed," as the phrase still runs in the acts of Parliament, and in the royal proclamations; not England's, not Scotland's. Our town, the King's town.

For it is an independent borough (1551) since the men who fared before us could not determine which should possess it, and so our very own time records that history in an actual fact. I do not suppose the present serious-looking, trades-minded people of the city, with their dash of fair Danish, remember their singular situation day by day. The tumult and the shouting have died which made "the Border" the most embattled place in the empire, and Berwick-upon-Tweed the shuttlecock in this international game of badminton.

It is a dual town at the best. But what has it not witnessed, what refuge, what pawn, has it not been, this capital of the Debatable Land, this Key of the Border.

The Tweed is here spanned by the Royal Border Bridge, opened in 1850, and called "the last Act of Union." But there is another bridge, a Roman bridge of many spans, antique looking as the Roman-Moorish-Spanish bridge at Cordova, and as antique as 1609, an Act of Union following swiftly on the footsteps of King James VI—who joyously paused here to fire a salute to himself, on his way to the imperial throne.

The walls of Berwick, dismantled in 1820 and become a promenade for peaceful townsfolk and curious sightseers, date no farther back than Elizabeth's time. But she had sore need of them; for this "our town," was the refuge for her harriers on retaliatory Border raids, particularly that most terrible Monday-to-Saturday foray of 1570, that answer to an attempt to reassert the rights of Mary, when fifty castles and peels and three hundred villages were laid waste in order that Scotland might know that Elizabeth was king.

It was her kingly father, the Eighth Henry, who ordered Hertford into Scotland—"There to put all to fire and sword, to burn Edinburgh town, and to raze and deface it, when you have sacked it and gotten what you can of it, as there may remain forever a perpetual memory of the vengeance of God lighted upon it for their falsehood and disloyalty. Sack Holyrood House and as many towns and villages about Edinburgh as ye conveniently can. Sack Leith and burn it and subvert it, and all the rest, putting man, woman and child to fire and sword without exception, when any resistance is made against you. And this done, pass over to the Fife land, and extend like extremities and destructions in all towns and villages whereunto ye may reach conveniently, not forgetting among the rest, so to spoil and turn upside down the Cardinal's town of St. Andrews, as the upper stone may be the nether, and not one stick stand by another, sparing no creature alive within the same, especially such as either in friendship or blood be allied to the Cardinal. The accomplishment of all this shall be most acceptable to the Majesty and Honour of the King."

Berwick has known gentler moments, even marrying and giving in marriage. It was at this Border town that David, son of the Bruce,

QUEEN MARY.

and Joanna, sister of Edward III, were united in marriage. Even then did the kingdoms seek an Act of Union. And Prince David was four, and Princess Joanna was six. There was much feasting by day and much revelry by night, among the nobles of the two realms, while, no doubt, the babies nodded drowsily.

At Berwick John Knox united himself in marriage with Margaret Stewart, member of the royal house of Stewart, cousin, if at some remove, from that Stewart queen who belonged to "the monstrous regiment of women," and to whose charms even the Calvinist John was sensitive. One remembers that at Berwick John was fifty, and Margaret was sixteen.

There is not much in Berwick to hold the attention, unless one would dine direct on salmon trout just drawn frae the Tweed. There are memories, and modern content with what is modern.

Perhaps the saddest eyes that ever looked on the old town were those of Queen Mary, as she left Jedburgh, after her almost fatal illness, and after her hurried ride to the Hermitage to see Bothwell, and just before the fatal affair in Kirk o' Field. Even then, and even with her spirit still unbroken, she felt the coming of the end. "I am tired of my life," she said more than once to Le Croc, French ambassador, on this journey as she circled about the coast and back to Edinburgh.

She rode toward Berwick with an escort of a thousand men, and looked down on the town from Halidon Hill, on the west, where two hundred years before (1333) the Scots under the regent Douglass had suffered defeat by the English.

It was an old town then, and belonged to Elizabeth. But it looked much as it does today; the gray walls, so recently built; the red roofs, many of them sheltering Berwickians today; the church spires, for men worshiped God in those days in churches, and according to the creeds that warred as bitterly as crowns; masts in the offing, whence this last time one might take ship to France, that pleasant smiling land so different from this dour realm. At all these Mary must have looked wistfully and weariedly, as the royal salute was fired for this errant queen. She looked also, over the Border, then becoming a hard-and-fast boundary, and down the long, long road to Fotheringay, and to peace at last and honour, in the Abbey.

It is well to stand upon this hill, before you go on to the West and the Border, or on to the North and the gray metropolis, that you may appreciate both the tragedy and the triumph that is Scotland's and was Mary's. The North Sea is turning purple far out on the horizon, and white sea birds are flying across beyond sound. The long level light of the late afternoon is coming up over England. In the backward of the Border a plaintive curlew is crying in the West, as he has cried since the days of Mary, and æons before.

Flodden

You may go westward from here, by train and coach, and carriage and on foot, to visit this country where every field has been a battlefield, where ruined peel towers finally keep the peace, where castles are in ruins, and a few stately modern homes proclaim the permanence of Scottish nobility; and where there is no bird and no flower unsung by Scottish minstrelsy, or by Scott. Scott is, of course, the poet and prose laureate of the Border. "Marmion" is the lay, almost the guide-book. It should be carried with you, either in memory or in pocket.

If the day is not too far spent, the afternoon sun too low, you can make Norham Castle before twilight, even as Marmion made it when he opened the first canon of Scott's poem—

"Day set on Norham's castle steep
And Tweed's fair river, broad and deep,
And Cheviot's mountains lone;
The battled towers, the donjon keep,
The loophole grates, where captives weep,
The flanking walls that round it sweep,
In yellow luster shone."

There is but a fragment of that castle remaining, and this, familiar to those who study Turner in the National Gallery. A little village with one broad street and curiously receding houses attempts to live in the shadow of this memory. The very red-stone tower has stood there at the top of the steep bank since the middle Eleven Hundreds. Henry II held it as a royal castle, while his craven son John—not so craven in battle—regarded it as the first of his fortresses. Edward I made it his headquarters while he pretended to arbitrate the rival claims of the Scottish succession, and to establish himself as the Lord Superior. On the green hill of Holywell nearby he received the submission of Scotland in 1291—the submission of Scotland!

Ford castle is a little higher up the river, where lodged the dubious lady with whom the king had dalliance in those slack days preceding Flodden—the lady who had sung to him in Holyrood the challenging ballad of "Young Lochinvar!" James was ever a Stewart, and regardful of the ladies.

> "What checks the fiery soul of James,
> Why sits the champion of dames
> Inactive on his steed?"

The Norman tower of Ford (the castle has been restored), called the King's tower, looks down on the battlefield, and in the upper room, called the King's room, there is a carved fire-place carrying the historic footnote—

> "King James ye 4th of Scotland did lye
> here at Ford castle, A. D. 1513."

Somehow one hopes that the lady was not sparring for time and Surrey, and sending messages to the advancing Earl, but truly loved this Fourth of the Jameses, grandfather to his inheriting granddaughter.

Coldstream is the station for Flodden. But the village, lying a mile away on the Scotch side of the Tweed, has memories of its own. It was here that the most famous ford was found between the two countries, witness and way to so many acts of disunion; from the time when Edward I, in 1296, led his forces through it into

Scotland, to the time when Montrose, in 1640, led his forces through it into England.

> "There on this dangerous ford and deep
> Where to the Tweed Leet's eddies creep
> He ventured desperately."

The river was spanned by a five-arch bridge in 1763, and it was over this bridge that Robert Burns crossed into England. He entered the day in his diary, May 7, 1787. "Coldstream—went over to England—Cornhill—glorious river Tweed—clear and majestic—fine bridge."

It was the only time Burns ever left Scotland, ever came into England. And here he knelt down, on the green lawn, and prayed the prayer that closes "The Cotter's Saturday Night"—

> "O Thou who pour'd the patriot tide
> That streamed through Wallace's undaunted heart,
> Who dared to nobly stem tyrannic pride
> Or nobly die, the second glorious part,
> (The patriot's God, peculiarly Thou art,
> His friend, inspirer, guardian and reward!)
> O never, never, Scotia's realm desert;
> But still the patriot and the patriot bard,
> In bright succession raise, her ornament and guard!"

Surely a consecration of this crossing after its centuries of unrest.

General Monk spent the winter of 1659 in Coldstream, lodging in a house east of the market-place, marked with its tablet. And here he raised the first of the still famous Coldstream Guards, to bring King Charles "o'er the water" back to the throne. Coldstream is the Gretna Green of this end of the Border, and many a runaway couple, noble and simple, has been married in the inn.

Four miles south of Coldstream in a lonely part of this lonely Border—almost the echoes are stilled, and you hear nothing but remembered bits of Marmion as you walk the highway—lies Flodden Field. It was the greatest of Scotch battles, not even excepting Bannockburn; greatest because the Scotch are greatest in defeat.

It was, or so it seemed to James, because his royal brother-in-law Henry VIII was fighting in France, an admirable time wherein to advance into England. James had received a ring and a glove and a message, from Anne of Brittany, bidding him

> "Strike three strokes with Scottish brand
> And march three miles on Scottish land
> And bid the banners of his band
> In English breezes dance."

James was not the one to win at Flodden, notwithstanding that he had brought a hundred thousand men to his standard. They were content to raid the Border, and he to dally at Ford.

> "O for one hour of Wallace wight,
> Or well skill'd Bruce to rule the fight,
> And cry—'Saint Andrew and our right!'
> Another sight had seen that morn
> From Fate's dark book a leaf been torn,
> And Flodden had been Bannockburn!"

The very thud of the lines carries you along, if you have elected to walk through the countryside, green now and smiling faintly if deserted, where it was brown and sere in September, 1513. One should be repeating his "Marmion," as Scott thought out so many of its lines riding over this same countryside. It is a splendid, a lingering battle picture—

> "And first the ridge of mingled spears
> Above the brightening cloud appears;
> And in the smoke the pennon flew,
> As in the storm the white sea mew,
> Then mark'd they, dashing broad and far,
> The broken billows of the war;
> And plumed crests of chieftains brave,
> Floating like foam upon the wave,
> But nought distinct they see.
> Wide ranged the battle on the plain;
> Spears shook, and falchions flash'd amain,
> Fell England's arrow flight like rain,
> Crests rose and stooped and rose again
> Wild and disorderly."

Thousands were lost on both sides. But the flower of England was in France, while the flower of Scotland was here; and slain—the king, twelve earls, fifteen lords and chiefs, an archbishop, the French ambassador, and many French captains.

You walk back from the Field, and all the world is changed. The green haughs, the green woodlands, seem even in the summer sun to be dun and sere, and those burns which made merry on the outward way—can it be that there are red shadows in their waters? It is not "Marmion" but Jean Elliott's "Flower of the Forest" that lilts through the memory—

"Dule and wae was the order sent our lads to the Border,
The English for once by guile won the day;
The Flowers of the Forest that foucht aye the foremost,
The pride of our land are cauld in the clay.

"We'll hear nae mair liltin' at the eve milkin',
Women and bairns are heartless and wae;
Sighin' and moanin' on ilka green loanin'—
The Flowers of the Forest are a' wede away."

I know not by what alchemy the Scots are always able to win our sympathy to their historic tragedies, or why upon such a field as Flodden, and many another, the tragedy seems but to have just happened, the loss is as though of yesterday.

CHAPTER II

SCOTTS-LAND

IT is possible to enter the Middle Marches from Berwick; in truth, Kelso lies scarcely farther from Flodden than does Berwick. But Flodden is on English soil to-day, and memory is content to let it lie there. These Middle Marches however are so essentially Scottish, the splendour and the romance, the history and the tragedy, that one would fain keep them so, and come upon them as did the kings from David I, or even the Celtic kings before him, who sought refuge from the bleak Scottish north in this smiling land of dales and haughs, of burns and lochs. Not at any moment could life become monotonous even in this realm of romance, since the Border was near, and danger and dispute so imminent, so incessant.

Preferably then one goes from Edinburgh (even though never does one go from that city, "mine own romantic town," but with regret; not even finally when one leaves it and knows

JAMES II.

one will not return till next time) to Melrose; as Scottish kings of history and story have passed before. There was James II going to the siege of Roxburgh, and not returning; there was James IV going to the field of Flodden and not returning; there was James V going to hunt the deer; there was James VI going up to London to be king; Mary Queen on that last journey to the South Countrie; Charles I and Charles II losing and getting a crown; Charles III—let us defy history and call the Bonnie Prince by his title—when he went so splendidly after Prestonpans.

It is a royal progress, out of Edinburgh into the Middle Marches; past Dalkeith where James IV rode to meet and marry Margaret of England; past Borthwick, where Queen Mary spent that strange hot-trod honeymoon with Bothwell—of all place of emotion this is the most difficult to realize, and I can but think Mary's heart was broken here, and the heart-break at Carberry Hill was but an echo of this; past Lauder, where the nobles of ignoble James III hung his un-noble favourite from the stone arch of the bridge; into the level rays of a setting sun—always the setting sun throws a more revealing light than that of noonday over this Scotland.

Melrose

I remember on my first visit to Melrose, of course during my first visit to Scotland, I sebeduled my going so as to arrive there in the evening of a night when the moon would be at the full. I had seen it shine gloriously on the front of York, splendidly on the towers of Durham. What would it not be on fair Melrose, viewed aright?

I hurried northward, entered Edinburgh only to convey my baggage, and then closing my eyes resolutely to all the glory and the memory that lay about, I went southward through the early twilight. I could see, would see, nothing before Melrose.

The gates of the Abbey were, of course, closed. But I did not wish to enter there until the magic hour should strike. The country round about was ineffably lovely in the rose light of the vanishing day.

> "Where fair Tweed flows round holy Melrose
> And Eildon slopes to the plain."

The Abbey was, of course, the center of thought continually, and its red-gray walls caught the light of day and the coming shadows of night in a curious effect which no picture can report; time has dealt wondrously with this stone, leaving the rose for the day, the gray for the night.

I wandered about, stopping in the empty sloping market-place to look at the Cross, which is as old as the Abbey; looking at the graveyard which surrounds the Abbey, where men lie, common men unsung in Scottish minstrelsy, except as part of the great hosts, men who heard the news when it was swift and fresh from Bannockburn, and Flodden, and Culloden; and where men and women still insert their mortality into this immortality—Elizabeth Clephane who wrote the "Ninety and Nine" lies there; and out into the country and down by the Tweed toward the Holy Pool, the Haly Wheel, to wonder if when I came again in the middle night, I, too, should see the white lady rise in mist from the waters, this lady of Bemersyde who had loved a monk of Melrose not wisely but very well, and who drowned herself in this water where the monk in penance took daily plunges, come summer, come winter. How often this is the Middle-Age penalty!

Far across the shimmering green meadows and through the fragrant orchards came the sound of bagpipes—on this my first evening in Scotland! And whether or not you care for the pipes, there is nothing like them in a Scottish twilight, a first Scottish twilight, to reconstruct all the Scotland that has been.

The multitudes and the individuals came trooping back. At a time of famine these very fields were filled with huts, four thousand of them, for always the monks had food, and always they could perform miracles and obtain food; which they did. That for the early time. And for the late, the encampment of Leslie's men in these fields before the day when they slaughtered Montrose's scant band of royalists at Philipshaugh, and sent that most splendid figure in late Scottish history as a fugitive to the north, and to the scaffold.

I knew that in the Abbey before the high altar lay the high heart of The Bruce, which had been carried to Spain and to the Holy Land, by order of Bruce, since death overtook him before he could make the pilgrimage. Lord James Douglass did battle on the way against the Moslems in southern Spain, where "a Douglass! a Douglass!" rang in battle clash against "Allah, illah, allah," and the Douglass himself was slain. The heart of The Bruce flung against the infidel, was recovered and sent on to Jerusalem, and then back to Melrose. The body of Douglass was brought back to Scotland, to St. Bride's church in Douglass, and his heart also lies before the high altar of Melrose. "In their death they were not divided."

There lies also buried Michael Scot

> "Buried on St. Michael's night,
> When the bell toll'd one and the moon was bright."

On such a night as this, I hoped. And Scot is fit companion for the twilight. This strange wizard of a strange time was born in Upper Tweedale, which is the district of Merlin—the older wizard lies buried in a green mound near Drummelzier. Michael traveled the world over, Oxford, Paris, Bologna, Palermo, Toledo, and finally, perhaps because his wizardry had sent him like a wandering Jew from place to place, back to the Border, his home country, where he came and served the Evil One. Dante places him in the Purgatory of those who attempt blasphemously to tear the veil of the future. The thirteenth century was not the time in which to increase knowledge, whether of this world or the next. Even to-day perhaps we save a remnant of superstition, and we would not boast

> "I could say to thee
> The words that cleft the Eildon hills in three."

Very dark against the gathering dark of the night sky rose the Eildon hills above, cleft in three by the wizardry of Scot. To that height on the morrow I should climb, for it is there that Sir Walter Scott, a later wizard, had carried our Washington Irving, just a century ago, and shown him all this Borderland—which lay about me under the increasing cover of night.

"I can stand on the Eildon Hill and point out forty-three places famous in war and verse," Sir Walter said to our Irving. "I have brought you, like a pilgrim in the Pilgrim's Progress, to the top of the Delectable Mountains, that I may show you all the goodly regions hereabouts. Yonder is Lammermuir and Smailholm; and there you have Galashiels and Torwoodelee and Gala Water; and in that direction you see Teviotdale and the Braes of Yarrow; and Ettrick stream winding along like a silver thread to throw itself into the Tweed. It may be pertinacity, but to my eye, these gray hills and all this wild Border country have beauties peculiar to themselves. When I have been for some time in the rich scenery about Edinburgh, which is like an ornamented garden land, I begin to wish myself back again among my own honest gray hills; and if I did not see the heather at least once a year, I think I should die."

On the morrow. But for to-night it was enough to remember that perfect picture as imagination painted it in Andrew Lang's verse—

"Three crests against the saffron sky,
Beyond the purple plain,
The kind remembered melody
Of Tweed once more again.

"Wan water from the Border hills,
Dear voice from the old years,
Thy distant music lulls and stills,
And moves to quiet tears.

"Like a loved ghost thy fabled flood
Fleets through the dusky land;
Where Scott, come home to die, has stood,
My feet returning, stand.

"A mist of memory broods and floats,
The Border waters flow;
The air is full of ballad notes
Borne out of long ago.

"Old songs that sung themselves to me,
Sweet through a boy's day dream,
While trout below the blossom'd tree
Plashed in the golden stream.

"Twilight, and Tweed, and Eildon Hill,
Fair and too fair you be;
You tell me that the voice is still
That should have welcomed me."

I did not miss the voice, any of the voices. They whispered, they sang, they crooned, they keened, about me. For this was Melrose, *mael ros,* so the old Celtic goes, "the naked headland in the wood." And I was seeing, was hearing, what I have come to see and hear; I, a Scot, if far removed, if in diluted element, and Scott's from the reading days of Auld Lang Syne.

And should I not within the moonlight see the white lady rise from the Haly Wheel? And should I not see the moonlight flooding the Abbey, Melrose Abbey? Out of a remembered yesterday, out of a confident midnight—surely there was a budding morrow in this midnight—I remembered the lines—

> "If thou would'st view fair Melrose aright,
> Go visit it by the pale moonlight;
> For the gay beams of lightsome day
> Gild but to flout the ruins gray.
> When the broken arches are black in night,
> And each shafted oriel glimmers white,
> When the cold light's uncertain shower
> Streams on the ruined central tower;
> When buttress and buttress alternately
> Seem framed of ebon and ivory;
> When silver edges the imagery,
> And the scrolls that teach thee to live and die;
> When distant Tweed is heard to rave,
> And the owlet to hoot o'er the dead man's grave,

> Then go—but go alone the while—
> Then view St. David's ruined pile;
> And, home returning, soothly swear
> Was never scene so sad and fair."

The moon did not rise that night.

I walked about the fields, lingered about the Cross in the market, looked expectantly at the Abbey, until two in the morning.

> "It was near the ringing of matin bell,
> The night was well nigh done."

The moon did not rise, and neither did the white lady. It was not because there was a mist, a Scottish mist, over the heavens; they were clear, the stars were shining, and the pole star held true, Charles' wain—as Charles should in Bonnie Scotland—held true to the pole. But it was a late July moon, and those Eildon hills and their circling kin rose so high against the night sky—daytime they seemed modest enough—that the moon in this latitude as far north as Sitka did not circle up the sky. Neither does the sun in winter, so the guardian explained to me next day.

Fair Melrose is fairest, o' nights, at some later or earlier time of the year. It was then that I resolved to return in December, on December 27, when the festival of St. John's is celebrated with torch lights in the ruins of the

Abbey—and Michael Scot comes back to his own! But then I reflected that the moon is not always full on the Eve of St. John's.

> "I cannot come, I must not come,
> I dare not come to thee,
> On the Eve of St. John's, I must walk alone,
> In thy bower I may not be."

I chose, years later, an October moon, in which to see it "aright."

Viewed by day, Melrose is surely fair; fair enough to enchant mortal vision. It is the loveliest ruin in the land where reform has meant ruin, and where from Kelso to Elgin, shattered fanes of the faith proclaim how variable is the mind of man through the generations, and how hostile when it forsakes.

Melrose is an old foundation. In truth the monastery was established at old Melrose, two miles farther down the Tweed, and is so lovely, so dramatic a corner of the Tweed, that Dorothy Woodsworth declared, "we wished we could have brought the ruins of Melrose to this spot." She missed the nearby murmur of the river as we do.

This oldest harbour of Christianity was founded in the pagan world by monks from Iona. Therefore by way of Ireland and not from Rome, blessed by Saint Columba sixty

MELROSE ABBEY.

years before Saint Augustine came to Canterbury. It was the chief "island" between Iona and Lindisfarne. Very haughty were these monks of the West. "Rome errs, Alexandria errs, all the world errs; only the Scots and the Britons are in the right." There is surely something still left of the old spirit in Scotia, particularly in spiritual Scotia.

Near Melrose was born that Cuthbert who is the great saint of the North, either side the Border, and who lies in the midst of the splendour of Durham. A shepherd, he watched his sheep on these very hills round about us, and saw, when abiding in the fields, angels ascending and descending on golden ladders. Entering Melrose as a novice he became prior in 664, and later prior at Lindisfarne. When the monks were driven from the Holy Island by the Danes they carried the body of St. Cuthbert with them for seven years, and once it rested at Melrose—

"O'er northern mountain, march and moor,
From sea to sea, from shore to shore,
Seven years St. Cuthbert's corpse they bore,
They rested them in fair Melrose;
But though alive he loved it well,
Not there his relics might repose."

When King David came to the making of

Scotland, he came into the Middle Marches, and finding them very lovely—even as you and I—this "sair sanct to the Croon," as his Scottish royal descendant, James VI saw him—and James would have fell liked to be a saint, but he could accomplish neither sinner nor saint, because Darnley crossed Mary in his veins—David determined to build him fair Abbeys. Of which, Melrose, "St. David's ruined pile," is the fairest. He brought Cistercians from Rievaulx in Yorkshire, to supplant the Culdees of Iona, and they builded them a beautiful stone Melrose to supplant the wooden huts of old Melrose. It centered a very active monastic life, where pavements were once smooth and lawns were close-clipped, and cowled monks in long robes served God, and their Abbot lorded it over lords, even equally with kings.

But it stood on the highway between Dunfermline and London, between English and Scottish ambitions. And it fell before them. Edward I spared it because the Abbots gave him fealty. But Edward II, less royal in power and in taste, destroyed it. The Bruce rebuilded it again, greater splendour rising out of complete ruin. When Richard II came to Scotland he caused the Abbey to be pillaged and burned. And when Hertford came for Henry VIII, after the Thirty

Nine Articles had annulled respect for buildings under the protection of Rome, the final ruin came to St. David's church-palace. Yet, late as 1810, church service, reformed, of course, was held in a roofed-over part of the Abbey ruin. To-day it is under the protection of the Dukes of Buccleuch. And, we remember as we stand here, while the beams of lightsome day gild the ruin, the mottoes of the great family of the Border, *Luna Cornua Reparabit,* which being interpreted is, "There'll be moonlight again." Then to light the raids, the reiving that refilled the larder. But to-morrow for scenic effect.

Examined in this daylight, the beauty of Melrose surely loses very little. It is one of the most exquisite ruins in the United Kingdom, perhaps second to Tintern, but why compare? It is of finest Gothic, out of France, not out of England. In its general aspect it is nobly magnificent—

"The darken'd roof rose high aloof
On pillars, lofty, light and small;
The keystone that locked each ribbed aisle
Was a fleur de lys or a quatre feuille,
The corbels were carved grotesque and grim;
And the pillars with clustered shafts so trim,
With base and with capital flourish'd around
Seem'd bundles of lances which garlands had bound."

And, as a chief detail which yields not to Tintern or any other, is the east window over the high altar, through which the moon and sun shines on those buried hearts—

> "The moon on the east oriel shone
> Through slender shafts of shapely stone,
> By foliaged tracery combined.
> Thou would'st have thought some fairy'd hand
> 'Twixt poplars straight the osier wand
> In many a freakish knot had twined,
> The*n* framed a spell when the work was done,
> And changed the willow wreaths to stone.
> The silver light, so pale and faint,
> Showed many a prophet and many a saint,
> Whose image on the glass was dyed,
> Full in the midst his cross of red
> Triumphant Michael brandish'd,
> And trampled on the Apostate's pride;
> The moonbeams kissed the holy pane,
> And threw on the pavement a bloody stain."

Abbotsford

If "Scott restored Scotland," he built the "keep" which centers all the Scott-land of the Border side.

Two miles above Melrose, a charming walk leads to Abbotsford; redeemed out of a swamp into at least the most memory-filled mansion of all the land. Scott, like the monks, could not leave the silver wash of the Tweed; and, more loving than those who dwelt at Melrose and Dryburgh, he placed his Abbot's House where the rippling sound was within a stone's throw.

The Tweed is such a storied stream that as you walk along, sometimes across sheep-cropped meadows, sometimes under the fragant rustling bough and athwart the shifting shadows of oak, ash, and thorn—Puck of Pook's hill must have known the Border country in its most embroidered days—you cannot tell whether or not the deep quiet river is the noblest you have seen, or the storied hills about are less than the Delectable mountains.

The name "Tweed" suggests romance—unless instead of having read your Scott you have come to its consciousness through the homespun, alas, to-day too often the factory-spun woolens, which are made throughout all Scotland, but still in greatest length on Tweedside.

Dorothy Wordsworth, winsome marrow, who loved the country even better than William, I trow—only why remark it when he himself recognized how his vision was quickened through her companionship?—has spoke the word Tweed—"a name which has been sweet in my ears almost as far back as I can remember anything."

The river comes from high in the Cheviot hills, where East and West Marches merge and where—

> "Annan, Tweed, and Clyde
> Rise a' out o' ae hillside."

And down to the sea it runs, its short hundred miles of story—

> "All through the stretch of the stream,
> To the lap of Berwick Bay."

As you walk along Tweedside, you feel its enchantment, you feel the sorrow of the thousands who through the centuries have exiled themselves from its banks, because of war, or because of poverty, or because of love—

> "Therefore I maun wander abroad,
> And lay my banes far frae the Tweed."

But now, you are returned, you are on your way to Abbotsford, there are the Eildons, across the river you get a glimpse of the Catrail, that sunken way that runs along the boundary for one-half its length, and may have been a fosse, or may have been a concealed road of the Romans or what not. Scott once leaped his horse across it, nearly lost his life, and did lose his confidence in his horsemanship.

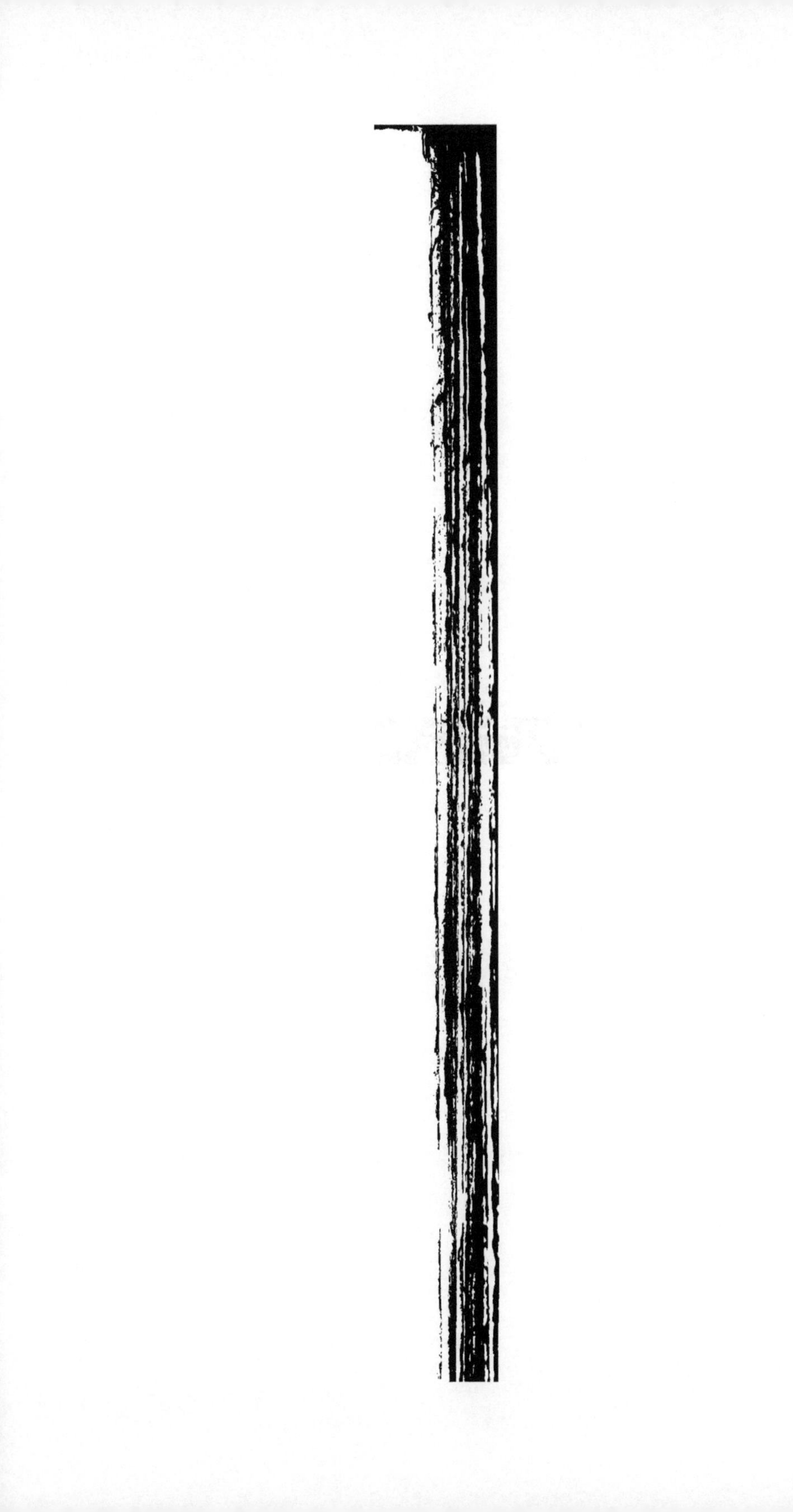

Abbotsford

"And all through the summer morning
I felt it a joy indeed
To whisper again and again to myself,
This is the voice of the Tweed."

It is not possible to approach Abbotsford, as it should be approached, from the riverside, the view with which one is familiar, the view the pictures carry. Or, it can be done if one would forego the walk, take it in the opposite direction, and come hither by rail from Galashiels—that noisy modern factory town, once the housing place for Melrose pilgrims, which to-day speaks nothing of the romance of Gala water, and surely not these factory folk "can match the lads o' Gala Water." It is a short journey, and railway journeys are to be avoided in this land of by-paths. But there, across the water, looking as the pictures have it, and as Scott would have it, rises Abbotsford, turreted and towered, engardened and exclusive.

It stands on low level ground, for it is redeemed out of a duckpond, out of Clarty hole. Sir Walter wished to possess the Border, or as much of it as might be, so he made this first purchase of a hundred acres in 1811. As he wrote to James Ballantyne—

"I have resolved to purchase a piece of ground sufficient for a cottage and a few fields.

There are two pieces, either of which would suit me, but both would make a very desirable property indeed, and could be had for between 7,000 and 8,000 pounds, or either separate for about half that sum. I have serious thoughts of one or both."

He began with one, and fourteen years later, when the estate had extended to a thousand acres, to the inclusion of many fields, sheep-cropped and story-haunted, he entered in his diary—

"Abbotsford is all I can make it, so I am resolved on no more building, and no purchases of land till times are more safe."

By that time the people of the countryside called him "the Duke," he had at least been knighted, and was, in truth, the Chief of the Border; a royal ambition which I doubt not he cherished from those first days when he read Percy under a platanus.

He paid fabulous prices for romantic spots, and I think would have bought the entire Border if the times had become safer, in those scant seven years that were left to him. Even Scott could be mistaken, for he bought what he believed was Huntlie Bank, where True Thomas had his love affair with the fair ladye—

"True Thomas lay on Huntlie Bank;
A ferlie he spied wi' his e'e;
And there he saw a ladye bright
Come riding down by the Eildon tree.

"Her skirt was o' the grass-green silk,
Her mantle o' the velvet fyne;
At ilka tett o' her horse's mane
Hung fifty siller bells and nine."

And now the experts tell us that it is not Huntlie Bank at all, but that is in an entirely different direction, over toward Ercildoune and the Rhymer's Tower.

There is a satisfaction in this to those of us who believe in fairies and in Scott. For fairies have no sense of place or of time. And of course if they knew that Scott wished them to have lived at his Huntlie Bank, they straightway would have managed to have lived there. Always, as you go through this land of romance, or any romance land, and wise dull folk dispute, you can console yourself that Scott also was mistaken(?).

The castle began with a small cottage, not this great pile of gray stone we can see from the railway carriage across the Tweed, into which we make our humble way through a wicket gate, a restrained walk, and a basement doorway. "My dreams about my cottage go on,'' he wrote to Joanna Baillie, as we all dream of building cottages into castles. "My present intention is to have only two spare bedrooms," but "I cannot relinquish my Border principles of accommodating all the cousins and duniwastles, who will rather sleep on chairs, and on the floor, and in the hay-loft, than be absent when folks are gathered together."

So we content ourselves with being duniwastles, whatever that may be, and are confident that Sir Walter if he were alive would give us the freedom of the castle.

In any event, if we feel somewhat robbed of any familiar intercourse, we can remember that Ruskin called this "perhaps the most incongruous pile that gentlemanly modernism ever designed." This may content the over-sensitive who are prevented ever hearing the ripple of the Tweed through the windows.

Scott was a zealous relic hunter, and if you like relics, if you can better conjure up persons through a sort of transubstantiation of personality that comes by looking on what the great have possessed, there can be few private collections more compelling than this of Abbotsford.

In the library are such significant hints for reconstruction as the blotting book wherewith Napoleon cleared his record, the crucifix on

THE STUDY, ABBOTSFORD.

which Queen Mary prayed, the quaigh of her great great and last grandson, the tumbler from which Bobbie Burns drank—one of them—the purse into which Rob Roy thrust his plunder, the pocket book of Flora MacDonald, which held nothing I fear from the generosity of the Bonnie Prince.

In the armoury are Scott's own gun, Rob Roy's gun, dirk and skene dhu, the sword of Montrose, given to that last of the great Cavaliers by his last king, Charles I, the pistol of Claverhouse, the pistol of Napoleon, a hunting flask of James III; and here are the keys of Loch Leven castle, dropped in the lake by Mary Queen's boatman; and the keys of the Edinburgh Tolbooth turned on so many brave men, yes, and fair women, in the old dividing days, of Jacobite and Covenanter.

The library of Scott, twenty thousand volumes, still lines the shelves, and one takes particular interest in this place, and its little stairway whereby ascent is made to the balcony, also book-lined, and escape through a little doorway. When Scott first came to the cottage of Abbotsford he wrote, furiously, in a little window embrasure with only a curtain between him and the domestic world. Here he had not only a library, but a study, where still stands the desk at which the Waverleys were written, and the well-worn desk chair.

After he had returned from Italy, whither he went in search of health and did not find it, he felt, one day, a return of the old desire to write, the ruling passion. He was wheeled to the desk, he took the pen,—nothing came. He sank back and burst into tears. As Lockhart reports it—"It was like Napoleon resigning his empire. The scepter had departed from Judah; Scott was to write no more."

Scott has always seemed like a contemporary. Not because of his novels; I fear the Waverleys begin to read a little stilted to the young generation, and there are none left to lament with Lowell that he had read all of Scott and now he could never read him all over again for the first time. It is rather because Scott the man is so immortal that he seems like a man still living; or at least like one who died but yesterday. Into the dining-room where we cannot go—and perhaps now that we think it over it is as well—he was carried in order that out of it he might look his last on "twilight and Tweed and Eildon hill." And there he died, even so long ago as September, 1832.

"It was a beautiful day," that day we seem almost to remember as we stand here in the vivid after glow, "so warm that every window was wide open, and so peacefully still that the sound of all others most delicious to his ear, the gentle ripple of the Tweed, was distinctly audible."

Dryburgh

Five days after they carried him to rest in the Abbey—rival certainly in this instance of The Abbey of England, where is stored so much precious personal dust. The time had become thrawn; dark skies hung over the Cheviots and the Eildon, and over the haughs of Ettrick and Yarrow; the silver Tweed ran leaden, and moaned in its going; there was a keening in the wind.

The road from Abbotsford past Melrose to Dryburgh is—perhaps—the loveliest walk in the United Kingdom; unless it be the road from Coventry past Kenilworth to Stratford. It was by this very way that there passed the funeral train of Scott, the chief carriage drawn by Scott's own horses. Thousands and thousands of pilgrims have followed that funeral train; one goes to Holy Trinity in Stratford, to the Invalides in Paris, but one walks to Dryburgh through the beautiful Tweedside which is all a shrine to Sir Walter.

The road runs away from the river to the little village of Darnick, with its ivy-shrouded tower, across the meadows to the bridge across the river, with the ringing of bells in the ear. For it was ordered on that September day of 1832, by the Provost, "that the church bell shall toll from the time the funeral procession reaches Melrose Bridge till it passes the village of Newstead."

I do not suppose the people of this countryside, who look at modern pilgrims so sympathetically, so understandingly, have ever had time to forget; the stream of pilgrims has been so uninterrupted for nearly a century. Through the market-place of Melrose it passed, the sloping stony square, where people of the village pass and repass on their little village errands. And it did not stop at the Abbey.

The day was thickening into dusk then; it is ripening into sunset glory to-day. And the Abbey looks very lovely, and very lonely. And one wonders if Michael Scot did not call to Walter Scott to come and join the quiet there, and if the dust that once was the heart of Bruce did not stir a little as the recreator of Scotland was carried by.

To the village of Newstead you move on; with the sound of immemorial bells falling on the ear, and pass through the little winding street —and wonder if the early Roman name of Trimontium, triple mountains, triple Eildon, was its first call name out of far antiquity as Scott believed.

Then the road ascends between hedgerows, and begins to follow the Tweed closely—and perhaps you meet pilgrims on Leaderfoot bridge who have come the wrong way. There is a steep climb to the heights of Bemersyde, where on the crest all Melrose Glen lies beautifully storied before you. And here you pause —as did those horses of Scott's, believing their master would fain take one last look at his favourite view.

There is no lovelier landscape in the world, or in Scotland. The blue line of the Cheviots bars back the world, the Dunion, the Ruberslaw, the Eildon rise, and in the great bend of the river with richly wooded braes about is the site of Old Melrose. Small wonder he paused to take farewell of all the country he had loved so well.

The road leads on past Bemersyde village with woodlands on either side, and to the east, near a little loch, stands Sandyknowe Tower.

Near the tower lies the remnant of the village of Smailholm, where Scott was sent out of Edinburgh when only three years old. It is in truth his birthplace, for without the clear air of the Border he would have followed the other Scott children; and without the romance of the Border he might have been merely a barrister.

Sandyknowe is brave in spite of its ruin, for it is built of the very stone of the eternal hills, and has become part of the hills. From its balcony, sixty feet high, a beautiful Scottish panorama may be glimpsed, and here Scott brought Turner to make his sketch of the Border. And here, because a kinsman agreed to save Sandyknowe Tower from the mortality that comes even to stone if Scott would write a ballad and make it immortal, is laid the scene of "Eve of St. John's"—with these last haunting intangible lines—

> "There is a nun in Dryburgh bower
> Ne'er looks upon the sun;
> There is a monk in Melrose tower
> He speaketh a word to none."

Then, back to the Tweed, where the river sweeps out in a great circle, and leaves a peninsula for Dryburgh. The gray walls of the ruin lift above the thick green of the trees; yew and oak and sycamore close in the fane.

ST. MARY'S AISLE AND TOMB OF SIR WALTER SCOTT, DRYBURGH ABBEY.

Druid and Culdee and Roman have built shrines in this lovely spot, but to-day pilgrimage is made chiefly because in the quiet sheltered ruined St. Mary's aisle sleeps Sir Walter. It would make one-half in love with death to think of being buried in so sweet a place.

Dryburgh is also one of St. David's foundations, in the "sacred grove of oaks," the Darach Bruach of the worship that is older than Augustus or Columba. These were white monks that David brought up from Alnwick where his queen had been a Northumbrian princess, and their white cloaks must have seemed, among these old old oaks, but the white robes of the Druids come back again.

It is a well-kept place, vines covering over the crumbling gray stone, kept by the Lords of Buchan. And, perhaps too orderly, too fanciful, too "improved"; one likes better the acknowledged ruin of Melrose, and one would prefer that Sir Walter were there with his kin, instead of here with his kindred. But this is a sweet place, a historic place, begun by Hugh de Moreville, who was a slayer of Thomas à Becket, and was Constable of Scotland. His tomb is marked by a double circle on the floor of the Chapter House, and there is nothing of the Chapter House; it is open to beating rain and scorching sun—fit retribution for his most foul deed.

It is not this remembrance you carry away, but that of St. Mary's aisle, in

> "Dryburgh where with chiming Tweed
> The lintwhites sing in chorus."

CHAPTER III

BORDER TOWNS

Kelso

IT is a very great little country which lies all about Melrose, with never a bend of the river or a turn of the highway or a shoulder of the hill, nay, scarce the shadow of any hazel bush or the piping of any wee bird but has its history, but serves to recall what once was; and because the countryside is so teeming seems to make yesterday one with today. The distances are very short, even between the places the well-read traveler knows; with many places that are new along the way, each haunted with its tradition, soon to haunt the traveler, while the people he meets would seem to have been here since the days of the Winged Hats.

Perhaps in order to get into the center of the ecclesiastical country—for after this being a Borderland, and a Scott-land, it is decidedly Abbots-land, even before Abbotsford came into being with its new choice of old title—the traveler will take train to Kelso, or walk there, a scant dozen miles from Melrose.

The journey is down the Tweed, which opens ever wider between the gentle hills that are more and more rounding as the flow goes on to the sea. There is not such intense loneliness; here is the humanest part of the Scottish landscape, and while even on this highway the cottages are not frequent, and one eyes the journeymen with as close inspection as one is eyed, still it is a friendly land. The southern burr—we deliberately made excuse of drinking water or asking direction in order to hear it—is softer than in the North; yet, you would not mistake it for Northumberland. We wondered if this was the accent Scott spoke with; but to him must have belonged all the dialect-voices.

It was at Roxburgh Castle that King David lived when he determined to build these abbeys of the Middle Marches, of which the chief four are Melrose, Dryburgh, Jedburgh and Kelso, with Holyrood as their royal keystone.

Roxburgh was a stronghold of the Border, and therefore met the fate of those strongholds, when one party was stronger than the other; usually the destruction was by the English because they were farther away and could hold the country only through making it desolate.

Who would not desire loveliness and desire to fix it in stone, if he lived in such a lovely spot as this where the Tweed and Teviot meet? David had been in England. He was brother to the English queen Maude, wife of Henry I, and had come in contact with the Norman culture. Or, as William of Malmesbury put it, with that serene assurance of the Englishman over the Scot, he "had been freed from the rust of Scottish barbarity, and polished from a boy from his intercourse and familiarity with us." Ah, welladay! if residence at the English court and Norman culture resulted in these lovely abbeys, let us be lenient with William of Malmesbury. Incidentally David added to the Scotland of that time certain English counties, Northumberland and Cumberland and Westmoreland—as well as English culture!

David was son to Saxon Margaret, St. Margaret, and from her perhaps the "sair sanct" inherited some of his gentleness. But also he had married Matilda of Northumberland, wealthy and a widow, and he preferred to remain on the highway to London rather than at Dunfermline. So he was much at Roxburgh.

But the castle did not remain in Scottish or English hands. It was while curiously interested in a great Flemish gun that James II was killed by the explosion—and the siege of Roxburgh went on more hotly, and the castle was razed to its present low estate.

To-day the silly sheep are cropping grass about the scant stones that once sheltered kings and defied them; and ash trees are the sole occupants of the once royal dwelling. To the American there is something of passing interest in the present seat of the Duke of Roxburgh, Floors castle across the Teviot. For the house, like many another Scottish house, still carries direct descent. And an heiress from America, like the heiress from Northumberland, unites her fortune with this modern splendour—and admits American's and others on Wednesdays!

The town of Kelso is charming, like many Tweed towns. It lies among the wooded hills; there is a greater note of luxury here. Scott called it "the most beautiful if not the most romantic village in Scotland." Seen from the bridge which arches the flood, that placid flood of Tweed, and a five-arched bridge ambitiously and successfully like the Waterloo bridge of London, one wonders if after all perhaps Wordsworth wrote his Bridge sonnet here—"Earth hath not anything to show more fair." Surely this bridge, these spires and the great tower of the Abbey, "wear the beauty of the morning," the morning of the world. The hills, luxuriously wooded, rise gently behind, the persistent Eildons hang over, green meadows are about, the silver river runs—and the skies are Scottish skies, whether blue or gray.

The Abbey, of course, is the crown of the place, bolder in design and standing more boldly in spite of the havoc wrought by men and time, and Hertford and Henry VIII; calmer than Melrose, less ornamental, with its north portal very exquisite in proportion.

The Abbot of Kelso was in the palmy early days chief ecclesiastic of Scotland, a spiritual lord, receiving his miter from the Pope, and armoured with the right to excommunicate.

There have been other kings here than David and the Abbot. The latter days of the Stewarts are especially connected with Kelso, so near the Border. Baby James was hurried hither and crowned in the cathedral as the III after Roxburgh. Mary Queen lodged here for two nights before she rode on to Berwick. Here in the ancient market-place, looking like the square of a continental town, the Old Chevalier was proclaimed King James VIII on an October Monday in 1715, and the day preceding the English chaplain had preached to the troops from the text—"The right of the first born is his." Quite differently minded from that Whig minister farther north, who later prayed "as for this young man who has come among us seeking an earthly crown, may it please Thee to bestow upon him a heavenly one."

When this Rising of the Forty Five came, and he who should have been Charles III (according to those of us who are Scottish, and royalist, and have been exiled because of our allegiance) attempted to secure the throne for his father, he established his headquarters at Sunilaw just outside Kelso; the house is in ruins, but a white rose that he planted still bears flowers. To the citizens of Kelso who drank to him, the Prince, keeping his head, and having something of his royal great uncle's gift of direct speech, replied, "I believe you, gentlemen, I believe you. I have drinking friends, but few fighting ones in Kelso."

Scott knew Kelso from having lived here, from going to school here, and it was in out of the Kelso library—where they will show you the very copy—that he first read Percy's Reliques.

"I remember well the spot . . . it was beneath a huge platanus, in the ruins of what had been intended for an old fashioned arbour in the garden. . . . The summer day had sped onward so fast that notwithstanding the sharp appetite of thirteen, I forgot the dinner hour. The first time I could scrape together a few shillings I bought unto myself a copy of the beloved volumes; nor do I believe I ever read a book half so frequently or with half the enthusiasm.''

Was it not a nearer contemporary to Percy, and a knight of romance, Sir Philip Sidney, who said, ''I never read the old song of Percie and Douglas that I found not my heart moved more than with a trumpet''?

For myself I have resolutely refused to identify the word, Platanus, lest it should not be identical with the spot where I first read my Percy.

Scott also knew Kelso as the place of his first law practice, and of his honeymoon. Here flowered into maturity that long lavish life, so enriched and so enriching of the Border.

Horatio Bonar was minister here for thirty years—I wondered if he wrote here, ''I was a wandering sheep.''

While James Thomson, who wrote ''The Seasons,'' but also ''Rule, Britannia''—if he was a Scotsman; perhaps this was an Act of Union—

"Rule, Britannia, rule the waves;
Britons never will be slaves!"

was born at a little village nearby, back in the low hills of Tweed, in 1700, seven years before the Union.

Jedburgh

From Kelso I took train to the Border town which even the Baedeker admits has had "a stormy past," and where the past still lingers; nay, not lingers, but is; there is no present in Jedburgh. It is but ten miles to the Border; more I think that at any other point in all the blue line of the Cheviot, is one conscious of the Border; consciousness of antiquity and of geography hangs over Jedburgh.

It lies, a hill town, on the banks of the Jed; "sylvan Jed" said Thomson, "crystal Jed" said Burns; a smaller stream than the Tweed, more tortuous, swifter, rushing through wilder scenery, tumultuous, vocative, before Border times began—if ever there were such a time before—and disputatious still to remind us that this is still a division in the kingdom.

One of the most charming walks in all Scotland—and I do not know of any country where foot-traveler's interest is so continuous (I wrote this before I had read the disastrous walking trip of the Pennell's)—is up this valley of the Jed a half dozen miles, where remnants of old forest, or its descendants, still stand, where the bracken is thick enough to conceal an army crouching in ambush, where the hills move swiftly up from the river, and break sharply into precipices, with crumbling peel towers, watch towers, to guard the heights, and where outcropping red scars against the hill mark sometimes the entrance to caves that must have often been a refuge when Border warfare tramped down the valley.

In Jedburgh we lodged not at the inn; although the name of Spread Eagle much attracted us; but because every one who had come before us had sought lodging, we, too, would "lodge," if it be but for a night.

Mary Queen had stayed at an old house, still standing in Queenstreet, Prince Charles at a house in Castlegate, Burns in the Canongate, the Wordsworths, William and Dorothy, in Abbey Close, because there was no room in the inn. I do not know if it were the Spread Eagle then, but the assizes were being held, Jethart justice was being administered, or, juster justice, since these were more parlous times, and parley went before sentence. Scott as a sheriff and the other officials of the country were filling the hostelry. But Sir Walter, then the Sheriff of Selkirk, sheriff being a position of more "legality" than with us, and no doubt remembering his first law case which he had pled at Jedburgh years before, came over to Abbey Close after dinner, and according to Dorothy Wordsworth "sate with us an hour or two, and repeated a part of the 'Lay of the Last Minstrel.' "

Think of not knowing whether it was an hour or two hours, with Scott repeating the "Lay," and in Jedburgh.

We lodged in a little narrow lane, near the Queen in the Backgate, with a small quaint garden plot behind; there would be pears in season, and many of them, ripening against these stone walls. The pears of the Border are famous. Our landlady was removed from Yetholm only a generation. Yetholm is the gipsy capital of this countryside. And we wondered whether Meg Faa, for so she ambitiously called herself, by the royal name of Scottish Romany, was descended from Meg Merrilies. Mrs. Faa had dark flashing eyes in a thin dark face, and they flashed like a two-edged dagger. She was a small woman, scarce taller than a

JEDBURGH ABBEY.

Jethart ax as we had seen them in the museum at Kelso. I should never have dared to ask her about anything, not even the time of day, and, in truth, like many of the Scotch women, she had a gift of impressive silence. All the night I had a self-conscious feeling that something was going to happen in this town of Jed, and in the morning when I met Mrs. Faa again and her eyes rather than her voice challenged me as to how I had slept, I should not have dared admit that I slept with one eye open lest I become one more of the permanent ghosts of Jed.

The Abbey is, in its way, its individual way, most interesting of the chief four of "St. David's piles." It is beautifully lodged, beside the Jed, near the stream, and the stream more a part of its landscape; smooth-shaven English lawns lie all about, a veritable ecclesiastical close. It is simpler than Melrose, if the detail is not so marvelous, and there is substantially more of it. The Norman tower stands square; if witches still dance on it they choose their place for security. The long walls of the nave suggest almost a restoration—almost.

When the Abbey flourished, and when Alexander III was king, he was wedded here (1285) to Joleta, daughter of the French Count de Dreux. Always French and Scotch have felt a kinship, and often expressed it in royal marriage. The gray abbey walls, then a century and a half old, must have looked curiously down on this gay wedding throng which so possessed the place, so dispossessed the monks, Austin friars come from the abbey of St. Quentin at Beauvais.

Suddenly, in the midst of the dance, the King reached out his hand to the maiden queen—and Death, the specter, met him with skeleton fingers. It may have been a pageant trick, it may have been a too thoughtful monk; but the thirteenth century was rich with superstition. Six months later Alexander fell from his horse on a stormy night on the Fife coast—and the prophetic omen was remembered, or constructed.

The Abbey was newly in ruin when Mary Queen rode down this way, only twenty-one years after Hertford's hurtful raid. Court was to be held here, the assizes of October, 1566, at this Border town. For the Border had been over-lively and was disputing the authority of the Scottish queen as though it had no loyalty. Bothwell had been sent down as Warden of the Marches to quell the marauding free-booters.

He had met with Little Jock Elliott, a Jethart callant, a Border bandit, to whom we can forgive much, because of the old ballad.

"My castle is aye my ain,
  An' herried it never shall be;
For I maun fa' ere it's taen,
  An' wha daur meddle wi' me?
Wi' my kuit in the rib o' my naig,
  My sword hangin' doun by my knee,
For man I am never afraid,
  An' wha daur meddle wi' me?
    Wha daur meddle wi' me,
    Wha daur meddle wi' me?
    Oh, my name is little Jock Elliott,
    An' wha daur meddle wi' me?

"I munt my gude naig wi' a will
  When the fray's in the wind, an' he
Cocks his lugs as he tugs for the hill
  That enters the south countrie,
Where pricking and spurring are rife,
  And the bluid boils up like the sea,
But the Southrons gang doon i' the strife,
  An' wha daur meddle wi' me?"

And perhaps we can forgive the reiver, since he dealt a blow to Bothwell that those of us who love Mary have longed to strike through the long centuries. Bothwell took Elliott in custody, Elliott not suspecting that a Scot could prove treacherous like a Southron, and was carrying him to the Hermitage. Jock asked pleasantly what would be his fate at the assize.

"Gif ane assyises wald mak him elene, he was hertlie contentit, but he behuvit to pas to the Quenis grace."

This was little promise to little Jock Elliott. He fled. Bothwell chased. Bothwell fired, wounded Jock, overtook him, and Jock managed to give Bothwell three vicious thrusts of his skene dhu—"Wha daur meddle wi' me!"—before Bothwell's whinger drove death into little Jock Elliott.

Bothwell, wounded, perhaps to death, so word went up to Edinburgh, was carried to the Hermitage.

Buchanan, the scandalous chronicler of the time—there were such in Scotland, then, and always for Mary—set down that "when news thereof was brought to Borthwick to the Queen, she flingeth away in haste like a madwoman by great journeys in post, in the sharp time of winter, first to Melrose, and then to Jedworth."

It happened to be the crisp, lovely, truly Scottish time, October, and Mary opened court at Jedburgh October 9, presiding at the meetings of the Privy Council, and then rode to the Hermitage October 16. She rode with an escort which included the Earl of Moray, the Earl of

HERMITAGE CASTLE.

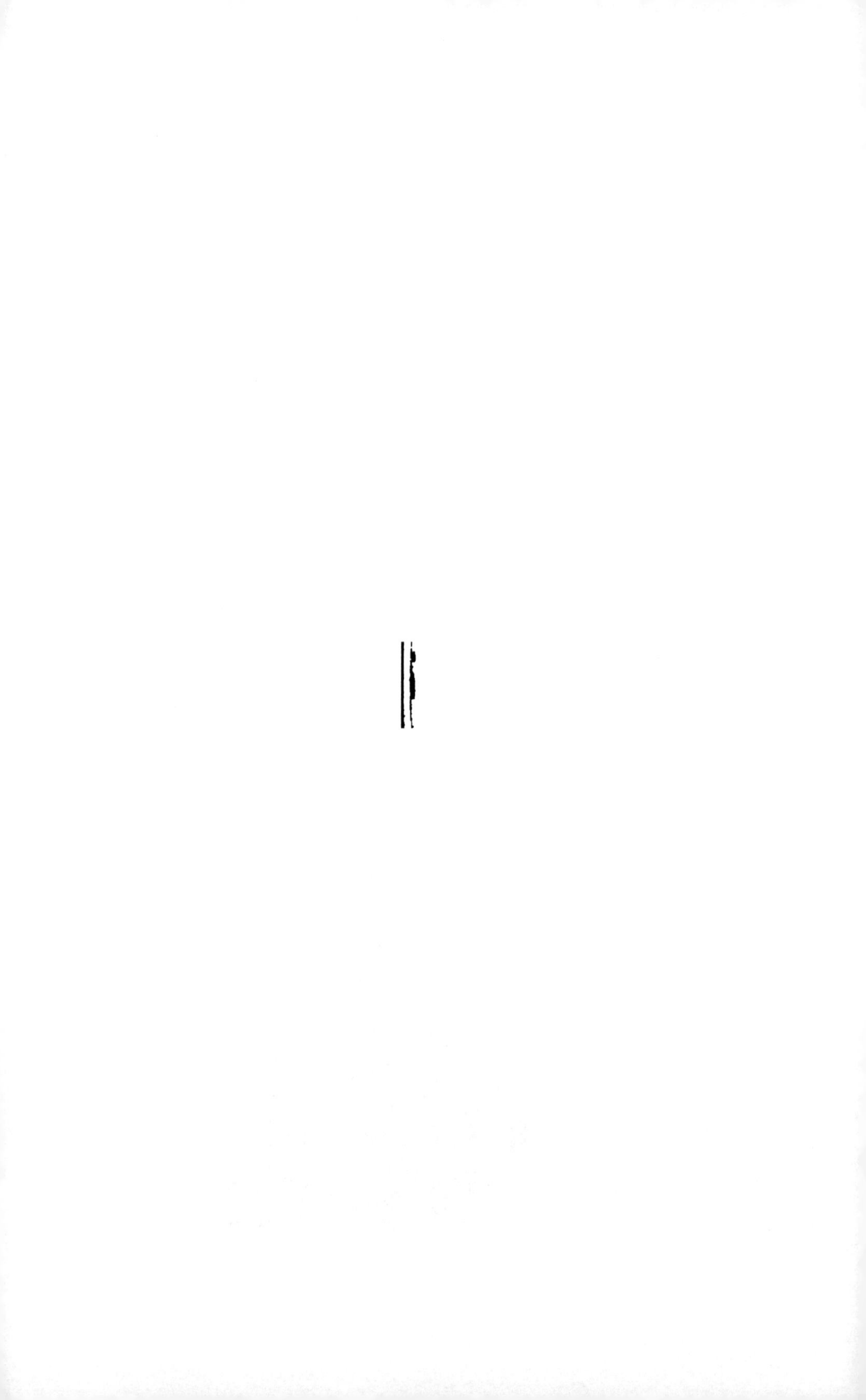

Huntley, Mr. Secretary Lethington, and more men of less note. For six days the girl queen (Mary was only twenty-four in this year of the birth of James, year before the death of Darnley, the marriage with Bothwell, the imprisonment at Loch Leven) had been mewed to state affairs, and a ride through the brown October woods, thirty miles there and thirty miles back again, must have lured the queen who was always keen for adventure, whether Bothwell was the goal, or just adventure.

The mist of the morning turned to thick rain by night, and the return ride was made in increasing wet and darkness. Once, riding ahead and alone and rapidly, the Queen strayed from the trail, was bogged in a mire, known to-day as the Queen's Mire, and rescued with difficulty.

Next day Mary lay sick at Jedburgh, a sickness of thirty days, nigh unto death. News was sent to Edinburgh, and bells were rung, and prayers offered in St. Giles. On the ninth day she lay unconscious, in this little town of Jedburgh, apparently dead, twenty years before Fotheringay. "Would God I had died at Jedburgh."

She did not die. Darnley visited her one day, coming from Glasgow. Bothwell came as soon as he could be moved, and the two made convalescence together in this old house of Jedburgh, perhaps the happiest house of all those where the legend of Mary persists. Even to-day it has its charm. The windowed turret looks out on the large fruit garden that stretches down to the Jed, very like that very little turret of "Queen Mary's Lookout" at Roscoff where the child queen had landed in France less than twenty years before.

Five years later, when Mary was in an English prison, a proclamation was read in her name at the town cross of Jedburgh, the herald was roughly handled by the Provost who received his orders from England, and Buccleuch and Ker of Fernihurst revenged themselves by hanging ten loyal (?) citizens who stood with the Provost.

Later, a century later, when at the town cross the magistrates were drinking a health to the new sovereign, a well-known Jacobite came by. They insisted on his joining in the toast. And he pledged—"confusion to King William, and the restitution of our sovereign and the heir!" Bravo, the Borderers!

Selkirk

The sentimental journeymen—with whom I count myself openly—may hesitate to visit Yarrow. It lies so near the Melrose country, and is so much a part of that, in song and story, that it would seem like leaving out the fragrance of the region to omit Yarrow. And yet—. One has read "Yarrow Unvisited," one of the loveliest of Wordsworth's poems. And one has read "Yarrow Visited." And the conclusion is too easy that if the unvisitings and visitings differ as much as the poems it surely were better not to "turn aside to Yarrow," to accept it as

> "Enough if in our hearts we know
> There's such a place as Yarrow. . . .
> For when we're there although 'tis fair,
> 'Twill be another Yarrow."

There is peril at times in making a dream come true, in translating the dream into reality, in lifting the mists from the horizon of imagination. Should one hear an English skylark, an Italian nightingale? should one see Carcassonne, should one visit Yarrow?

Ah, welladay. I have heard, I have seen.

Just at first, because no dream can ever quite come true, not the dream of man in stone, or of song in bird-throat, or even of nature in trees and sky and hills, there is a disappointment. But after the reality these all slip away into the misty half-remembered things, even Carcassonne, even Yarrow; the dream enriched by the vision, the vision softened again into dream.

And so, I will down into Yarrow.

Coaches run, or did before the war, and will after the war, through the pleasant dales of Yarrow and Moffat, dales which knew battles long ago and old unhappy far off things, but very silent now, too silent; almost one longs for a burst of Border warfare that the quiet may be filled with fitting clamour. The coaches meet at Tibbie Shiel's on St. Mary's and it is to Tibbie's that you are bound, as were so many gallant gentlemen, especially literary gentlemen, before you.

Selkirk is the starting point. And Selkirk is a very seemly, very prosperous town, looking not at all like an ecclesiastic city, as it started to be in the dear dead days of David the saint, looking very much as a hill city in Italy will look some day when Italy becomes entirely "redeemed" and modern, and exists for itself instead of for the tourist. Selkirk is indifferent to tourists, as indeed is every Scottish town; Scotland and Scotsmen are capable of existing for themselves. Selkirk hangs against the hillside above the Ettrick, and its show places are few; the spot where Montrose lodged the night before the defeat at Philipshaugh, the statue of Scott when he was sheriff, "shirra," the statue of Mungo Park near where he was given his medical training, and the home of Andrew Lang.

There is no trace of the "kirk o' the shielings," founded by the religious from Iona, from which by way of Scheleschyrche came Selkirk. Nor is there trace of Davis's pile, ruined or unruined, in this near, modern, whirring city. It is the sound of the looms one remembers in Selkirk, making that infinity of yards of Scotch tweed to clothe the world. Selkirk and Galashiels and Hawick form the Glasgow of the Border.

Always industrious, in the time of Flodden it was the "souters of Selkirk" who marched away to the Killing—

"Up wi' the Souters of Selkirk
And down wi' the Earl o' Home."

These same souters—shoemakers—were busy in the time of Prince Charles Edward and contracted to furnish two thousand pair of shoes to his army; but one does not inquire too closely into whether they furnished any quota of the four thousand feet to go therein.

It was a warm sunny day when I made my pilgrimage up the Yarrow to St. Mary's. Although Yarrow has always sung in my ears, I think it was rather to see one sight that I came for the first time to Scotland, to see

> "The swan on still St. Mary's Lake
> Float double, swan and shadow."

I rather think it was for this I had journeyed across the Atlantic and up the East coast route. Such a sentimental lure would I follow. But then, if that seems wasteful and ridiculous excess of sentiment, let us be canny enough, Scotch enough, to admit that one sees so many other things, incidentally.

The "wan waters" of the Yarrow were shimmering, glimmering, in the morning light as I coached out of Selkirk, and by Carterhaugh.

> "I forbid ye, maidens a',
> That wear gowd in your hair,
> To come or gae by Carterhaugh;
> For young Tamlane is there."

These round-shouldered hills, once covered with the Wood of Caledon, and the Forest of

Ettrick, and the Forest of Yarrow, are very clear and clean in their green lawns to-day, scarce an ancient tree or a late descendant standing; here and there only gnarled and deformed, out of the centuries, out of perhaps that "derke forest" of James IV. His son, the Fifth James, thought to subdue the Border and increase his revenue by placing thousands of sheep in this forest; and these ruining the trees have decreased the tourists' rightful revenue. It is because of this absence of trees that one is perhaps more conscious of the shining ribbon of river; longer, clearer stretches may be seen in the green plain:

"And is this—Yarrow? This the stream
  Of which my fancy cherished
So faithfully a waking dream?
  An image that has perished!
O that some minstrel's harp were near
  To utter notes of gladness,
And chase this silence from the air
  That fills my heart with sadness!"

About Philipshaugh, two miles from Selkirk, the trees are in something of large estate, with oak and birch and fir and rowan, making dark shadows in the fair morning, as the historically minded traveler would fain have it. For it was there that Montrose met defeat, his small band against Leslie's many men. All about there lie legends of his fight and his flight across the Minchmoor and on to the North.

And through here Scott loved to wander. Here he let the Minstrel begin his Last Lay—

> "He paused where Newark's stately Tower
> Looks down from Yarrow's birchen bower."

And it was hither the Scotch poet came with Wordsworth, as the English poet describes it—

> "Once more by Newark's Castle gate
> Long left without a warder,
> I stood, looked, listened, and with Thee
> Great Minstrel of the Border."

Nearby, and near the highways, is the deserted farm cottage, the birthplace of Mungo Park, who traveled about the world even as you and I, and I fancy his thought must often have returned to the Yarrow.

The driver will point out the Trench of Wallace, a redout a thousand feet long, on the height to the North; and here will come into the Border memories of another defender of Scotland who seems rather to belong to the North and West.

Soon we reach the Kirk of Yarrow, a very austere "reformed" looking basilica, dating back to 1640, which was a reformed date, set among pleasant gardens and thick verdure.

NEWARK CASTLE.

Scott and Wordsworth and Hogg have worshiped here, and from its ceiling the heraldic devices of many Borderers speak a varied history.

Crossing the bridge we are swiftly, unbelievingly, on the Dowie Dens of Yarrow.

> "Yestreen I dream'd a dolefu' dream;
> I fear there will be sorrow!
> I dream'd I pu'd the heather green,
> Wi' my true love on Yarrow.
>
> "But in the glen strive armed men;
> They've wrought me dole and sorrow;
> They've slain—the comeliest knight they've slain—
> He bleeding lies on Yarrow.
>
> "She kiss'd his cheek, she kaim'd his hair,
> She search'd his wounds all thorough;
> She kiss'd them till her lips grew red,
> On the dowie houms of Yarrow."

Then we come into the country of Joseph Hogg. The farm where he was tenant and failed, for Hogg was a shepherd and a poet, which means a wanderer and a dreamer. And soon to the Gordon Arms, a plain rambling cement structure, where Hogg and Scott met by appointment and took their last walk together.

Hogg is the spirit of all the Ettrick place. Can you not hear his skylark—"Bird of the wilderness, blithesome and cumberless"—in that far blue sky above Altrive, where he died —"Oh, to abide in the desert with thee!"

And now the driver tells us we are at the Douglass Glen, up there to the right lies the shattered keep of the good Lord James Douglass, the friend of Bruce. Here fell the "Douglass Tragedy," and the bridle path from Yarrow to Tweed is still to be traced.

> "O they rade on and on they rade,
> And a' by the light of the moon,
> Until they came to yon wan water,
> And there they lighted down."

St. Mary's

And soon we are at St. Mary's Loch—which we have come to see. To one who comes from a land of lakes, from the Land of the Sky Blue Water, there must be at first a sudden rush of disappointment. This is merely a lake, merely a stretch of water. The hills about are all barren, rising clear and round against the sky. They fold and infold as though they would shield the lake bereft of trees, as though they would shut out the world. Here and there, but very infrequent, is a cluster of trees; for the most part it is water and sky and green heathery

INTERIOR VIEW, TIBBIE SHIEL'S INN.

hills. The water is long and narrow, a small lake as our American lakes go, three miles by one mile; but large as it looms in romance, rich as it bulks in poetry.

Tibbie Shiel's is, of course, our goal. One says Tibbie Shiel's, as one says Ritz-Carlton, or the William the Conqueror at Dives. For this is the most celebrated inn in all Scotland, and it must be placed with the celebrated inns of the world. There is no countryside better sung than this which lies about St. Mary's, and no inn, certainly not anywhere a country inn, where more famous men have foregathered to be themselves. Perhaps the place has changed since the most famous, the little famed days, when Scott stopped here after a day's hunting, deer or Border song and story, up Meggatdale; and those famous nights of Christopher North and the Ettrick shepherd, nights deserving to be as famous as the Arabian or Parisian or London. The world has found it out, and times have changed, as a local poet complains—

"Sin a' the world maun gang
And picnic at St. Mary's."

The inn, a rambling white house, stands on a strip between two waters, added to no doubt since Tibbie first opened its doors, but the closed beds are still there—it was curious enough to see them the very summer that the Graham Moffatts played "Bunty" and "The Closed Bed"—and the brasses which Tibbie polished with such housewifely care.

For Tibbie was a maid in the household of the Ettrick shepherd's mother. She married, she had children, she came here to live. Then her husband died, and quite accidentally Tibbie became hostess to travelers, nearly a hundred years ago. For fifty-four years Tibbie herself ran this inn; she died in what is so short a time gone, as Scottish history goes, in 1878.

During that time hosts of travelers, partienlarly, wandered through the Border, came to this "wren's nest" as North called it. Hogg, of course, was most familiar, and here he wished to have a "bit monument to his memory in some quiet spot forninst Tibbie's dwelling." He sits there, in free stone, somewhat heavily, a shepherd's staff in his right hand, and in his left a scroll carrying the last line from the "Queen's Wake"—"Hath tayen the wandering winds to sing."

Edward Irving, walking from Kirkcaldy to Annan, was here the first year after Tibbie opened her doors so shyly. Carlyle, walking from Ecclefechan to Edinburgh, in his student days, caught his first glimpse of Yarrow from here—and slept, may it be, in one of these closed beds? Gladstone was here in the early '40's during a Midlothian campaign. Dr. John Brown—"Rab"—came later, and even R. L. S. knew the hospitality of Tibbie Shiel's when Tibbie was still hostess.

It is a long list and a brave one. In this very dining-room they ate simply and abundantly, after the day's work; in this "parlour" they continued their talk. And surely St. Mary's Lake was the same.

Down on the shore there stands a group of trees, not fir trees, though these are most native here. And here we loafed the afternoon away —for fortunately we were the only ones who "picnic at St. Mary's." There were the gentleman and his wife whom we took for journalistic folk, they were so worldly and so intelligent and discussed the world and the possibilities of world-war—that was several years ago—until at the Kirk of Yarrow the local minister, Dr. Borlund, uncovered this minister, James Thomson, from Paisley. If all the clergy of Scotland should become as these, austerity of reform would go and the glow of culture would come.

We all knew our history and our poetry of

this region, but none so well as the minister. It was he who recited from Marmion that description which is still so accurate—

"By lone St. Mary's silent Lake;
Thou know'st it well—nor fen nor sedge
Pollute the clear lake's crystal edge;
Abrupt and sheer the mountains sink
At once upon the level brink;
And just a trace of silver strand
Marks where the water meets the land.
Far in the mirror, bright and blue,
Each hill's huge outline you may view;
Shaggy with heath, but lonely, bare,
Nor tree nor bush nor brake is there,
Save where of land, yon silver line
Bears thwart the lake the scatter'd pine.
Yet even this nakedness has power,
And aids the feelings of the hour;
Nor thicket, dell nor copse you spy,
Where living thing conceal'd might lie;
Not point, retiring, hides a dell
Where swain, or woodman lone might dwell;
There's nothing left to fancy's guess,
You see that all is loneliness;
And silence aids—though the steep hills
Send to the lake a thousand rills;
In summer time, so soft they weep.
The sound but lulls the ear asleep;
Your horse's hoof-tread sounds too rude,
So stilly is the solitude."

Across the water is the old graveyard of vanished St. Mary's kirk. And it was the low-

ST. MARY'S LAKE.

voiced minister's wife—a Babbie a little removed—who knew

> "What boon to lie, as now I lie,
> And see in silver at my feet
> St. Mary's Lake, as if the sky
> Had fallen 'tween those hills so sweet,
> And this old churchyard on the hill,
> That keeps the green graves of the dead,
> So calm and sweet, so lone and wild still,
> And but the blue sky overhead."

We sat in the silences, the still silent afternoon, conscious of the folk verse that goes—

> "St. Mary's Loch lies shimmering still,
> But St. Mary's kirkbell's lang dune ringing."

Suddenly, over the far rim of the water, my eye caught something white, and then another, and another. And I knew well that were I but nearer, as imagination knew was unnecessary, I might see the swan on still St. Mary's Lake, and their shadow breaking in the water.

CHAPTER IV

THE EMPRESS OF THE NORTH

I SUPPOSE the Scotsman who has been born in Edinburgh may have a pardonable reluctance in praising the town, may hesitate in appraising it; Stevenson did; Scott did not. And I suppose if one cannot trace his ancestry back to Edinburgh, or nearly there, but must choose some of the other capitals of the world as his ancestral city, one might begrudge estate to Edinburgh.

I have none of these hesitations, am hampered by none of these half and half ways. Being an American, with half a dozen European capitals to choose from if I must, and having been born in an American capital which is among the loveliest—I think the loveliest—I dare choose Edinburgh as my dream city. I dare fling away my other capital claims, and all modification, ever Scotch moderation, to declare without an "I think" or "they say," Edinburgh is the most beautiful, the most romantic, the singular city of the world.

Those who come out of many generations of migration grow accustomed to choosing their quarter of the world; they have come from many countries and through nomadic ancestors for a century, or two, or three. And perhaps they, themselves, have migrated from one state to another, one city to another. Every American has had these phases, has suffered the sea change and the land. Surely then he may adopt his ancestral capital, as correctly as he adopts his present political capital.

It shall be Edinburgh. And while Constantinople and Rio and Yokohama may be splendid for situation, they have always something of foreign about them, they can never seem to touch our own proper romance, to have been the setting for our play. Edinburgh is as lovely, and then, the chalice of romance has been lifted for centuries on the high altar of her situation.

Edinburgh is a small city, as modern cities go; but I presume it has many thousands of population, hundreds of thousands. If it were Glasgow numbers would be important, fixative. But Edinburgh has had such a population through the centuries that to cast its total with only that of the souls now living within her precincts were to leave out of the picture those shadowy and yet brilliant, ever present generations, who seem all to jostle each other on her High street, without respect to generations, if there is very decided respect of simple toward gentle.

Edinburgh is, curiously, significantly, divided and scarce united, into Old Town and New Town. And yet, the Old Town with its ancient *lands* so marvelously like modern tenements, and its poverty which is of no date and therefore no responsibility of ours, is neither dead nor deserted, and is still fully one-half the town. While New Town, looking ever up to the old, looking across the stretch to Leith, and to the sea whence came so much threatening in the old days, and with its memories of Hume and Scott who are ancient, and of Stevenson, who, in spite of his immortal youth, does begin to belong to another generation than ours —New Town also, to a new American, is something old. It has all become Edinburgh, two perfect halves of a whole which is not less perfect for the imperfect uniting.

There is no city which can be so "observed." I venture that when you have stood on Castle Hill—on the High Street with its narrow opening between the *lands* framing near and far pictures—on Calton Hill—when you have been able to "rest and be thankful" at Corstorphine Hill—when you have climbed the Salisbury crags—when you have mounted to Arthur's Seat and looked down as did King Arthur before there was an Edinburgh—you will believe that not any slightest corner but fills the eye and soul.

There is, of course, no single object in Edinburgh to compare with objects of traveler's interest farther south. The castle is not the Tower, Holyrood is a memory beside Windsor, St. Giles is no Canterbury, St. Mary's is not St. Paul's, the Royal Scottish art gallery is meager indeed, notwithstanding certain rare riches in comparison with the National. But still one may believe of any of these superior objects, as T. Sandys retorted to Shovel when they had played the game of matching the splendours of Thrums with those of London and Shovel had named Saint Paul's, and Tommy's list of native wonders was exhausted, but never Tommy—"it would like to be in Thrums!" All these lesser glories go to make up the singular glory which is Edinburgh.

The Castle

And there is the castle. Nowhere in all the world is castle more strategically set to guard the city and to guard the memories of the city and the beauty.

For the castle is Edinburgh. It stood there, stalwart in the plain, thousands and thousands of years ago, this castle hill which invited a castle as soon as man began to fortify himself. It has stood here a thousand years as the bulwark of man against man. Certain it will stand there a thousand years to come. And after—after man has destroyed and been destroyed, or when he determines that like night and the sea there shall be no more destruction. Castle Hill is immortal.

Always it has been the resort of kings and princes. First it was the keep of princesses, far back in Pictish days before Christian time, this "Castell of the Maydens." From 987 B. C. down to 1566, when Mary was lodged here for safe keeping in order that James might be born safe and royal, the castle has had royalties in its keeping. It has kept them rather badly in truth. While many kings have been born here,

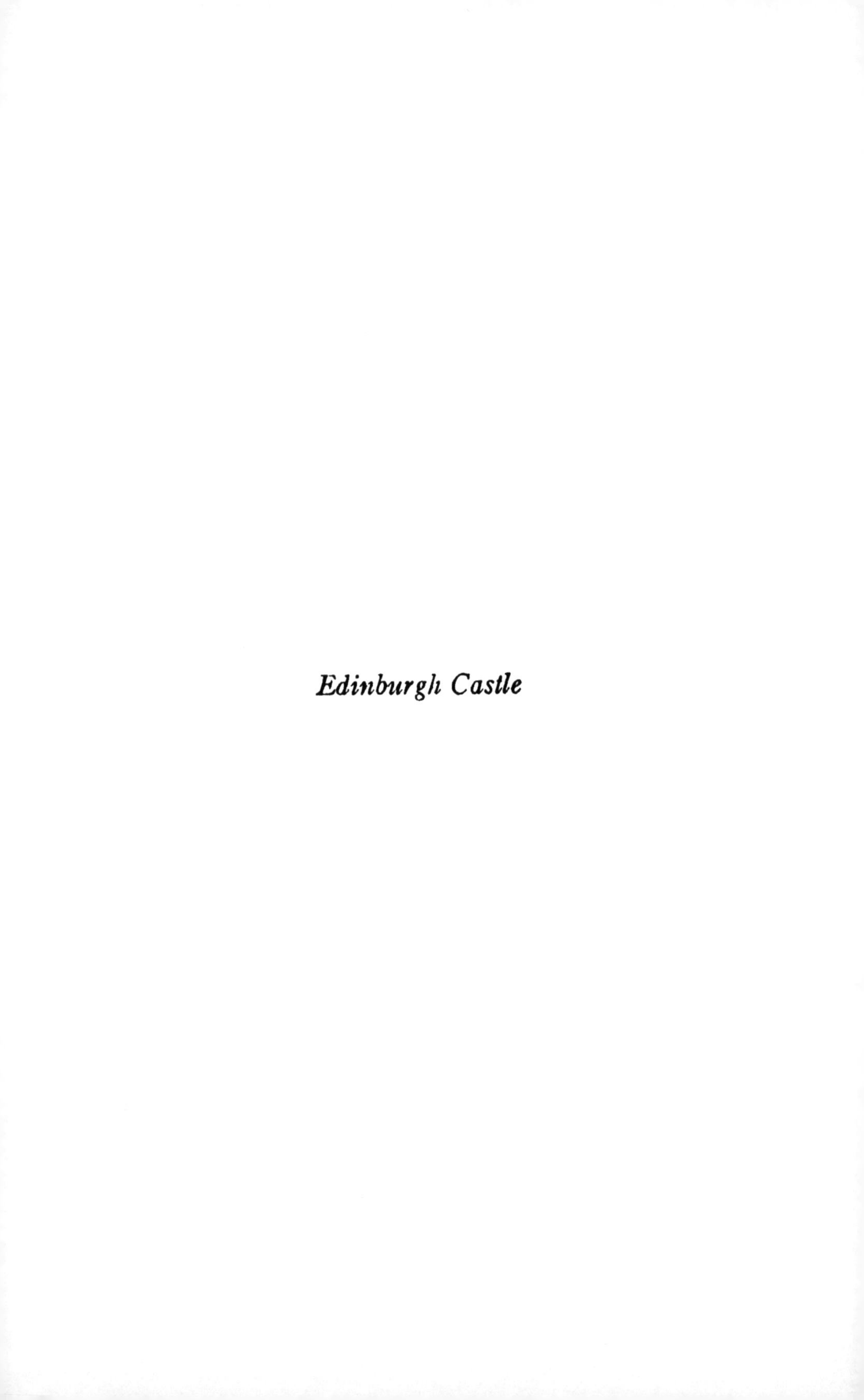

Edinburgh Castle

few kings have died in its security; almost all Scottish kings have died tragically, almost all Scottish kings have died young, and left their kingdom to some small prince whose regents held him in this castle for personal security, while they governed the realm, always to its disaster.

There is not one of the Stewart kings, one of the Jameses, from First to Sixth, who did not come into the heritage of the kingdom as a baby, a youth; even the Fourth, who rebelled against his father and won the kingdom—and wore a chain around his body secretly for penance. And these baby kings and stripling princes have been lodged in the castle for safe keeping, prologues to the swelling act of the imperial theme.

History which attempts to be exact begins the castle in the seventh century, when Edwin of Deira fortified the place and called it Edwin's burgh. It was held by Malcolm Canmore, of whom and of his Saxon queen Margaret, Dunfermline tells a fuller story; held against rebels and against English, until Malcolm fell at Alnwick, and Margaret, dead at hearing the news, was carried secretly out of the castle by her devoted and kingly sons.

After Edward I took the castle, for half a

century it was variously held by the English as a Border fortress. Once Bruce retook it, a stealthy night assault, up the cliffs of the west, and The Bruce razed it. Rebuilt by the Third Edward, it was taken from this king by a clever ruse planned by the Douglass, Black Knight of Liddesdale. A shipload of wine and biscuits came into harbour, and the unsuspecting castellan, glad to get such precious food in the far north, purchased it all and granted delivery at dawn next morning. The first cart load upset under the portcullis, the gate could not be closed, the cry "A Douglass," was raised, and the castle entered into Scottish keeping, never to be "English" again until the Act of Union.

Henry IV and Richard II attempted it, but failed. Richard III entered it as friend. For three years it was held for Mary by Kirkcaldy, while the city was disloyal. Charles I held it longer than he held England, and Cromwell claimed it in person as part of the Protectorate. Prince Charles, the Third, could not take it, contented himself with the less castellated, more palatial joys, of Holyrood; a preference he shared with his greatest grandmother.

To-day perhaps its defense might be battered down, as some one has suggested, "from the Firth by a Japanese cruiser." But it looks like a Gibraltar, and it keeps impregnably the treasures of the past; as necessary a defense, I take it, as of any material treasure of the present.

If you are a king you must wait to enter; summons must be made to the Warder, and it must be certain you are the king; even Edward VII, most Stewart of recent kings had to prove himself not Edward I, not English, but "Union." If you are a commoner you know no such difficulties.

First you linger on the broad Esplanade where a regiment in kilts is drilling, perhaps the Black Watch, the Scots Greys. No doubt of late it has been tramped by regiments of the "First Hundred Thousand" and later, in training for the wars.

As an American you linger here in longer memory. For when Charles was king—the phrase sounds recent to one who is eternally Jacobite—this level space was a part of Nova Scotia, and the Scotsmen who were made nobles with estates in New Scotland were enfeoffed on this very ground. So close were the relations between old and new, so indifferent were the men of adventuring times toward space.

Or, you linger here to recall when Cromwell

was burned in effigy, along with "his friend the Devil."

You pass through the gate, where no wine casks block the descent of the portcullis, and the castle is entered. There are three or four points of particular interest.

Queen Margaret's chapel, the oldest and smallest religious house in Scotland, a tiny place indeed, where Margaret was praying when word was brought of the death of Malcolm in battle, and she, loyal and royal soul, died the very night while the enemies from the Highlands, like an army of Macbeth's, surrounded the castle. The place is quite authentic, Saxon in character with Norman touches. I know no place where a thousand years can be so swept away, and Saxon Margaret herself seems to kneel in the perpetual dim twilight before the chancel.

There is Mons Meg, a monstrous gun indeed, pointing its mouth toward the Forth, as though it were the guardian of Scotland. A very pretentions gun, which was forged for James II, traveled to the sieges of Dumbarton and of Norham, lifted voice in salute to Mary in France on her marriage to the Dauphin, was captured by Cromwell and listed as "the great iron murderer, Muckle Meg," and "split its throat" in

MONS MEG.

saluting the Duke of York in 1682, a most Jacobite act of loyalty. After the Rising of the Forty Five this gun was taken to London, as though to take it from Scotland were to take the defense from Jacobitism. But Sir Walter Scott, restoring Scotland, and being in much favour with George IV, secured the return of Mons Meg. It was as though a prince of the realm has returned. Now, the great gun, large enough to shoot men for ammunition, looks, silently but sinisterly, out over the North Sea.

History comes crowding its events in memory when one enters Old Parliament Hall. It is fitly ancestral, a noble hall with an open timbered roof of great dignity, with a collection of armour and equipment that particularly reequips the past. And in this hall, under this roof, what splendour, what crime! Most criminal, the "black dinner" given to the Black Douglasses to their death. Unless one should resent the dinner given by Leslie to Cromwell, when there was no black bull's head served.

By a secret stair, which commoners and Jacobites may use to-day, communication was had with the Royal Lodgings, and often must Queen Mary have gone up and down those stairs, carrying the tumult of her heart, the perplexity of her kingdom; for Mary was both woman and sovereign.

The Royal Lodgings contain Queen Mary's Rooms, chiefly; the other rooms are negligible. It is a tiny bedchamber, too small to house the eager soul of Mary, but very well spaced for the niggard soul of James. One merely accepts historically the presence of Mary here; there is too much intertwining of "H" and "M." No Jacobite but divorces Darnley from Mary, even though he would not effect divorce with gunpowder. King James I, when he returned fourteen years after to the place where he was VI, made a pilgrimage to his own birthroom on June 19, 1617. I suppose he found the narrow space like unto the Majesty that doth hedge a king.

Mary must have beat her heart against these walls as an eagle beats wings against his cage. She never loved the place. Who could love it who must live in it? It was royally hung; she made it fit for living, with carpets from Turkey, chairs and tables from France, gold hangings that were truly gold for the bed, and many tapestries with which to shut out the cold—eight pictures of the Judgment of Paris; four pictures of the Triumph of Virtue!

Here she kept her library, one hundred and

fifty-three precious volumes—where are they now? "The Queen readeth daily after her dinner," wrote Randolph, English envoy, to his queen, "instructed by a learned man, Mr. George Buchanan, somewhat of Lyvie."

And I wondered if here she wrote that Prayer which but the other day I came upon in the bookshop of James Thin, copied into a book of a hundred years back, in a handwriting that has something of Queen Mary's quality in it—

"O Domine Deus!
Speravi in te;
O care mi Iesu!
Nunc libera me:
In dura catena,
In misera poena
Desidero te;
Languendo, gemendo,
Et genuflectendo
Adoro, imploro,
Ut liberes me!"

Her windows looked down across the city toward Holyrood. Almost she must have heard John Knox thunder in the pulpit of St. Giles, and thunder against her. And, directly beneath far down she saw the Grassmarket. Sometimes it flashed with gay tournament folk; for before and during Mary's time all the world came to measure lances in Edinburgh. Sometimes it swarmed with folk come to watch an execution; in the next century it was filled in the "Killing Time," with Covenanter mob applauding the execution of Royalists, with Royalist mob applauding the execution of Covenanters; Mary's time was not the one "to glorify God in the Grassmarket."

At the top of the market, near where the West Bow leads up to the castle, was the house of Claverhouse, who watched the killings. At the bottom of the market was the West Port through which Bonnie Dundee rode away.

"To the Lords of Convention, 'twas Claverhouse spoke,
Ere the king's crown go down there are crowns to be broke,
So each cavalier who loves honour and me,
Let him follow the bonnet of Bonnie Dundee.
Come fill up my cup, come fill up my can,
Come saddle my horses and call up my men,
Fling all your gates open, and let me gae free,
For 'tis up with the bonnets of Bonnie Dundee."

And to-day, but especially on Saturday nights, if you care to take your life, or your peace in hand, you can join a strange and rather awful multitude as it swarms through the Grassmarket, more and more drunken as midnight comes on, and not less or more drunken than the mob which hanged Captain Porteous.

It is a decided relief to look down and find

the White Hart Inn, still an inn, where Dorothy and William Wordsworth lodged, on Thursday night, September 15, 1803—"It was not noisy, and tolerably cheap. Drank tea, and walked up to the Castle."

The Cowgate was a fashionable suburb in Mary's time. A canon of St. Andrews wrote in 1530, "nothing is humble or lowly, everything magnificent." On a certain golden gray afternoon I had climbed to Arthur's Seat to see the city through the veil of mist—

> "I saw rain falling and the rainbow drawn
> On Lammermuir. Harkening I heard again
> In my precipitous city beaten bells
> Winnow the keen sea wind."

It was late, gathering dusk and rain, when I reached the level and thinking to make a short cut—this was once the short cut to St. Cuthbert's from Holyrood—I ventured into the Cowgate, and wondered at my own temerity. Stevenson reports, "One night I went along the Cowgate after every one was a-bed but the policeman." Well, if Scott liked to "put a cocked hat on a story," Stevenson liked to put it on his own adventures. The Cowgate, in dusk rain, is adventure enough.

Across the height lies Greyfriar's. The church is negligible, the view from there superb, the place historic. One year after Jenny Geddes threw her stool in St. Giles and started the Reformation—doesn't it sound like Mrs. O'Leary's cow?—the Covenant was signed (Feb. 28, 1638) on top of a tomb still shown, hundreds pressing to the signing, some signing with their blood. The Reformation was on, not to be stopped until all Scotland was harried and remade.

I like best to think that in this churchyard, on a rainy Sunday, Scott met a charming girl, fell in love with her, took her home under his umbrella, and, did not marry her—his own romance!

Because no king shall ever wear the crown again, nor wave the scepter, nor wield the sword of state, the Regalia, housed in the Crown Room, and guarded from commoner and king by massive iron grating, is more interesting than any other appanage of royalty in the world. The crown which was worn by Bruce, and which sat rather uneasily on the very unsteady head of Charles II at what time he was crowned at Scone and was scolded, is of pure gold and much bejeweled. The scepter, made in Paris for James V, carries a beryl, come from Egypt three thousand years ago, or, from a Druid priest in the mist of time. The sword

GREYFRIARS' CHURCHYARD.

was a gift from Pope Julius to James IV; in those days the Scottish sovereign was surely the "Most Catholic Majesty."

England has no ancient regalia; hers were thrown into the melting pot by Cromwell. The Protector—and Destructor—would fain have grasped these "Honours," but they were spirited away, and later concealed in the castle. Here they remained a hundred and ten years, sealed in a great oak chest. The rumour increased that they had gone to England. And finally Sir Walter Scott secured an order from George IV to open the chest (Feb. 4, 1818).

It was a tremendous moment to Scott. Could he restore the Honours as well as the country? There they lay, crown of The Bruce, scepter of James V, sword of Pope and King. The castle guns thundered—how Mons Meg must have regretted her lost voice!

And still we can hear the voice of Scott, when a commissioner playfully lifted the crown as if to place it on the head of a young lady near—"No, by God, no!" Never again shall this crown rest on any head. That is assured in a codicil to the Act of Union. And—it may be that other crowns shall in like manner gain a significance when they no longer rest on uneasy heads.

The view from the King's bastion is royal. Where is there its superior? And only its rival from Calton Hill, from Arthur's Seat. The Gardens lie below, the New Town spreads out, the city runs down to Leith, the Firth shines and carries on its bosom the Inchkeith and the May; the hills of Fife rampart the North; the Highlands with Ben Lomond for sentinel form the purple West; and south are the Braid hills and the heathery Pentlands—the guide has pointed through a gap in the castle wall to the hills and to the cottage at Swanston.

"City of mists and rain and blown gray spaces,
Dashed with the wild wet colour and gleam of tears,
Dreaming in Holyrood halls of the passionate faces
Lifted to one Queen's face that has conquered the years.
Are not the halls of thy memory haunted places?
Cometh there not as a moon (where blood-rust sears
Floors a-flutter of old with silks and laces)
Gilding a ghostly Queen thro' the mist of tears?

"Proudly here, with a loftier pinnacled splendour
Throned in his northern Athens, what spells remain
Still on the marble lips of the Wizard, and render
Silent the gazer on glory without a stain!
Here and here, do we whisper with hearts more tender,
Tusitala wandered thro' mist and rain;
Rainbow-eyes and frail and gallant and slender,
Dreaming of pirate isles in a jeweled main.

"Up the Canongate climbeth, cleft a-sunder
Raggedly here, with a glimpse of the distant sea,

Flashed through a crumbling alley, a glimpse of wonder,
  Nay, for the City is throned in Eternity!
Hark! from the soaring castle a cannon's thunder
  Closeth an hour for the world and an æon for me,
Gazing at last from the martial heights whereunder
  Deathless memories roll to an ageless sea."

High Street

If the Baedeker with a cautious reservation, declares Princes Street "Perhaps" the handsomest in Europe, there is no reservation in the guide-book report of Taylor, the "Water Poet," who wrote of the High Street in the early Sixteen Hundreds, "the fairest and goodliest streete that ever my eyes beheld." Surely it was then the most impressive street in the world. Who can escape a sharp impression to-day? It was then the most curious street in the world, and it has lost none of its power to evoke wonder.

A causeway between the castle and Holyrood, a steep ridge lying between the Nor' Loch (where now are the Princes' Gardens) and the Sou' Loch (where now are the Meadows, suburban dwelling) the old height offered the first refuge to those who would fain live under the shadow of the castle. As the castle became more and more the center of the kingdom, dwelling under its shadow became more and more important, if not secure. The mightiest lords of the kingdom built themselves town houses along the causeway. French influence was always strong, and particularly in architecture. So these tall *lands* rose on either side of the long street, their high, many-storied fronts on the High Street, their many more storied backs toward the Lochs. They were, in truth, part of the defense of the town; from their tall stories the enemy, especially the "auld enemy," could be espied almost as soon as from the castle. And the closes, the wynds, those dark tortuous alleys which lead between, and which to-day in their squalor are the most picturesque corners of all Europe, were in themselves means of defense in the old days when cannon were as often of leather as of iron, and guns were new and were little more reaching than arrows, and bludgeons and skene dhus and fists were the final effective weapon when assault was intended to the city.

The ridge divides itself into the Lawnmarket, the High Street, and the Canongate; St. Giles uniting the first two, and the Netherbow port, now removed, dividing the last two.

The Lawnmarket in the old days was near-royal, and within its houses the great nobles lodged, and royalty was often a guest, or a secret guest. The High Street was the business street, centering the life of the city, its trade, its feuds—"a la maniére d'Edimborg" ran the continental saying of fights—its religion, its executions, its burials. The Canongate, outside the city proper and outside the Flodden wall and within the precincts of Holyrood, therefore regarded as under the protection of Holy Church, became the aristocratic quarters of the later Stewarts, of the wealthy nobles of the later day.

I suppose one may spend a lifetime in Edinburgh, with frequent days in the Old Town, wandering the High Street, with the eye never wearying, always discovering the new. And I suppose it would take a lifetime, born in Old Town and of Old Town, to really know the quarter. I am not certain I should care to spend a lifetime here; but I have never and shall never spend sufficient of this life here. It is unsavoury of course; it is slattern, it is squalid, danger lurks in the wynds and drunkenness spreads itself in the closes. If the old warning cry of "Gardey loo!" is no longer heard at ten o' the night, one still has need of the answering "Haud yer hand!" or, your nose. Dr. Samuel

Johnson, walking this street on his first night in Edinburgh, arm in arm with Boswell, declared, "I can smell you in the dark!" No sensitive visitor will fail to echo him to-day. There are drains and sewers, there is modern sanitation in old Edinburgh. But the habits of the centuries are not easily overcome; and the Old Town still smells as though with all the old aroma of the far years. Still, it is high, it is wind-swept—and what of Venice, what of the Latin Quarter, what of Mile End, what of the East Side?

But there is still splendour and power, bequeathed as Taylor said, "from antiquitie to posteritie," in spite of the decline and the decay. If the palace of Mary of Lorraine on Castle Hill is fallen and the doorways are in the Museum—Mary who was mother to Mary Queen, and contemporary worthy to Catherine of Medici—there are still, at the end of the long street, Moray House and Queensberry House. Moray is where Cromwell lodged in 1648, and gave no hint of what was coming in 1649; if he had, history might have been different; to-day Moray House is the United Free Church Training college! Queensberry House is where lived those Queensberry marquises of fighting and sporting renown, and where the Marquis lived

MORAY HOUSE.

who forced through the Act of Union—"There ended an old song"; and now it is the Refuge for the Destitute!

There is still beauty shining through the dust and the cobwebs; here a doorway with bold insignia and exquisite carving, leading to—nowhere; here a bit of painting, Norrie's perhaps, or a remnant of timbered ceiling; and everywhere, now as then—more now than then, since sanitary destruction has had its way here and there—glimpses of the city and the moors and the mountains.

It is invidious to compare, to choose from these closes. Each has its history, its old habitations, its old associations, its particular picturesqueness; Lady Stair's, Baxter's, Byer's, Old Stamp Office, White Horse, and many more.

Through this street what glory that was Scotland has not passed and what degradation, what power has not been displayed and what abasement? To see it now, filled with people and with marching troops in honour of the visiting king, is to get back a little of ancient history, of greater glory. It lends itself to such majesty, dull and deserted as it is for the most part.

When the King came to Edinburgh following

on his coronation, making a pilgrimage of his realm, he came to St. Giles, as has come every sovereign of Scotland, from Malcolm who may have worshiped in the Culdee church, to George in whose honour the chapel of the Thistle and the Rose was unveiled.

> "For noo, unfaithfu' to the Lord
> Auld Scotland joins the rebel horde;
> Her human hymn-books on the board
> She noo displays,
> An' Embro Hie Kirk's been restored
> In popish ways."

On a Sunday morning I hurried to St. Giles to see the trooping of the colours. (Later, listening to Dr. White, in a recently built reformed church on Princes Street, I heard a sermon from the text, "You shall see the king in all his beauty." But, no mention of King George! It was even as it was in the old days.)

In truth it was a brave sight to find the High Street thronged with people, and the regiments marching down from St. Giles to Holyrood. The king did not enter town till next day. (I saw, with some resentment, over the door of a public house, the motto, "Will ye no come back again?") But, somehow, so many kings gone on, the play was rather better staged with the sovereign not there. I learned then how gor-

INTERIOR OF ST. GILES.

geons the old days must have been with their colour and glitter and flash.

I suppose there was a tall *land* where in my day stood and still stands Hogg's hotel, just above the Tron Kirk; the *lands* on the south side the High burned a century ago. But, to the American gazing down on ancient memories and present sovereignties, there was a wonderful courtesy shown by the hotel. I had interrupted their quiet Sabbath; it can still be quiet in Edinburgh notwithstanding that a tram car carried me on my way hither. The dining-room of this hotel looked out on the High, and it was breakfast time for these covenanting-looking guests from the countryside. But I, an invader, was made welcome and given the best seat on the balcony; a stranger and they took me in. Sometime I shall take up residence in this Latin Quarter, and if not in Lady Stair's Close, then in Hogg's hotel. The name sounds sweeter if you have just come up from Ettrick.

Nor did I miss the King. For

> "I saw pale kings, and princes too,
> Pale warriors, death-pale were they all;
> Who cry'd—'La Belle Dame sans merci
> Hath thee in thrall!'"

It was the Belle Dame, it was the Queen, I saw most often on the High Street, riding to and fro from the time of the "haar" on her return from France, till that last terrible night and the ride to Loch Leven.

After that you may visit the John Knox house if you will, and read for your edification its motto. "Lyfe God abonne al and yi nichtbour as yi Self," and buy a book or two in its book shop. I took particular pleasure in buying a girlish picture of Mary Queen, and a book of the poems of Robert Fergusson, neither of which would have pleasured John.

After that you may look at the "I. K." in the pavement, and realize that Dr. Johnson's wish for Knox has been fulfilled—"I hope in the highway."

After that you may look on the heart stamped in the pavement near St. Giles, where once stood the Heart of Midlothian, the Old Tolbooth.

There is only one other memory of High Street and of Scotland that for me equals that of Mary. It is Montrose. Up the Canongate comes the rumbling of a tumbril, like the French Revolution. And out of the high *lands* there look the hundreds of Covenanting folk, triumphant for the moment. And on the balcony of Moray House, within which the marriage of Lady Mary Stewart to the Marquis of

JOHN KNOX'S HOUSE.

Lorne has just been celebrated, there stands the wedding party, and among them the Earl of Argyle. Up the street comes the cart. And within it clad like a bridegroom—"fyne scarlet coat to his knee, trimmed with silver galoons, lined with taffeta, roses in his shoon, and stockings of incarnet silk"—stands the Marquis of Montrose, the loyalest Scotsman that ever lived.

After the field of Kylsyth, after the field of Philipshaugh, and the flight to the North and the betrayal, he has been brought back to Edinburgh, to a swift and covenanting sentence, and to death at the Tron.

His eyes meet proudly those of Argyle who has deserted his king and who thinks to stand in with the Covenant and with the future. It is the eyes of Argyle which drop. And Montrose goes on.

His head is on the picket of the Netherbow Port. His four quarters are sent to the four corners of the kingdom, Glasgow, Perth, Aberdeen, Inverness.

But the end is not yet. The tables turn, as they turned so often in those unstable times. It is Argyle who goes to the scaffold. Charles is king, the Second Charles. There is an edict. The body of Montrose is dug up out of the

Boroughmoor. It is buried in Holyrood. The four quarters are reassembled from Glasgow and Perth and Aberdeen and Inverness. A procession fairly royal moves from Holyrood to St. Giles. At the Netherbow it pauses. The head is taken down from the pike. The body of Montrose is whole again. An honourable burial takes place in the cathedral sanctuary.

Even though when search was made at the restoring of the church and the erection of the effigy the remains could not be found, there has been that justification by procession and by faith, that justification of loyalty that we remember when we remember Montrose—

> "He either fears his fate too much,
> Or his deserts are small,
> That dares not put it to the touch,
> To gain or lose it all."

Holyrood

Holyrood, ruined as it is, empty as it is, spurious as it is, still can house the Stewarts. Nowhere else are they so completely and splendidly Stewart. It is the royalest race which ever played at being sovereign; in sharp contrast with the heavier, more successful Tudors;

JAMES GRAHAM, MARQUIS OF MONTROSE.

crafty but less crafty than the Medici; amorous but more loyal than the Bourbons.

Never did kings claim sovereignty through a more divine right—and only one (whisper sometimes intimates that he was not Stewart, but substitute; but he left a Stewart descent) failed to pay the penalty for such assertion. It was the splendour which was Stewart while they lived, the tragedy that was Stewart when they came to die, which makes them the royal race.

There were born in Holyrood not one of them, unless it be James V. But almost all of them were married in Holyrood, held here their festive days, and, not one of them died in Holyrood. It is their life, the vivid intense flash of it, across those times that seem mysterious, even legendary in remembered times north of the Border. Life was a holiday to each of the Stewarts, and he spent it in the palace and in the pleasance of Holyrood.

The Abbey, with the monastery which was attached to it, begins far back before the Stewarts. It was founded by David I, the abbey-builder. Legend has it that he went a-hunting on a holy day, and straying from the "noys and dyn of Bugillis," a white stag came against him. David thought to defend himself, but a hand bearing a cross came out of the cloud, and the stag was exorcised. David kept the cross. In dream that night within the castle he was commanded to build an abbey where he had been saved, and the hunting place being this scant mile and a quarter from the castle—then a forest where now it is treeless—David placed this convenient abbey where it has stood for six centuries, defying fire and war and reformation, until the citizens of Edinburgh ravaged it when the roof fell in in the middle of the eighteenth century.

There is a curious feeling when one crosses the Girth stones at the lower end of the Canongate. It is a century and more since this was sanctuary. But it is impossible to step across these stones, into the "Liberty of Holyrood," and not wonder if there may not perhaps be some need in your own soul of sanctuary. Thousands and thousands of men—"abbey lairds" as they were pleasantly called—have stepped across this line before me, through the centuries. Who am I to be different, unneedful? May I not need inviolate sanctuary? May it not be that at my heels dogs some sinister creditor who will seize me by the skirts before I reach the boundary beyond which there is no exacting for debt? A marvelous thing, this ancient idea of sanctuary. It made an oasis

HOLYROOD PALACE.

of safety in a savage world. Surely it was super-christian. And here, at Holyrood, as the medieval statute declares, "qukilk privelege has bene inviolabie observit to all maner of personis cuman wythin the boundes . . . past memorie of man." What has the modern world given itself in place of ancient sanctuary? Justice, I suppose, and a jury trial.

But, once across the Girth, one becomes, not a sanctuarian, but a Stewart.

The situation is a little dreary, a little flat. And the palace, as a palace, is altogether uninteresting to look on. It is not the building of David or of the earlier Stewarts. But of that Merry Monarch who harboured so long in France, when England was determining whether it would be royal or republican, and Scotland was determining whether it would be covenanted or uncovenanted. The Merry Monarch was ever an uncovenanted person, not at all Scottish, although somewhat like the errant James—whose errancy was of his own choosing. Charles had acquired a French taste at the court of his cousin, Louis the Grand. So the new Holyrood was built in French baronial style. And no monarch has ever cared to inhabit it for any length of time. Only King Edward VII, who would have been a happy successor to James, but Edward was very studious in those days of 1859, when he lodged here and studied under the direction of the Rector of the Royal High School. Still I can but think that it was in this Stewart place that Edward developed his Stewartship.

There is not a stone to speak of the magnificence, of the strength, of David. The Abbey was burned and burned again, by Edward and Richard the Second, and entirely rebuilt when the Stewarts were beginning to be splendid and assured. Over the west doorway, high-arched and deep-recessed, early English in its technique, Charles I, who was crowned here in 1633, caused the stone to be placed.

> "He shall build ane House for my name and I will stablish the throne of his kingdom forever."

The tablet still stands above the doorway. But Charles is lying for his sins in a vault at St. George's chapel at Windsor far in the south, having paid his penalty on the scaffold in Whitehall. And the House is in ruins, "bare ruined choir," where not even "the late birds sing." Although Mendelssohn in speaking of the impression the Abbey made on him, does say, "I think I found there the beginnings of my Scotch symphony."

This "magnificent Abbey-Kirk of Halirude"

was no doubt very splendid; although in architectural beauty it cannot compare with Melrose, not even the great east window with its rich quatrefoil tracing. But what scenes have been staged in that historic drama, that theatrical piece, we call the history of the Stewarts!

Before the high altar, under that east window, when James I was kneeling before God in prayer, there appeared the Lord of the Isles, come repentant from burning Inverness and other rebellion, to kneel before the king, his own sword pointed at his breast.

Before this altar James II was married to Mary of Gueldres. James III was married to Margaret of Denmark, who brought the Orkneys as her dower. James IV was married to Margaret Tudor, the union of the "Thistle and the Rose." James V was not married here, he went to France for his frail bride, Magdalene, who lived but seven weeks in this inhospitable land, this hospitable Holyrood. She was buried in Holyrood chapel, only to be dug up and tossed about as common clay when the Edinburgh citizens made football of royal skulls.

The two sons of James VI, Henry who should have been king and who might have united royalist and commoner had fate granted it, and Charles who was to become king, were both christened here. James VII, brother to Charles II, restored this Chapel Royal and prepared it for the Roman ritual. James VIII was never here, or but as a baby. Charles III—did the Bonnie Prince in that brief brilliant Edinburgh moment of his, ever kneel before this then deserted altar and ask divine favour while he reasserted the divine right of kings?

Here—or was it secretly, in Stirling?—the Queen—one says The Queen and all the world knows—gowned in black velvet, at five o'clock on a July morning, was married to her young cousin, Henry Darnley. A marriage that endured two long terrible tumultuous years.

Here—or was it in the drawing-room?—at two o'clock on a May morning, the Queen was married to Bothwell, by Adam Bothwell, Bishop of Orkney, not with mass as she had been wed to her boy-cousin, but with preaching as she wed the Bishop's cousin. And "at this marriage there was neither pleasure nor pastime used as use was wont to be used when princes were married." So says the Diurnal Occurents of Scotland. A marriage that endured a brief, perhaps happy, tragedy-gathering month.

And the Queen beautiful was destroyed, by the Reformation, like an Abbey.

The bones of Darnley were ravaged by the

JAMES IV.

citizens of Edinburgh out of the ruins of this chapel. Or were they carried to Westminster by that unroyal son who was so laggard in caring for the remains of his queenly mother? I hope that Darnley does not rest beside her. For I think those exquisite marble fingers of the effigy in Henry VII's chapel, looking I fain believe as those of Mary looked, tapering, lovely, sinister, would not so fold themselves in prayer without unfolding through the long centuries.

In the old palace the most glorious days were those when James IV was king. As the most glorious days of Scotland were those which are almost legendary. The palace still had the grandeur that was Norman and the grace that was early English under David. Its front, towered and pinnacled, suggesting more fortress security than this dull château, opened upon a great outer court that lay between the palace and the walls. Coming down the Canongate from the castle it must have looked very splendid to James. And yet he did not care to remain in it long. All the Stewarts had errant souls, and they loved to wander their kingdom through. It presented ample opportunity for adventure; scarce a Stewart ever left Scotland. That last Prince, who flashed across Scotland in one last Stewart sword thrust—"My friends," he said in Holyrood the night before Prestonpans, "I have thrown away the scabbard"—was but treading in the steps of his royal forebears, the royal fore-errants.

In the days of James IV—we say it as one should say in the days of Haroun al Raschid, and indeed Edinburgh was in those early years of the Fifteen Hundreds the Bagdad of the world, and her days as well as her nights were truly Arabian—the world must have looked much as it does on the pleasant morning when we make our royal entry into Holyrood.

The Abbey grounds, a regal area then, and still a regality, were rich with woodland and orchard, and terraced and flowered into southern beauty. The red crags of the Salisbury ridge rose bold above as they do to-day, and crowning the scene the leonine form of Arthur's Seat above the green slopes, the lion keeping guard against the invading lion of England! I think James must often have climbed to that height to look forth over his domain, over his city, to watch the world, as King Arthur—whom he did not resemble—did legendary centuries before.

It was a busy time in Edinburgh; men's hands and wits were working. In Leith, then as now the port, then as now a separate burgh, there was much shipping and much building of ships; King James dreamed of a navy, and he had an admirable admiral in Sir Anthony Wood. In the castle there was the forging of guns, the "seven sisters of Brothwick," under direction of the king's master gunner, while Mons Meg looked on, and perhaps saw the near terrible future when these sisters of hers should be lost at Flodden.

In the city there was the splendid beginning of that intellectual life which has ever been quick in Edinburgh. It was a joyous time; witness the account from the lord High treasurer—

"On the 11th of February, 1488, we find the king bestowing nine pounds on gentil John, the English fule; on the 10th of June we have an item to English pipers who played to the king at the castle gate, of eight pounds eight shillings; on the thirty-first of August Patrick Johnson and his fellows, that playit a play to the king, in Lithgow, receives three pounds; Jacob the lutar, the king of bene, Swanky that brought balls to the king, twa wemen that sang to his highness, Witherspoon the foular, that told tales and brought fowls, Tom Pringill the trumpeter, twa fithelaris that sang Grey Steill to the king, the broken-bakkit fiddler of St.

Andrew's, Quhissilgyllourie a female dancer, Willie Mercer who lap in the stank by the king's command."

Oh, a royal and democratic and merry time. It was Flodden that made men old, that tragic climax to this splendour.

"In the joyous moneth tyme of June," in the pleasant garden of the town-house of the great Earl of Angus, looking down on the still waters of the Nor' Loch, and across the woods and moors to the glittering blue Firth, there sat the pale stripling, Gavin Douglass, third son of Douglass, Archibald Bell-the-Cat, late in orders at Mony musk, but now come up to St. Giles as prior in spite of his youth, and more absorbed in poetry than men.

> "More pleased that in a barbarous age
> He gave rude Scotland Virgil's page,
> Than that beneath his rule he held
> The bishopric of fair Dunkeld."

Here I would dispute Scott. After all, Dark Ages are not always as dark as they look to those who come after. And if the "Dark Ages" of Europe were brilliantly luminous in Moslem capitals, Bagdad and Cordova, so "rude Scotland" was more polished under James IV than England under Henry VII, or France under Louis XII.

As Gavin has recorded in "The Palice of Honour," he had interview with Venus in her proper limbo, and she had presented him with a copy of Virgil, bidding him translate it. And so, quite boldly, before any Englishman had ventured, and all through the winter, forgetful—except when he wrote his prefaces of

scharp soppis of sleit and of the snypand snaw

he had worked over his translation, from the Latin into the Scottish, and now it was nearly ready "to go to the printer," or more like, to be shown to the king. In sixteen months he had completed thirteen books; for he had added a book of Maphæus Vegius, without discrimination.

He was certain of the passage *facilis descensus Averni,* for Gavin was Scotch, the time was Stewart. It ran in this wise—

"It is richt facill and eithgate, I tell thee
For to descend, and pass on down to hell,
The black zettis of Pluto, and that dirk way
Stand evir open and patent nicht and day.
But therefore to return again on hicht
And heire above recovir this airis licht
That is difficul werk, thair labour lyis,
Full few thair bene quhom hiech above the skyis,
Thare ardent vertue has raisit and upheit
Or zit quhame equale Jupiter deifyit,
Thay quhilkie bene gendrit of goddes may thy oder attane
All the mydway is wilderness unplane

Or wilsum forest; and the laithlie flude
Cocytus, with his drery bosom unrude
Flows environ round about that place."

But he was not quite certain that he had been splendid enough, and daring enough, in his application of the royal lines—

"Hic Cæsar et omnis Iuli
Progenies, magnum caeli ventura sub axem."

So he had sent for his friend, William Dunbar, Kynges Makar, laureate to the sovereign. And Dunbar was never loath for a "Flyting," a scolding. He had them on every hand, with every one, and not only those he held with "gude maister Walter Kennedy," and published for the amusement of the King and his Court. It was a more solemn event when the future Bishop of Dunkeld summoned him. Though Gavin was fifteen years younger than William, he was more serious with much study, and under the shadow of future honours, and then, too, he was a Douglass.

So Dunbar came, striding up the Canongate between the tall inquisitive houses—even he found them "hampered in a honeycaim of their own making"—a very handsome figure, this Dunbar, in his red velvet robe richly fringed with fur, which he had yearly as his reward from the King, and which I doubt not he preferred to the solemn Franciscan robe he had renounced when he entered the King's service.

James was away at Stirling. James was a poet also. Surely, on internal evidence, it is the Fourth James and not the Fifth, who wrote those charming, and improper poems, "The Gaberlunzieman" and "The Jolly Beggar."

"He took a horn frae his side, and blew baith loud and shrill,
And four and twenty belted knights came skipping o'er the hill.

"And he took out his little knife, loot a' his duddies fa';
And he was the brawest gentleman that was amang them a'."

"And we'll gang nae mair a roving,
So late into the night;
And we'll gang nae mair a roving, boys,
Let the moon shine ne'er so bright."

Dunbar, official Makar, would fain secure the criticism of young Gavin on this joyous lament he had writ to the King in absence—

"We that here in Hevenis glory . . .
I mean we folk in Paradyis
In Edinburgh with all merriness."

And perhaps the young Gavin and the old Dunbar in their common fellowship of poetry, would drink a glass of red wine in memory of friends passed into death's dateless night—*Timor Mortis conturbat me.*

> "He has Blind Harry and Sandy Traill
> Slaine with his schour of mortall haill. . . .
> In Dunfermelyne he had done rovne
> With Maister Robert Henrisoun."

And Dunbar, who was so much more human than Gavin, if older, would quote those immortal new lines of Henryson—

> "Robene sat on gude grene hill
> Kepand a flok of fe,
> Mirry Makyne said him till,
> Robene, thow pity on me."

While Gavin, so much elder than his looks, and mindful of Scottish as well as of Trojan history, would quote from Blind Harry in the name of Wallace—

> "I grant, he said, part Inglismen I slew
> In my quarrel, me thocht nocht halff enew.
> I mowyt na war but for to win our awin (own).
> To God and man the rycht full weill is knawin (known)."

Then Dunbar would wrap his rich red robe about him—I hope he wore it on ordinary days, or were there any when James the Fourth was king?—and stride back, through the Canongate to Holyrood, back to the court, where he would meet with young David Lindsay, of a different sort from young Gavin Douglass. And they would chuckle over "Kitteis Confessioun," a dialogue between Kitty and the curate, which Lindsay had just written—and would not Dunbar be gracious and show it to the King?

> Quod he, "Have ye na wrangous geir?"
> Quod scho, "I staw ane pek o' beir."
> Quod he, "That suld restorit be,
> Tharefore delyver it to me."
> Quod he, "Leve ye in lecherie?"
> Quod scho, "Will Leno mowit me."
> Quod he, "His wyfe that sall I tell,
> To mak hir acquentance with my-sell."
> Quod he, "Ken ye na heresie?"
> "I wait nocht quhat that is," quod scho.
> Quod he, "Hard he na Inglis bukis?"
> Quod scho, "My maister on thame lukis."
> Quod he, "The bischop that sall knaw,
> For I am sworne that for to schaw."
> Quod he, "What said he of the King?"
> Quod scho, "Of gude he spak naething."
> Quod he, "His Grace of that sall wit,
> And he sall lose his lyfe for it."

Perhaps Warbeck was listening, Perkin Warbeck who pretended to be Duke of York, pretended to the English crown. So Scotland harboured him, and Holyrood was hospitable to him. James married him to Lady Jane Gordon, and for years, until he wearied of it, maintained a protectorate over this pinchbeck Pretender.

I am certain that Dom Pedro de Ayala did not linger in the court to gossip with Dunbar, or with the hangers-on. Dom Pedro had come up from Spain on a strange ambassadorial errand, to offer to James in marriage a Spanish princess, knowing well that there might be no Spanish princess (Maria was betrothed to Portugal); but no doubt believing that there ought to be, since James was slow in marrying, and surely a Spanish princess would best mate this royalest of the Stewarts. Dom Pedro better liked the extravagant kingly court at Holyrood than the niggardly court at Windsor. He wrote home to Ferdinand and Isabella, "The kingdom is very old, and very noble, and the king possessed of great virtues, and no defects worth mentioning." No defects! Certainly not. James had the qualities of his defects, and these were royal. James could speak—not keep still—in eight languages, and could and did say "all his prayers." So Dom Pedro reports to his Most Catholic Majesty.

When he was thirty years old, this King Errant married, not the hypothetical daughter of Spain, but the substantial youthful Margaret Tudor, aged fourteen. The Scottish king would none of the alliance for years; James preferred hypothetical brides and errant affairs. But the

MARGARET TUDOR, QUEEN OF JAMES IV.

English king saw the advantage and pressed it. He had united the roses, red and white, of England; he would fain join the thistle to the rose.

So James, in August, 1503, journeyed out to Dalkeith, whither Margaret had come. He returned to "hys bed at Edinborg varey well countent of so fayr a meetyng." A few days later, Margaret made her entry into Edinburgh, James having met her, gallantly dressed in "a jacket of crimson velvet bordered with cloth of gold." Leaving his restive charger, "mounting on the pallefroy of the Qwene, and the said Qwene behind hym, so rode throw the towne of Edinburgh." Their route lay through the Grassmarket up to the Castle Hill, and down the High Street and the Canongate, to the Abbey. Here they were received by the Archbishop of St. Andrews. Next day they were married by the Archbishop of Glasgow, the Archbishop of York joining in the solemn and magnificent celebration.

It is the most splendid moment in Edinburgh history, within the Abbey and the palace, and within the city. The Town Cross ran with wine, the high *lands* were hung with banners and scarlet cloth, and morality plays were performed before the people. In the palace there was a royal scene. And our friend, William Dunbar, Kynges Makar, read his allegory of "The Thrissl and the Roiss," which is still worth reading, if Chaucer is worth reading.

But, at night, in the royal apartment, the night before the wedding, perhaps in the fragment of the old palace which remains, the gallant king played to the little princess upon the virginal; and then, on bended knee and with unbonneted head, he listened while she played and sang to him. Out of the dark of the time it is a shining scene; and out of the splendour of the moment it brings a note of tenderness.

Another decade, another August, and the Boroughmoor (where now run the links of Burntland) was covered with the white of a thousand tents, Scotland was gathered for war, the "ruddy lion ramped in gold" floated warlike over all, and James and all Scotland prepared to march down to Flodden, heeding not the warning which had sounded at midnight in ghostly voice at the Town Cross; a warning no doubt arranged by Margaret, never a Stewart, always a Tudor. And—all Scotland was turned into a house of mourning.

Half a century later the history of Scotland came to a climax, and Mary Stewart came to Holyrood; that queen who then and ever since held half the world in thrall, like another Iseult. The covenanted world has rejected her, as no doubt it would reject Iseult.

Shrouded in a gray "haar" from off the North Sea, rising like a Venus out of the mists of the sea, Mary Stewart, Dowager of France, Queen of Scotland, Heiress of England, came unto her own. And, her own received her, and, received her not.

The castle hanging high in air no longer hung there. The palace lying low on the plain was not there, on that August 19, 1561. There was nothing but what was near at hand; Mary could not see a hundred feet into her kingdom. In truth she arrived at port a week before the ship was expected—and Mary also flashed through her kingdom; witness the ride across the Marches to the Hermitage, and the ride through the North to punish Huntley. Hers was a restless soul, a restless body.

On her return to the kingdom she was accompanied by a great retinue, three of her French uncles of Guise and of Lorraine, her four Maries, and many ambassadors. It was a suspended moment in the world, the sixth decade of the sixteenth century. And nowhere were affairs in such delicate balance, or so like to swing out of balance as in Scotland; where religion, sovereignty, feudalism, morality, were swaying dizzily. So all the world sent their keenest ambassadors to observe, to foresee if possible, to report.

Yet Mary rode through the mists.

"Si grand brouillard," says the Sieur de Brantome, that gossipy chronicler, and Mary and her French courtiers and Scotch Maries, rode through the "haar," from Leith up whatever was the Leith Walk of that day to Holyrood.

The palace must have rung with French chatter, of these wondering and inquisitive and critical folk; for all the cultured world was French in those days, and Mary and her Maries had been only five or six when they left stormy Scotland for the pleasant smiling land of France.

Not for long was she permitted to believe she had brought France back with her and there was no reality in Scotland but as she made it. Reformation pressed in upon her, even through the windows of this turret where again she seems to listen to that prophetic and pious serenade, Scottish protestant psalms accompanied by fiddles and sung to a French Catholic queen. "Vile fiddles and rebecks," complains Brantome, hesitating to call vile the mob of five hundred gathered in the Scotch mists; but they sang "so ill and with such bad accord that there could be nothing worse. Ah, what music, and what a lullaby for the night!"

The rooms of Mary are still inclosed, the walls still stand about them, and a romantic care withholds the ravages of time from those tapestries and silken bed hangings, dark crimson damask, which Mary drew about her on that night of her return. And here hangs a picture of Queen Elizabeth, authentic, Tudoresque, which did not hang here when Mary returned; but what dark shadow of Elizabeth lurked behind these hangings! The very guard to whom you protest the picture understands—"I think it an insult to her memory."

It is here that Queen Mary still reigns. All the old palace was burned, carelessly, by Cromwell's soldiers, at what time men were caring nothing for palaces, and less for royalty. But, fate was royal, was Jacobite, and this gray turret of the northwest corner a building of James V on a foundation of James IV—perhaps where he had listened in the evening to Margaret and her virginal—was saved from the wrath of the Commonwealth. Within these very walls Mary played on the virginal, perhaps on the rebeck, and many sought to know her stops—"you can fret me, yet you cannot play upon me."

Here she was loved, as she still is loved. Here she made love, the mystery!—as always. Here she flashed those bright eyes on courtiers and commoners and straightway these fell into bondage—the Stewarts never drew the line of division. Here those eyes battled with John Knox as he met her in Dialogues, as John has faithfully recorded. And here those bright eyes filled with a storm of tears at his denunciation; but Knox felt their power. Here she met Darnley, in the chapel married him, and Knox called after dinner to declare that the Reformation did not approve. Here by the very stairs of the turret Darnley led the murderers on Rizzio, from his private apartments to hers. (I find it fit that Ker of Fawdonside, one of the murderers, should have married later the widow of Knox.) Mary was held here a prisoner; they would "cut her into collops and cast her over the wall" if she summoned help. But Mary could order that the blood stains of the fifty-six wounds of Rizzio should remain "ane memoriall to quychen her revenge." They quicken our thought of Mary to-day—if we accept them. From Holyrood Mary went to Kirk o' Field on a Sunday night in Febru-

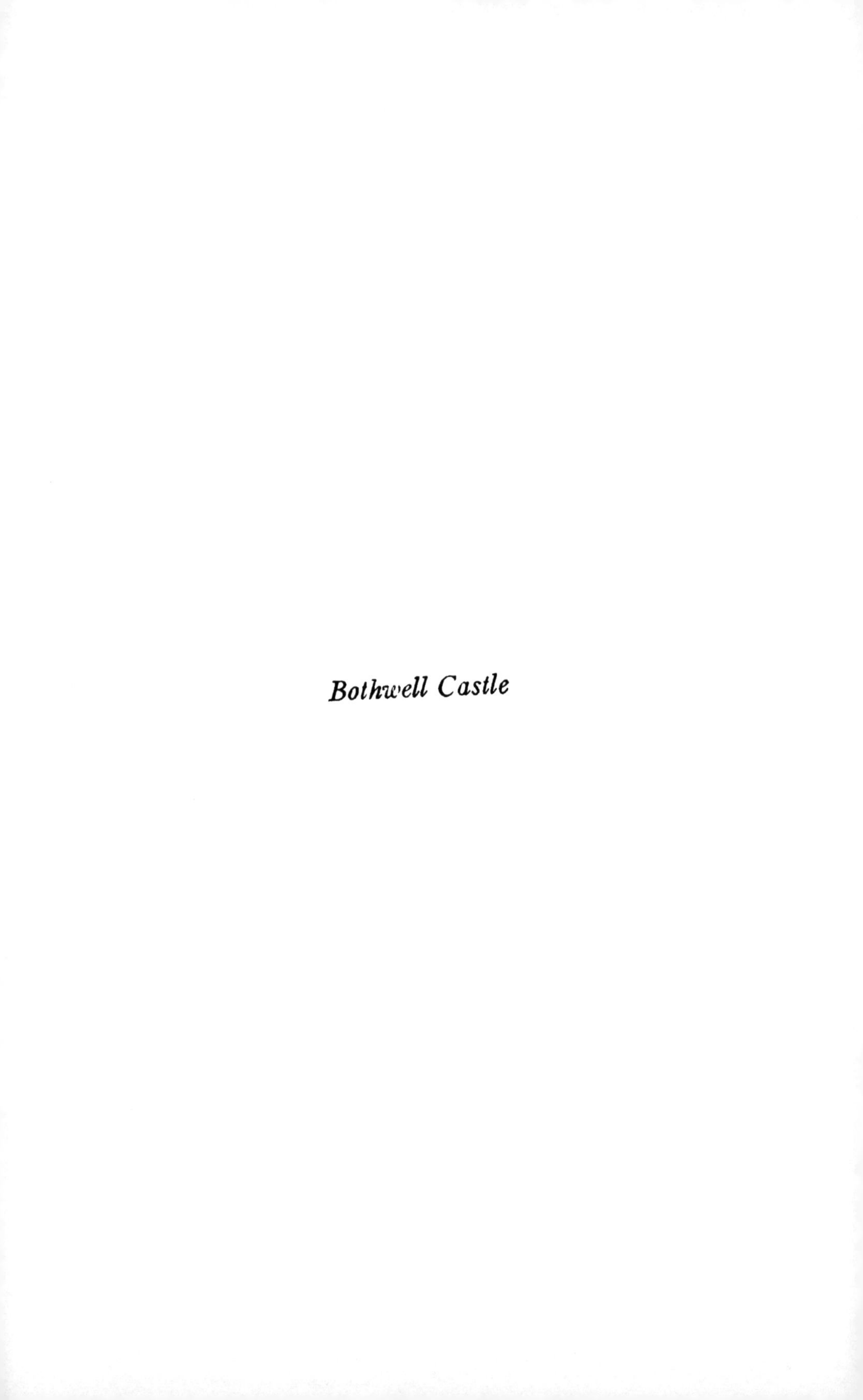

Bothwell Castle

ary, to visit Darnley who lay "full of the small pox." He had come back from Bothwell castle on Mary's urging; but he had gone to Bothwell to escape her revenge for Rizzio. She returned to Holyrood—"the Queen's grace gang and with licht torches up the Black Friar's Wynd"—where the wedding festivities of a member of her household were in progress. And, I doubt not, devoted to Mary as I am, that she was the merriest of the company.

Then the dark.

Then, at two in morning, an explosion that shook all Edinburgh, that astonished the world, that still reverberates through the world.

Then—the dark.

A marriage, at two in the morning, a flight to Borthwick, a meeting at Carberry, one more night in Edinburgh, in a house as mean as that of Kirk o' Field, a day at Holyrood, and a forced ride with ruffian nobles, Lindsay and Ruthven on each hand, to Loch Leven, thirty miles in the night of June 16, 1567—and Edinburgh and Holyrood and the Crown of Scotland know her no more.

> "Helen's lips are drifting dust,
> Ilion is consumed in rust."

And Mary. And Holyrood.

There is one more Holyrood scene descending from this. On a Saturday evening, March 26, 1603, the son of Mary, the King of Scotland, supped with the Queen, perhaps in that small supper room where Rizzio was supping with a queen; and they had retired. "The palace lights were going out, one by one." And Sir Robert Carey, three days out from London, clattered into the courtyard, the King was roused, Sir Robert knelt before him—

"Queen Elizabeth is dead, and Your Majesty is King of England!"

James I of England, James VI of Scotland, son of Mary, son of Darnley, son of the ninth generation from Bruce, The Bruce. The "auld enemy" is finally defeated; and to borrow again from Rosaline Masson, "the lights of Holyrood went out, one by one."

In the long picture gallery of this dull modern palace, nothing of which either Mary or James ever saw, there hangs a series of portraits, one hundred pictures of Scottish kings, painted under order of Charles II in 1680, by the Fleming, DeWitt, who agreed to furnish the pictures in two years for one hundred and twenty pounds. They begin with Fergus I, 330 B. C. They are the kings who passed before the prophetic vision of Banquo. Enough to frighten Macbeth!

One brief brilliant ghost of Stewart glory returns. In this gallery was held the ball of Prince Charles Edward, described in "Waverley."

And after this theatric moment, and after the Prince had defeated the "royalists" at Falkirk, Hardy's dragoons slashed these pictures of Scottish kings, since the Prince they could not reach.

Princes Gardens

There are certain public places of beauty where the beauty is so enveloping that the place seems one's very own, seems possessed. That, I take it, is the great democratic triumph, in that it has made beauty a common possession and places of beauty as free to the people as is the air.

Chief of these is Princes Street Gardens.

I could, in truth I have, spent there days and half-days, and twilights that I would willingly have lengthened to midnights, since the northern night never quite descends, but a romantic gray twilight veils everything, and evokes more than everything. For any lengthened visit in Edinburgh I dare not inhabit a hotel room on the Garden side, since all my time would be spent at the window. For a shorter visit, such a room lengthens the day, defies the closed gate of the Gardens.

It was from such a window as this, "From a Window in Princes Street" that Henley looked forth—

"Above the crags that fade and gloom
Starts the bare knee of Arthur's Seat;
Ridged high against the evening bloom
The Old Town rises, street on street;
With lamps bejeweled, straight ahead,
Like rampird walls the houses lean,
All spired and domed and turreted,
Sheer to the valley's darkling green;
Ranged in mysterious array,
The Castle menacing and austere,
Looms through the lingering last of day;
And in the silver dusk you hear,
Reverberated from crag and scar,
Bold bugles blowing points of war."

Princes Street is, I believe, not a mile long, a half-mile the part which is gardened. It is the loveliest street in the world. It seems infinite instead of half-mile.

Of course to the loyal American that praise is received half-way. For he remembers Riverside Drive with the majesty of the Hudson, North Shore Drive with the shoreless infinity of Lake Michigan, Summit Avenue with the

PRINCES STREET.

deep gorge of the Upper Mississippi, Quebec and its Esplanade. But even these "handsome streets" cannot match Princes for history and beauty in one, for the old and the new, for the Old Town and the New Town.

Princes Street, to speak briefly of its geography, is a broad thoroughfare, with a medley of buildings on the north side, but uniform in gray stone, where hotels and shops furnish the immediate life of the city. There are electric cars running the full length of the street; and it is the only street I know which is not spoiled through the presence of these necessary carriers.

There are cabs, and there are sight-seeing cars, from which in high advantage, and in half a day, you can see everything in Edinburgh. Yes, actually. I who speak to you have done it, partly for the greed of seeing it steadily and seeing it whole, and partly for the comment of these Scotch coach drivers and guards, who are not merely Scottish but the essence of Scotland. I shall never forget how an American traveler—of course they are all Americans in these tally-hos—commenting on the driver's remark that the "Old Queen" wanted to build a palace where Donaldson's Hospital now stands and she was refused—"but she was the Queen!" Nevertheless, asserted Mr. Sandy Coachman, "She was refused." Not so in the old days of Queenship.

The entire life of Edinburgh, of Scotland, streams through this broad straight street.

On the opposite side lie the Gardens, stretching their way parallel with the street, a wide, green-lawned, tree-forested purlieu, terraced and flowered, with a "sunken garden" near the Castle-side, through which trains are conveyed. The smoke, so much lamented, does often rest with grace and gray loveliness in the hollows of the place, so that one does not miss the waters of the Nor' Loch that once flowed here as moat.

Above rises the castle in greater majesty than from any other point. Down from the castle runs the ridge of the High Street, and the high *lands* with flags of washing hanging out the windows which answer the flags red and leoninely rampant, on the buildings of Princes Street. The crown of St. Giles and the spire of the Tronkirk hanging above all.

To the west is St. John's, where in the graveyard Raeburn is buried; and old St. Cuthbert's, where in the graveyard De Quincey is buried. There are Raeburns in the Royal gallery which stands on the island dividing the Gardens, and there are many Raeburns here and there, in private rooms of banks and other institutions, rare Raeburns with that casual, direct, human look he could give men and women. The galleries are worth a visit both for their best, and for their not-best. There are statues of famous Scotsmen on the terraces, and of course the Scott monument, beautifully Gothic, and as sacred as a shrine.

There are goods to be bought in the shops, pebbles and cairngorms in jewelry and kickshaws of that ilk; rugs and plaidies, sashes and ties, and Scott and Stevenson books bound in the Royal Stewart silk. Unhappy the traveler who has not provided himself beforehand with a tartan. Almost every one can if he will. And there is always the college of heraldry to help one out. Or the audacity of choosing the tartan you like best; an affront, I assure you, to all good Scots. For however unlovely a Scotch tartan may be in the eyes of the world—nominations are invidious—in the eyes of the clansman there is nothing so "right" as his own particular tartan. He would not exchange it for a Douglass or a Stewart.

These tartans have exerted a very marked effect on the Scottish sense of taste. On Princes Street you may not find such richly dressed women as on Regent Street, but the harmony of colouring will please you better. While no doubt this is due to the fact that for several hundred years the Scottish taste has had the benefit of intimate association with the French, it can also be traced to the longer centuries during which tartans have brought an understanding of colour harmonies. Because there has been this love of colour, there has come with it vanity. With vanity there has come that rare ability of the women of the race to maintain a unity, a harmony, a complete relationship between skirts and waists. There is no country in Europe where the "act of union" at the feminine waistline is so triumphant as in Scotland, particularly in Edinburgh. The universal American achievement has been equaled in Europe only in Scotland.

There are teashops which invite you in, when the wind sweeps too harshly, or the rain beats itself into more than a Scotch mist, or even when the sun shines too hot. There is a garden tea place on top of a high hotel which confronts the Castle. Even in this Far North there is much open air dining, and more especially open air tea-ing. I am not certain that Dr. Johnson would have much cared for this modern tea room, where he might review the world. It seems that he drank much tea when he was the guest of Boswell, especially when he was the guest of Mrs. Boswell, in James Court the other side the Gardens. "Boswell has handsome and very spacious rooms, level with the ground on one side of the house, and the other four stories high." And Boswell says of Johnson, "My wife had tea ready for him, which it is well known he delights to drink at all times, particularly when sitting up late." From this roof tea garden one can see James's Court at the top of the Mound, although the Boswell lodgings are burned down. And one can almost see Holyrood, where tea was introduced by James VII.

After you have shopped and had your tea, and the past retakes possession, you will return to the green valley of the Gardens, to forget the clang of the tram cars, to look up at the great Castle Hill, green until it meets the buff-coloured stone and the buff-coloured buildings that seem to grow out of the stone, if it is a clear day; while the ramparts seem temporarily to have blossomed with red geraniums, if red coats are leaning over the edge.

A clear day in Edinburgh is possible. I have spent a month of such days, and have longed for the mists, a touch of them, that the castle might turn to a purple wonder, and the deep blue shadows sink over it, and the gray precipice of the High Street look higher than ever. Gray is in truth the colour of Edinburgh, "the gray metropolis of the North." But it is never a dreary gray, never a heavy gray like London. There the gray is thick, charged with soot; one can rub it from his face. In Edinburgh the gray is luminous, a shifting playing colour, with deep shadows turning to deep blue, with rifts or thinnings of the cloud, through which yellow and brown glimmers make their way.

Above all, Edinburgh is never monotonous. That is perhaps its charm, a something that every feminine city knows; Edinburgh is feminine, and Paris, and Venice, and New Orleans.

And there hangs the castle, sometimes in midair—

> "Hast thou seen that lordly castle, that castle by the sea?
> Golden and red above it the clouds float gorgeously."

Sometimes standing stalwart and stern, a challenge to daring, a challenge to history. That farther edge of the Castle Hill as it is silhouetted against the west sky—if you walk around on Lothian Street you can see the full face of the Rock—has invited many an adventurer, both from within and without.

It was down that steep hill that the sons of

Margaret carried their queen mother, when the hosts of Donalbane were besieging the place, and a Scotch "haar" rolling in from the sea and shutting off the castle enabled the little procession to pass safely with its precious burden, and swiftly down to the Queen's ferry, and across to Dunfermline.

Up the face of that Rock when The Bruce did not hold this stronghold there stole in the night of a thirteenth century winter—it must have been much colder, even in Edinburgh, in the thirteenth century—a picked band of men; picked by Randolph afterward Earl of Moray, and led by Frank, who, years before when he had been a soldier in the castle garrison and night leave was forbidden, used to make his way down this cliff to visit a bonnie lassie in the West Bow. Now, on a wind-swept night, which can be very windy around that castle profile—the wind has not abated since the thirteenth century—Frank led the remembered way. I wonder if he remembered the lassie. But his footing was sure. Once, it is true, the sentinel seemed to have discovered them. But it was only the boast the sentinel makes to the night when he makes his last round. The men huddled against the face of the Rock. Then they moved onward. The ladders were too short to reach the rampart. Two were bound together. The men over, the cry "A Moray!" rings in the castle. Scotland has won it again.

Another century, and James III is king. This least royal of the Stewarts, jealous of his more royal brother, locked the Duke of Albany in the castle, and felt secure. But the Duke had friends. A French clipper came into Leith. It brought wine to Albany, and the wine cask contained a rope. Inviting his guardians to sup with him, he plied them with heated wine, perhaps drugged wine, then, the dagger. Albany's servant insisted on going down the rope first. It was short, he fell the rest of the distance. Albany hurried back for the sheets from his bed, made his safe way down. He carried the servant man all the way to Leith—he had just "whingered" the guard—found the boat, and safety, and France.

Up the Rock, in Covenanting days, stole Claverhouse, the Bonnie Dundee, to a secret conference with the Duke of Gordon, hoping to win him away to Stewart loyalty and the North.

I cannot remember that any of Scott's characters went this way. He thought it "scant footing for a cat." But Stevenson knew the way. Perhaps not actually, but he sent more

JOHN GRAHAM OF CLAVERHOUSE, VISCOUNT DUNDEE.

than one of his characters up or down the Rock —St. Ives with a rope that was long enough to reach.

Calton Hill

Perhaps the best view of Edinburgh—only perhaps, for each view differs, and you have not seen the whole city unless you have seen it from the various vantage points—is that from the Calton Hill. For a very good reason. The Hill itself is negligible enough, although it is impossible to understand Edinburgh, to understand Scotland, unless you have looked on the architectural remnants on this Hill, and considered them philosophically. But, as Stevenson said—"Of all places for a view, the Calton Hill is perhaps the best; since you can see the castle, which you lose from the castle, and Arthur's Seat, which you cannot see from Arthur's Seat." An excellent reason, which also places the castle and Arthur's Seat.

Calton Hill does not tower so high over the city as these other two points; one may still look up to Arthur's Seat, one may look across to the castle. Yet, the city lies near. Yet, the country rolls out to the Firth, and out to the Pentlands. Perhaps a gray-sea haze dulls the far edge of the far Kingdom of Fife. Perhaps a blue haze hangs over the Pentlands. Perhaps a smoke-cloud makes a nearer sky for the town itself, this Auld Reekie. Not only perhaps, but very probably. There are clear days in Edinburgh. They are to be treasured. There is no air more stimulating in all the world. October sometimes slips into the other months of the year, fills the air with wine, clears the air of filament. But, not often, not often for the tourist from beyond seas who makes Edinburgh in the summer. But still it is possible from Calton Hill to catch the farthest glory of the encircling hills, and the near glory of the ever glorious city.

The Hill itself is a place of monuments, and a very pretentious place. Also, very absurd. I suppose it is possible to be of two minds about the remnant of the Parthenon which stands so conspicuously on the highest plateau, a construction dating back to that royal time when George the Fourth came to this northern capital, and was—alas!—received as though he were Bonnie Prince Charlie himself; and was received—again alas!—by Sir Walter clad in a Campbell plaid, and as loyal to the Regent, the florid Florizel, as he had been to Prince Charles in the "Waverleys." Because of all these loyalties this never finished monument, with its twelve columns and architrave spread above, looks sufficiently pathetic, and sufficiently absurd. "A very suitable monument to certain national characteristics," said a later Scots writer, who perhaps never ceased being a Jacobite.

There are monuments; one to Dugald Stewart, and the visitor not philosophical is apt to ask, Who was Dugald Stewart? There is a memorial to Burns whose friend Willie that brewed a peek o' malt lies in the Old Calton burying ground near by. Hume lies there, too, and Dr. John Brown, and Stevenson's dead.

"There on the sunny frontage of a hill,
Hard by the House of Kings, repose the dead,
My dead, the ready and the strong of word.
Their works, the salt-encrusted, still survive;
The sea bombards their founded towers; the night
Thrills pierced with their strong lamps. The artificers
One after one, here in this grated cell,
Where the rain erases and the dust consumes,
Fell upon lasting silence."

There is a monument to Lord Nelson. And looking as though he belonged there is a bronze figure of Abraham Lincoln.

All this lies about, with casual sheep cropping the grass.

But, there lies the city. And there lies the country.

To the south rises Arthur's Seat, the lion. The much castellated jail, is beneath you, another absurd elaborate building, a castle after castle-days. Farther a-city lies Holyrood, with the ruined abbey, the Queen Mary wing, and the scarlet patch of the sentinel moving to and fro and guarding all this vanished greatness. Nothing more appeals than this sentinel-watch of the ghosts of the past.

Turn but a little and the Old Town lies before you, the castle splendid, still the guardian, the long ridge of the High Street with its jagged buildings that from here rise almost to the purple edge of the hilly Pentland background, with the spire of the Tolbooth and the crown of St. Giles breaking against the sky. And down at the foot of the vantage Hill stretches Princes Street with the Scott monument rising athwart the haze of city and sky.

From the north edge of Calton there is a more empty panorama, but still significant. Now it is bound in with tenements high and thick, but in the golden days it was a steep hillside leading down to a jousting ground. Tradition has it that Bothwell launched his horse down its almost-precipice, and so entered the tilting ground, while ladies' bright eyes rained influence and gave the prize; but most glowing were the eyes of Mary.

Beyond, the suburbs fill in the two miles that stretch to Leith, and to the Firth, glittering out to the far sea.

At night, if you have no fear of hobgoblins or of hooligans, Calton Hill is an experience. It is a still place, the silence the greater because the city lies so near, and looks so busy with its twinkling lights. A gulf of gloom lies between. The night is velvet black, a drop curtain against which is thrown the star-pricked map of the city. One can well believe how the young Stevenson, in those romantic days when he carried a lantern under his jacket, used to climb this hill venturesomely, and with the dog in "Chanticler," exclaim, "I shall never forget the first night I lapped up the stars." It is something to lap stars from the black pool which is Edinburgh by night.

If you have, happily, lived in a high city, Boston, Seattle, Duluth, Denver, St. Paul, San Francisco, with water and land combined, you, too, have lingered upon a heaven-kissed hill on such a night as this, and Edinburgh seems native.

Scott, of course, must have known Calton

Hill, although Salisbury Crags under Arthur's Seat, with its more feasible promenade, better appealed to him when he was writing the "Waverleys." There is an American who has written of the Hill, a young inland American whom the gods loved to an early death. I remember hearing Arthur Upson talk of days and nights on the Calton, and his sonnet catches the note—

"High and alone I stood on Calton Hill
Above the scene that was so dear to him
Whose exile dreams of it made exile dim.
October wooed the folded valleys till
In mist they blurred, even as our eye upfill
Under a too-sweet memory; spires did swim,
And gables, rust-red, on the gray sea's brim—
But on these heights the air was soft and still,
Yet, not all still; an alien breeze will turn
Here, as from bournes in aromatic seas,
As round old shrines a new-freed soul might yearn
With incense of rich earthly reveries.
Vanish the isles: Mist, exile, searching pain,
But the brave soul is freed, is home again."

CHAPTER V

THE KINGDOM OF FIFE

FROM Edinburgh as I looked out on the Forth from every vantage point, I was conscious of the hills of Fife ever backing in the prospect. And I kept repeating to myself the old rhyme of the witches—

> "The Thane of Fife had a wife,
> Ah, where is she now!"

I determined to set sail and find not the wife, but the kingdom.

It is a continuing splendour, this name—the Kingdom of Fife. Than the thing nothing could be less royal, more democratic. For Fifeshire is given over to farm lands and coal fields and treeless stretches, and the fringe of Fife is made up of fishing villages "a hodden gray plaid wi' a gowden fringe," said a King Jamie. It lies there, separate from Scotland, although very Scottish, between the firths of the Forth and the Tay, with the Ochil hills a barrier on the landside. The separating firths are now connected with Scotland by great bridges, over which the trains pass with reluctance. And the wind is always blowing in Fife, a cold, stern, relentless, Calvinistic wind, off the North Sea. Not by every wind of doctrine but by a disciplining Calvinistic wind is this Kingdom swept into conformity.

There is no end of castles and of historic memories lying like pebbles upon the seashore of the Firth. Pick up any sea shell—I do not remember seeing any, so combed have these beaches been from the memory of man—and it will whisper a tale in your ear.

But there is for me but one pilgrimage to be made in Fifeshire, to Kirkcaldy; to the place, not of Ravenscraig Castle, nor because Adam Smith and political economy were here born twins, nor because Carlyle taught here for two years, nor because Edward Irving preached here; their dwellings and schools and graves can be seen. But because Marjorie Fleming was born here, passed to and fro, from Granton to Burntisland, in those brief beautiful nine years that were granted to her, and to us, and lies buried in the old kirkyard of Abbotshall.

Perhaps you do not know Marjorie. She was the friend, the intimate friend of Sir Walter Scott. And I can but think how large and void the world was a century ago, in that Charles Lamb was living in London when Marjorie was living in Kirkcaldy, and was dreaming of his "Dream Children," when he might have known this most precious child, fit to be the friend of Lamb as she was of Sir Walter.

Other men who have loved her with a tenderness which can belong but to the living child, immortally living, are Dr. John Brown who wrote the wonder book about her fifty years ago, through which most of us have claimed Marjorie as our own, and Mark Twain, who only a month before he died—and joined her—wrote as tenderly and whimsically of her as he ever wrote of any child or any maid. Among such august company we almost hesitate to enter, but surely at this distance of time we may lay our love beside that of the great men who found Pet Marjorie one of the most precious human treasures the world has ever held.

She was but a little girl, and only nine years all told, when the last day came to her a hundred and more years ago, December 19, 1811. The first six years she lived in Kirkcaldy, "my native town which though dirty is elene in the country," Marjorie wrote this from Edinburgh a little patronizingly, and Marjorie was never strong on spelling. The next three years she lived with her aunt in the Scottish capital, where she wrote those journals and letters which have kept her memory warm to this day. In July of 1811 she returned to the town by the North Sea, and in December she was gone.

In the morning of the day on which I made my pilgrimage I went up to the Parliament buildings in the Old Town, looked them about, saw the lawyers pacing to and fro, as Stevenson had paced, but not for long—the absurdity of it!—and then down the hill in the shadow of three men.

"One November afternoon in 1810"—(the year in which the "Lady of the Lake" was published) "three men, evidently lawyers, might have been seen escaping like school boys from the Parliament House, and speeding arm in arm down Bank Street and the Mound, in the teeth of a surly blast of sleet." They were Lord Erskine, William Clerk—and the third we all know; what service of romance has he not performed for us! As the snow blattered in his face he muttered, "how it raves and drifts! On-ding o' snaw—aye, that's the word, on-ding." And so he approached his own door, Castle Street, No. 39. There, over the door, looking forth on the world, is his face to-day, looking up Young Street.

Then, as he grew restless and would awa, I followed him through Young Street up to No. 1, North Charlotte Street. It is a substantial building, still of dignified and fair estate; neighbourhoods are not transformed in a Scots century as they are in America. But it carries no tablet to tell the world that here Marjorie lived. It was here that at the age of six she wrote her first letter to Isa Keith. It was here that Marjorie saw "regency bonnets" and with eyes of envy; as indeed she envied and desired with the passionate depths of her nature all lovely and strange things. Here she read the Newgate calendar, and found it a fascinating affair—Marjorie less than nine! And here that Isabel Keith, her adored cousin, would not permit the little bookworm to read much of lovers or to talk of them. Marjorie says very gravely, "a great many authors have expressed themselves too sentimentally," but Isa was never able quite to cure Marjorie of her interest in love.

That evening Sir Walter carried her, through the "on-ding o' snaw," in a shepherd's plaid, over to Castle Street. I walked through the narrow stone-lined thoroughfare on a hot July morning—and I could feel the cold and snow of that winter a century back, and see the strong, lame, great man, carrying the wee wifie in the neuk of his plaid, to the warm firelight of his castle. Marjorie and he would romp there the evening long. She would hear him say his lessons, "Ziccoty, diccoty, dock," or "Wonery, twoery, tickery, seven," while Marjorie "grew quite bitter in her displeasure at his ill behaviour and stupidness."

Then they would read ballads together; and then "he would take her on his knee, and make her repeat Constance's speeches in King John till he swayed to and fro sobbing his fill. Fancy the gifted little creature, like one possessed, repeating—

"'For I am sick, and capable of fears,
Oppressed with wrongs, and therefore full of fears;
A widow, husbandless, subject to fears;
A woman, naturally born to fears.'"

I walked out through what used to be fields, and is now much suburban dwelling, toward Braehead.—"I am going to-morrow to a delightful place, Braehead by name, where there is ducks, cocks, bubblyjocks, 2 dogs, 2 cats and swine which is delightful"—to Ravelston—"I am at Ravelston enjoying nature's fresh air. The birds are singing sweetly, the calf doth frisk and nature shows her glorious face."

Ravelston is still a place of delight, with its

great cliffs breaking the surface of the park and a deep-lying lake with dark woodlands. I wish Marjorie might have known the ballad by Sydney Dobell; it has the magic quality she would have felt.

"Ravelston, Ravelston,
The merry path that leads
Down the golden morning hill,
And through the silver meads;

"She sang her song, she kept her kine,
She sat beneath the thorn,
When Andrew Keith of Ravelston
Rode thro' the Monday morn.

"Year after year, where Andrew came,
Comes evening down the glade,
And still there sits a moonshine ghost
Where sat the sunshine maid.

"She makes her immemorial moan,
She keeps her shadowy kine;
O Keith of Ravelston
The sorrows of thy line!"

In the late afternoon I took tram for Leith, changing of course at Pilrig, because Leith remains haughtily aloof from Edinburgh and emphasizes it through this break at the boundary. "When we came to Leith," says Boswell, "I talked perhaps with too boasting an air, how pretty the Frith of Forth looked; as indeed, after the prospect from Constantinople, of which I have been told, and that from Naples, which I have seen, I believe the view of the Frith and its environs from the Castle-hill of Edinburgh is the finest prospect in Europe, 'Aye,' replied Dr. Johnson, 'that is the state of the world. Water is the same everywhere.' "

And so, down to the pier, stopping on the way to look at a New Haven fishwife in her picturesque costume, which she has worn ever since the Danes came over. Yes, and looking for a suitable piece of earth for Queen Magdalene to kiss, "Scottis eard!" Well, if not here, there is Scottis eard worthy elsewhere.

I asked for the ferry to Burnt-is-land. The conductor of the tram looked, yes, and laughed. Burnt-island, he dared, *dared* to repeat. And so, I took ferry from Granton to—Burnt-island.

It is a long journey across the Firth. Far down the waters rises the bold rock of the Bass, around which I had sailed a day before, looking for a landing for some one more ponderous than solan geese or kittie wake, and not finding it; although I was told that from Canty bay—excellent Scots name—the innkeeper will row you o'er, and you may walk where James I was waiting for the boat which should carry him to safety in France, and getting instead the

TANTALLON CASTLE.

boat which carried him to prison in England. Still I like to remember that Henry IV declared in explanation that he "could speak very good French" himself, if that were what they were sending Scottish Jamie o'er the water for; Henry who had years of the Hundred Years' War behind him.

The rock is rent by a cavern running clean through. It's quite a terrific place, and seven acres of benty grass must have seemed small refuge for the Covenanters who were lodged here numerously in Killing Time.

On the mainshore, the Lothian, rises Tantallon Castle, where Marmion dared to beard Angus Bell-the-Cat. It still looks pretty tremendous, and still stands, like the Coliseum. "Ding doon Tantallon? Build a brig to the Bass!" runs the proud proverb.

But we are on our way across the Firth. There was a certain magic about it on my day of pilgrimage. The north shore lay sparkling in the late afternoon sun, blue shimmering land against a clear blue sky, the thin rim of the continent playing here and there with opalescent colour where man had builded village or castle, or where man had not destroyed the ancient green. The south shore lay vague and gray, and growing darker, against the falling afternoon, while the Lammermuirs stood up in paler dusk in the background, and the sun blazed behind them. And all about the Firth glittered like an inland lake, a Great Lake. I thought of how the Roman galleys and Norse fleets had come this way, and looked and departed. And how kings had brought their armies here, and looked, perhaps besieged, and departed. And how time and time and time again, French fleets had sailed in here to help their continuing ally, Scotland. And how kings had sailed out from here to France, and how Scots knights had sailed out from here for France, the Crusades, anywhere that promised adventure. And here Saxon Margaret had sailed in to be Scotland's queen. And here Scottish Mary had sailed in to be Scotland's queen, and not to be. Far out in the offing the sun shone golden upon the brown sails of a single fishing boat, tacking to catch a homing wind, a ghost where once had sailed the war and merchant fleets of nations.

At Burntisland I did not pause to visit Rossend Castle where Mary is supposed to have had her affair with Chastelard; certainly not. Nor at Kinghorn, where Alexander III, within a few months after he had married in haunted Kelso, and within a few hours perhaps after he had drunk the blude red wine in Dunfermline, came galloping by this way, the horse stumbled, the king fell, and

> "Quhen Alysandyr oure King was dede
> That Scotland led in luve and le . . .
> Succoure Scotland and remede
> That stands in perplexite."

Kirkcaldy

If Kirkcaldy was a "lang toun" in the olden days, it is longer to-day, stretching from Link-town to Dysart, and broadening inland to Gallatown, where they make the famous Wemyss pottery. To-day Kirkcaldy makes linoleum and jute and engineering works, and it is the center of a string of fishing villages, a "metropolitan borough system," hundreds of boats fishing the North Sea with KY marked as their home port, when their sailor men make home in any of these picturesque and smelling villages, St. Monan, Pittenweem, Cellardyke, Crail where Mary of Lorraine landed, Largo where Sir Andrew Wood the admiral lived, and where Alexander Selkirk lived what time he did not live as Crusoe in Juan Fernandez, and Anstruther—

> "Wha wad na be in love
> Wi' bonny Maggie Lauder,
> A piper met her gaen to Fife
> And speired what wast they ca'd her. . . .
> I've lived in Fife
> Baith maid and wife
> These ten years and a quarter,
> Gin ye should come to Anster Fair
> Speir ye for Maggie Lauder."

There is also some castellated splendour, Ravenscraig, and Wemyss on the site of the castle of MacDuff, then of Fife, this Wemyss being the ill-fated place where Mary first met Darnley.

Abbotshall kirkyard is at the right of the railway station as the train pulls in to Kirkcaldy. In his book of Scotch pilgrimages when William Winter was on his way to St. Andrews, past Kirkcaldy, he wrote "gazing as I pass at its quaint church among the graves." I suppose he did not know what grave.

But first I would find where she had lived. Kirkcaldy is close set against the sea. Here on winding High Street, I found the house in which she had lived, standing much as it did no doubt a hundred years ago, except for a new coat of tan on the stone. From those upper windows Marjorie looked out on the coach going away toward Edinburgh. The ground floor is occupied by a book store, where I could buy no book about Marjorie. Under a window you enter the archway and find yourself in a little green-grassed court, which is all that is left of Marjorie's garden. The house proper fronted the garden in that comfortable excluding way which British people still prefer for their places of habitation. It is still occupied as a dwelling, and the nursery still looks as it did in Marjorie's day, and the drawing-room, where she wrote that letter to Isa Keith— "I now sit down on my botom to answer all your kind and beloved letters." The door of the nursery was open. I remembered those last days, when lying ill, her mother asked Marjorie if there was anything she wished. "Oh, yes, if you would just leave the room door open a wee bit, and play 'The Land o' the Leal,' and I will lie still and think and enjoy myself."

"I'm wearin' awa', Jean,
Like snaw wreaths in thaw, Jean,
I'm wearin' awa',
To the Land o' the Leal."

The kirkyard lies on the outskirts of the town. It was a beautiful place as the Scotch sun sank behind the Fife hills and the Firth. The organist was playing and the music drifted out through the narrow lancet windows when I found the little white cross marked "Pet Marjorie," and the old gray tombstone with its simple token, "M. F. 1811."

For a hundred years then she has been lying there. But Marjorie has become one of the immortal dream children of the world. I laid my fresh flowers beside another's which had withered, and went my ways into the dusk.

St. Andrews

Past Kirkcaldy the road leaves the sea and runs northward through meadows between fields which have the look of centuries-old cultivation, at peace like the fields and villages of the English Midland, to St. Andrews.

> "St. Andrews by the Northern Sea,
> A haunted town it is to me!
> A little city, worn and gray,
> The gray North Ocean girds it round;
> And o'er the rocks, and up the bay,
> The long sea-rollers surge and sound;
> And still the thin and biting spray
> Drives down the melancholy street,
> And still endure, and still decay,
> Towers that the salt winds vainly beat.
> Ghost-like and shadowy they stand

Dim mirrored in the wet sea-sands.
"St. Leonard's Chapel, long ago
We loitered idly where the tall
Fresh-budded mountain ashes blow
Within thy desecrated wall;
The tough roots rent the tombs below,
And April birds sang clamorous,
We did not dream, we could not know
How hardly Fate would deal with us!

"O broken minster, looking forth
Beyond the bay, above the town,
O winter of the kindly North,
O college of the scarlet gown!"

Small wonder St. Andrews is the ecclesiastical capital of Scotland, and smaller wonder, remembering the Calvinistic wind, that here happened the brunt of the fight between the old faith and the new.

It is a clean and seemly town, with much historic memory and much present day dignity, a small gray town, "the essence of all the antiquity of Scotland in good clean condition," said Carlyle. Its ancient sights the cathedral and the castle; its living sight the university and the golf links.

The town stands on a promontory, three long streets converging on the cathedral and castle lying in ruins. The cathedral, a hundred years in the building, and very splendid in its wealth of detail, its vastness of space like that of York or Amiens, was dedicated in the days of The Bruce, with the king present to endow it with a hundred marks "for the mighty victory of the Scots at Bannockburn, by St. Andrew's, the guardian of the realm." For three hundred years its wax tapers lighted the old rites according to which The Bruce worshiped; he was not covenanted. Then the torch of the reformation was applied to it, the torch of the flaming tongue of John Knox.

To-day there are three towers left of the five —Dr. Johnson hoped that one which looked unstable on the day of his visit, would "fall on some of the posterity of John Knox; and no great matter!" There are massive walls. There is no roof between us and the sky, which, after all, does shelter the true faith, and if one misses the chanting of the monks echoing through these arches, under this roofless space, there is the moan of the sea, sobbing at the foot of the crag, the sea which is of no faith and never keeps faith. And if one misses the scarlet robes of Cardinal Beaton as he swept through these aisles in splendid procession with all the gorgeous trappings of his retinue, there are mosses and wild flowers to give glows of colour—one must content himself. Those were

ST. ANDREWS CASTLE.

evil days, whatever the faith; there was not much division in matters of conduct; there may have been in matters of morals.

The castle stands stalwart on the rock promoutory washed by the ocean, and the ocean breaks angrily at its base like a creature robbed over long of its prey. It is not the castle in which the Cardinal lived, but it was built soon after, and wrecked so thoroughly, and looks so very ancient, that one would fain believe; and the guide will tell, unless you prevent him, that it was at these windows that the Cardinal sat at his ease and witnessed the entertainment of the auto da fe of the non-conformist, George Wishart, burned alive on March 28, 1542; about the time Philip the Second was burning heretics in the Old Plaza at Madrid, and a little before Queen Mary spouse to Philip, was burning them in England. And it was only two months later, May 29, when workmen were strengthening the castle at the orders of the Cardinal against this very thing that happened, that the reformers made their way in, killed the Cardinal, and hung him "by the tane arm and the tane foot," from the very balcony where he had sat to enjoy Wishart's burning. A very barbarous time. As Wishart had lain in the Bottle Dungeon months before his burning, so

Beaton lay in the dungeon in salt, seven months before his burial.

John Knox joined the reformers, holding the town until it was taken by the French fleet—"defended their castle against Scotland, France, and Ireland all three"—surrendering to Strozzi, Prior of Capua, a Knight of Rhodes; so was the great world made small in those days by errant knights and captains and hired mercenaries. The French captain entered, "and spoiled the castle very rigorously," lest it should be "a receptacle for rebels." All this in the time of the Regency of Mary of Lorraine.

Knox was taken and sent to the galleys for a year. Then he returned, and was frequently in St. Andrews, preaching in the town kirk, founded, perhaps, by the confessor of Saint Margaret, preaching here some of his last sermons. "I saw him everie day of his doctrine go hulie and fear," wrote James Melville, "with a furrning of martriks about his neck, a staff in the an hand," and lifted up to the pulpit "whar he behovite to lean at his first entrie; bot or he had done with his sermont, he was so active and vigorus, that he lyk to ding that pulpit in blads and fly out of it." The pulpit held. And so did the doctrine of Knox.

The square tower of St. Regulus, a pre-Norman bit of architecture, perhaps Culdee, stands southeast of the cathedral. Dr. Johnson was indignant with Boswell that he missed it. This with the many other towers of church and college make St. Andrews a towered town.

There is an air, an atmosphere, in St. Andrews; it is an academic town, serene, certain of itself, quiet, with wide streets and gray stone buildings. It is full of dignity, full of repose, as a northern Oxford combined with a northern Canterbury should be. There is a spell of ancientry over the gray old walls, but it is unbroken ancientry; if there is a bar sinister, the present generation has forgotten it.

And, of course—oh, not of course, but primarily—there is golf. There is golf everywhere in Scotland. The golf ball and not the thistle is the symbol of Scotland to-day, and from the Tee at St. Andrews the Golf Ball has been driven round the world. James VI, careful Scot, recognized golf as an industry, and granted letters patent in 1618 for the manufacture of golf balls—the old leather, feather-stuffed sphere—to James Melville and William Berwick.

Edinburgh is ringed about with golf courses, public and private. So is Scotland. The

Firth of Forth is continuous with them, from North Berwick where the fleeting traveler is as certain to see golf balls as he is to see the Bass, up to St. Andrews. The Links of Leith are the most historic, for it was on these that Charles I was playing when news came of the Irish rebellion—and all that it led to. And here, his son, later James II, played against two English noblemen who had declared they could beat him, and James, cannily—true Scot!—chose the best player in Scotland, one Paterson an Edinburgh cobbler—and gave him the wager, and doubled it, out of which Paterson built for himself Golfer's *Land* in the Canongate. The Links of the Forth are not a golf course, although there may be some who assert that they were once an ancient course, say, for King Arthur and his Knights.

Sealand, shoreland, it seems, makes the ideal golf course, the soil growing with short crisp grass that makes a springy and slippery turf, and makes a keen game; the inlander, of course, and the American inlander, may not understand that golf can never quite be golf, certainly never be the true Scottish rite, unless it is played near the sea, with the tang of the sea and of golf entering into one's blood—and, preferably at St. Andrews.

At St. Andrews golf is a business, a sublimated business; or better, an education. Degrees are taken in it quite as high and requiring as thorough a training as at the University. It is to St. Andrews that the good golfer goes when he dies. And he aspires to go there before.

Or, rather at St. Andrews golf is a religion. Half the stories told of golf are, as might be expected of a game which came to its flowering in Scotland, religious, or irreligious. And one of the best of them is told in Stewart Dick's book on "The Forth." A Scots minister was playing and playing rather badly, and expressing himself in words if not in strokes. (Only those of you who have read "Sentimental Tommy" will understand that unconsciously I have played on the word "stroke!") The minister exclaimed bitterly as he emerged from his unholy battle with the bunker—is Bunker Hill, perhaps a hazard in golf?— "Ah maun gie it up! ah maun gie it up!" "What!" cried his partner alarmed, "gie up gowf?" "Naw, naw," returned the minister, "gie up the meenistry."

Perhaps to amend again, golf at St. Andrews is life. And in their death they are not divided. The graveyard near the Abbey, with stones hoary from the sixteenth century, is renowned to-day because it contains the graves of good golfers, Allan Robertson, old Tom Morris, and young Tom Morris, the greatest golfer since Paterson, dead at the pathetic age of 24; after that comes a man's best golfing years, that is, for his pleasure. Young Tom's grave is marked by an elaborate monument with an inscription that befits a king.

CHAPTER VI

TO THE NORTH

ONE leaves Edinburgh for the North—the haunted North—as in a royal progress. The train moves out of the Waverley station, and through the Gardens, under the very shadow of Castle Rock.

And it moves through the scant few miles of country, richly cultivated, suburban fairly, yet there are level wheatlands, and country cottages and orchards; it is southern, English, these few miles down to the Forth.

"The blackbird sang, the skies were clear and clean,
We bowled along a road that curved its spine
Superbly sinuous and serpentine
Thro' silent symphonies of summer green,
Sudden the Forth came on us—sad of mien,
No cloud to colour it, no breeze to line;
A sheet of dark dull glass, without a sign
Of life or death, two beams of sand between,
Water and sky merged blank in mist together,
The Fort loomed spectral, and the Guardship's spars
Traced vague, black shadows on the shimmery glaze:
We felt the dim, strange years, the gray, strange weather,
The still, strange land, unvexed of sun or stars,
Where Lancelot rides clanking thro' the haze."

To every one comes this sense of strange years and a strange land, even at Queensferry, even to Henley.

The inn, where we have all put up in imagination, with Scott, and again with Stevenson, lies under the bridge, as though it would escape the quick curious gaze from these iron girders so high above what Scott ever dreamed or Davy Balfour. And then, the train creeps out over this modern audacity, this very ugly iron spanning of the river. Fortunately we are upon it and cannot see its practical, monstrous being, "that monster of utility," as Lord Rosebery called it. He should know its phrase, since it is ever present in the view from his Dalmeny Park, lying east of the Bridge and south of the Forth.

This is precisely where Queen Margaret was ferried to and fro a thousand years ago. The monks who had charge of the ferry took from the toll every fourth and every fortieth penny—a delightful bit of geometric finance. Who could calculate and who would dispute the calculation, of fourth and fortieth?

Dunfermline

"The King sits in Dunfermline toun
Drinking the blude-red wine."

Because of such lines as these I would cross far seas, merely to have been, if far lonely destructive centuries after, in the very place of their being.

For Dunfermline is surely a very kingly name for a king's town, and "blude-red" wine is of such a difference from mere red, or blood-red wine. What wonder that Alexander III, of whom it is written, went to his death over at Kinghorn in such a tragic way!

But the king who forever sits in Dunfermline is that Malcolm of the eleventh century who brings hither something more than legend yet something as thrilling, as "authentic" as legend. Malcolm is the son of Duncan, in Shakespeare's play, and in history.

"The son of Duncan
From whom this tyrant holds the due of birth,
Lives in the English court; and is received
Of the most pious Edward with such grace
That the malevolence of fortune nothing
Takes from his high respect."

Malcolm, after "the deep damnation of his taking off," fled from the red wrath of Macbeth and into the far prophecy of Banquo, to the court of Edward the Confessor. There perhaps he met Margaret; or perhaps not, since she was grand-niece to the Confessor, and Malcolm was a middle-aged man when this first royal Scottish romance occurs. When he returned he built himself a castle here on the safe north side of the Forth; if ever any place were safe in that eleventh century. He waited here the coming of Margaret, and she came, the first Margaret of England.

It was the first year after the Conquest, and Princess Margaret with her brother and sister were fleeing to her mother's people in Bohemia. They were wrecked far north in the Firth of Forth—which thereby becomes part of the legendary coast of Bohemia. She landed at St. Margaret's Hope, the first bay to the west of North Queensferry. Malcolm saw her from his high tower—and they were married—and they lived happily ever after, and richly for a quarter of a century; and they live immortally now.

Their history is certain, but it reads like a romance. It may be read, very exquisitely set forth, in "The Tides of Spring," a one-act drama by Arthur Upson, the young American poet whose sonnet on Calton Hill I have just quoted; a poet who went to his death so tragically and so beautifully in Lake Bemidji in Minnesota, a few years ago.

The story in the play, of Malcolm and Margaret, is all apple blossoms and spring tides; it is very lovely. Margaret has met Malcolm before, and destiny brings her to Scotland and to the king. It is a beautiful beginning to a long enduring love story that through all the reality of history shows a tender devotion from this stern northern king to the saintly queen from the Saxon South.

They safeguarded themselves and their royal flock in Edinburgh, but they lived in Dunfermline. Margaret knew a richer and a more religious life than Malcolm, and she it was who laid the foundations of the kingdom, in court and church. "Whatever she refused, he refused also; whatever pleased her, he also loved, for the love of her," says her confessor. English Margaret, unlike the later English Margaret of Alexander III, did not find the North "a sad and solitary place"; and unlike the English Margaret of James IV she was saintly, a white pearl in this wild red time.

Malcolm and Margaret became the father

and mother of a royal brood, four kings of Scotland, and of Queen Matilda of England—surely Banquo saw clearly on that terrible night; his prophecy began with a royal rush.

But who would not live a lovely and pleasant life in this well-placed royal burg, serene upon her hill? Rich green fields spread down to the Forth, the red network of the bridge lifts itself into view, far to the left sweeps the Firth out to North Berwick Law and the Bass, and Edinburgh swims in the haze against the leonine mountain that is ever her guard.

The Abbey gives the town its special dignity. There is nothing left of the church built by Queen Margaret—where she robbed the box of the money the king had just given at mass if she found the poor requiring more immediate help. But this ancient nave built by Margaret's son David is so very ancient that one could well spare the accurate historic knowledge that it is a generation too late for emotion. There are ponderous round pillars that could have sustained all the history we require of them, high casements, a bare triforium, altogether a Davidic place, a simplicity, a truth about it, that we would not dispute.

The new church was built a century ago over the old, and the ancient nave is like an aisle in the new. Certain details, like the little Norman doorway, once walled-up in the time of Knox, reward us with their preserved beauty.

The tombs of Malcolm and Margaret are without the wall. Malcolm perhaps is there; they carried bodies far in those days of material resurrection, and would have brought Malcolm from Northumberland. But Margaret, canonized next century, was too precious to remain in Ultima Thule, so Spain carried her away—and who knows where she rests?

But within, before the high altar—or shall we say since this is a reformed place, before the pulpit?—rests the body of The Bruce. It is no doubt The Bruce. For Dunfermline was forgotten in rebellious times, and the tombs were undisturbed. Even in the North transept there rest the bones of eleven kings earlier than The Bruce.

Yes, it is very certain The Bruce, wrapped in gold cloth in the thirteenth century, his heart only missing and lying at Melrose. Scott who was everywhere and investigating everything saw the tomb opened and pronounced—King Robert Bruce. One could wish the great letters about the modern tower looking like an electric sign, were "reformed." But here within the quiet, to stand at the very spot where is the dust of so mighty a man, mighty in valour, mighty in sovereignty—I find it a more substantial emotion than I have felt in the Invalides.

Ancientry preserves its unbroken descent outside the church. The mother of Wallace is buried here, and the thorn be planted to mark her grave still flourishes, to the ninth century after.

The people who sit in Dunfermline town have not too much concern for King Robert and King Alexander. Nor do they do much sitting, these busy industrious Dunfermliners. They are living their own lives, and making for themselves profit through the generosity of a later fellow citizen.

Dunfermline is a center of great coal fields, and center of the Scotch linen making. So the town is modern, looks modern, and the people move briskly. If they know you are a tourist on ancient errand bent, they look curiously. You come from so far to recapture ancient life, when you might have so much modern life in your own country.

They know what America means. For Andrew Carnegie is their fellow citizen, or would be had he not become an American. Seventy years ago he was born in a cottage toward which the Dunfermline folk look with the attention we show the Abbey. And Carnegie has not only given a library to Dunfermline—yes, a library—Malcolm could not read Margaret's books, but he had them richly bound and bejeweled and kissed them in reverence of her. But the Laird has given a technical school, and the Pittencrieff Glen, which is a lovely pleasure ground with the scant stones of Malcolm's palace above, and a trust of two million and a half dollars, which the wise town corporation is busy utilizing for the advancement of Dunfermline town.

Loch Leven

And on to Loch Leven. I cannot think that any one can come upon this castle without emotion. Or he should never come to Scotland.

It is a famous fishing lake, a peculiar kind of trout are abundant, twenty-five thousand taken from it each year; rather I have given the round numbers, but an exact toll of the fish taken is required by law, and for the past year it was, with Scottish accuracy, something more or something less than twenty-five thousand. The lake is controlled altogether by an anglers association. No boat can row on it, no fisherman can cast his line, but by permission.

There is a small shop in Edinburgh where tickets and tackle can be taken, and much advice from the canny Scot who keeps the shop, and who would make your fishing expedition a success. "I don't know what your scruples are," he ventured, "but if ye want the Loch Leven boatmen to be satisfied, I'd advise ye to take wi' a bit o' Scotch. A wee bit drappie goes a long wa."

"Just a wee deoch and doris!"

We remembered Harry Lauder, and wondered if we could say "It's a braw bricht moon licht nicht." Or would those redoutable boatmen ken that we were but pretending to Scotch and even suspect our "Scotch"?

They did not.

The Green hotel is an excellent place to stay, kept by a Scotchman who knows that in America every one knows every one else. We slept in feather beds, and we inspected the collection of "stanes," one of the best I have ever seen in Scotland, a great variety, some of them natural boulders, some wood with iron weights—someday I must brave the rigours of a Scotch winter and see them curl on Duddingston or on Leven. And I should like to see Bob Dunbar of St. Paul, champion curler of America, measure his skill against the champion of Scotland.

And, of course, there was talk with the Scot host. "So ye're American. Well, maybe ye ken a mon that lives in Minn'apolis. He's twa sisters live here; and he's built a hoose for them." It happened that we did ken of this man, who came from Kinross to Minneapolis with only his Scotch canniness, and has built the Donaldson business into one of the great department stores of America.

And next day, after we had slept on feather beds, we had our fishing in Loch Leven, with thousands of wild swan disputing our possession; a big boat, with big oars, sweeps, one man to each oar, one a loquacious fellow with no dialect (he might as well have been English), and the other taciturn with a dialect thick as mud or as Lauder's. And we caught two of the twenty-five thousand odd which were credited to that year.

As the train came alongside Loch Leven on its way to Kinross station, suddenly I felt Mary as I never have realized her, before or since. There across the lake lay St. Serf's isle, and there rose the keep of the old castle. And over that water, as plainly—more plainly, than the fishing boats that lay at their ease—I saw her take boat on a still evening, May 2, 1568, at half past seven o'clock from prison—to liberty —to prison!

I was not mistaken. She who was with me saw it, as distinctly, as vividly. Perhaps it was that all our lives this had been to us one of the great adventuring moments—for which we would exchange any moment of our lives. We were idolaters always, Mariolaters. And now we know that places are haunted, and that centuries are of no account; they will give up their ghosts to those who would live in them.

"Put off, put off, and row with speed,
For now is the time and the hour of need,
To oars, to oars, and trim the bark,
Nor Scotland's queen be a warder's mark;
Yon light that plays 'round the castle moat,
Is only the warder's random shot;
Put off, put off, and row with speed,
For now is the time and the hour of need.

"Those pond'rous keys shall the kelpies keep,
And lodge in their caverns, so dark and deep,
Nor shall Loch Leven's tower and hall
Hold thee, our lovely lady, in thrall;
Or be the haunts of traitors sold,
While Scotland has hands and hearts so bold.
Then onward, steersman, row with speed,
For now is the time and the hour of need.

"Hark! the alarum bell has rung,
The warder's voice has treason sung,

The echoes to the falconets roar,
Chime sweetly to the dashing shore;
Let tower, hall, and battlement gleam,
We steer by the light of the taper's gleam,
For Scotland and Mary on with speed,
Now, now, is the time and the hour of need!"

Because of that experience, because of the feeling I have for Queen Mary, I have never landed upon St. Serf's island. It has happened, quite without my making intentional pilgrimage, that I have been in many places where Queen Mary has been; and willingly I have made my accidental pilgrimages of loyalty. I have stood in the turret at Roscoff where she landed when only five, hurried from Scotland that she might escape sinister England; in the chapel in Notre Dame where she was married to the Dauphin; in the château at Orleans where she lived with him much of that brief happy French life she loved so dearly; in the two small garret chambers where she lodged in Coventry; in Hardwick Hall, where Bess of Hardwick was her stern jailer; at Fotheringay where nothing remains of that ensanguined block but a low heap of stones which the grass covers; in Peterborough where she found her first resting place; in Westminster her last final resting place; and in many and many a haunted place of this Scottish land.

And just before starting north I made a little journey to Linlithgow which lies twenty miles west of Edinburgh. The palace overlooks a quiet blue loch, a blue smiling bit of water, on which much royalty has looked forth, and on which the eyes of Mary first looked. There, in the unroofed palace of Linlithgow, in the "drawing-room," in December, 1542, was born that queen who ever since has divided the world.

> "Of all the palaces so fair
> Built for the royal dwelling,
> In Scotland far beyond compare
> Linlithgow is excelling.
> And in the park in jovial June
> How sweet the merry linnet's tune,
> How blithe the blackbird's lay."

It was the dower-house of Scottish queens, and hither James V brought Mary of Lorraine after he had married her at St. Andrews. (I wondered if there was any haunting memory of Margaret of Denmark who sat here sewing when the nobles raged through the palace seeking the life of James III. Or of Margaret of England as she sat here waiting for James IV to return from Flodden.)

Of the regency of Mary of Lorraine, when James V died and Mary was a baby, Knox spluttered that it was "as semlye a sight (yf

DRAWING-ROOM, LINLITHGOW PALACE, WHERE QUEEN MARY WAS BORN.

men had eis) as to putt a sadill upoun the back of ane unrowly kow.'' Knox did not pick his language with any nicety when he said his say of women and the monstrous regiments of them. And to his Puritan soul there could come no approval of the love affairs of Mary of Lorraine, such as that one sung by the Master of Erskine, who was slain at Pinkiecleuch—

"I go, and wait not quhair,
I wander heir and thair,
I weip and sichis rycht sair
With panis smart;
Now must I pass away, away,
In wilderness and lanesome way,
Alace! this woeful day
We suld departe."

And now there is neither Margaret nor Mary, neither regent nor reformer, palace of neither Linlithgow nor Leven. How the destructions of man have thrown palaces and doctrines open to the winds of heaven. And how purifying this destruction. And what precious things have passed with them, what tears of women have been shed, and how are the mouths of men become dust.

Loch Leven has one lovely gracious memory of Mary in the days before everything was lost. She was lodging here, and had sent for Knox to come from Edinburgh.

"She travailed with him earnestly for two hours before her supper, that he would protect the Catholic clergy from persecution." Knox slept in the castle, but "before the sun," as he records, he was awakened by the sound of horns and of boats putting off to the mainland. For the queen would go a-hawking.

Presently Knox was roused. The queen would have him join her "be-west Kinross," to continue the conversation.

The reformer did not rise as early as the queen—the serenity of that righteous conscience! He rose reluctantly at her summons. His reforming eyes, no doubt, looked with displeasure on the exquisite beauties of the unreformed morning, the mists lying soft on the Lomonds, day just emerging from night.

So he joined her, and they rode together, she on her horse, he on his hackney.

And the morning came on, and the day was a glory.

Mary warned Knox that a certain Bishop sought to use him, and Knox afterward acknowledged the value of her warning. She asked him to settle a quarrel between Argyle and his wife, her half sister, as Knox had done before. And often no doubt she glanced at her hawk hanging in the high Scottish sky.

And finally she declared—"as touching our reasoning of yesternight, I promise to do as ye required. I shall summon the offenders and ye shall know that I shall minister justice."

And the reformer, softened by the morning, and by Mary's eyes—"I am assured then that ye shall please God and enjoy rest and prosperity within your realm."

And Knox rode off. And Mary rode hawking.

The time was not yet come when Mary should say—"Yon man gar me greet and grat never tear himself. I will see if **I** can gar him greet."

Or, for Knox to pray—"Oh, Lord, if thy pleasure be, purge the heart of the Queen's Majestic from the venom of idolatry, and deliver her from the bondage and the thralldom of Satan."

Perth

Perth may be the Fair City, but it is scarce fair among cities, and is chiefly regarded even by itself as a point of departure, the Gate of the Highlands. The railway platform is at least a third of a mile long, and very bewildering to the unsuspecting visitor who thought he was merely coming to the ancient Celtic capital.

For, very far backward, this was the chief city of the kingdom, before Scotland had spread down to the Forth, and down to the Border. Even so recently (?) as the time of James the First it was held the fairest city in the kingdom. But the assassination of that monarch must have led the Jameses to seek a safer city in which to be fair.

There is a touch of antiquity about the town. One is shown the house of the Fair Maid; in truth that being the objective of the casual traveler signs in the street point the way. It may or may not be. But we agreed to let Scott decide these things and he, no doubt, chose this house. Curfew Street that runs by, looking like a vennel—vennel? I am certain—was inhabited rather by lively boys, and no fair head looked out from the high window that would have furnished an excellent framing for the fair face of Catherine Glover.

The North Inch I found to be not an island in the Tay, but a meadow, where every possible out-door activity takes place among the descendants of Clans Chattan and Quhele—there is race-course, golf links, cricket field, football, grazing, washing. I trust the clans are somewhat evener now in numbers, although there were left but one Chattan to level the Quheles. Coming from the Chattan tribe I must hope the centuries since that strifeful day have brought reëxpansion to the Chattans.

Farther up the Inch, onto the Whin, the eye looks across to Scone. The foot does not cross, for there is nothing left of the old Abbey, not even of the old palace where Charles II, last king crowned in Scotland, suffered coronation —and was instructed in the ways of well doing according to the Covenant. Even the stone of destiny was gone then, brought from Dunstaffnage, and taken to Westminster.

There is nothing, or only stones, left of the Blackfriar's Monastery in which James, the poet-king, suffered death. Surely he was born too soon. As last instead of first of the Jameses, what might he not have done in the ways of intelligence and beauty, as England's king as well as Scotland's? Very beautifully runs his picture of Lady Joanna Beaufort, seen from a window in Windsor—

> "The fairest and the freshest flower,
> That ever I saw before that hour,
> The which o' the sudden made to start
> The blood of my body to my heart . . .
> Ah, sweet, are ye a worldly creature,
> Or heavenly thing in form of nature?"

He came back from his enforced habitation in England accompanied by Lady Joanna as Queen, and determined "if God gives me but a dog's life, I will make the key keep the castle and the brachen bush the cow." It was a dog's death the gods gave. The nobles, the Grahams, would not keep the castle. So in Blackfriars the king was "mercilessly dirked to death," notwithstanding that Catherine Douglass—the Douglasses were with James then—made a bar across the door with her arm where the iron had been sinisterly removed. A dark scene, with "the fairest flower" looking on.

So, I think it not so ill, even though time delayed over a hundred years, that John Knox (May, 1559) should have preached such an incendiary sermon that in three days there was nothing left of Black or Gray friary but the broken stones.

Nor is there anything left of Gowrie house, where James VI was almost entrapped and almost slain—"I am murdered—treason—treason"; the jail stands on its site. Huntington Tower still stands down the Tay; and there also James very nearly came to his death, at the plotting of the son of that Ruthven who killed Rizzio and forced Mary to abdicate.

Kinnoul Hill overlooks the town, and furnishes a very fair view of the Fair City. No

HUNTINGTON TOWER.

doubt it was from this height that the Roman looked down upon the Tay—

> "Behold the Tiber! the vain Roman cried,
> Viewing the ample Tay from Baiglie's side;
> But where's the Scot that would the vaunt repay,
> And hail the puny Tiber for the Tay?"

It is more wonderful to-day to know that salmon weighing seventy pounds are sometimes taken from this Tay. The river leads down through the rich Carse of Gowrie, toward Dundee and marmalade. Thither we shall not go; but it shall come to us.

Ruskin spent his childhood in Perth and did not like it. But Ruskin liked so little in the world, except—"that Scottish sheaves are more golden than are bound in other lands, and that no harvests elsewhere visible to human eye are so like the 'corn of heaven,' as those of Strath Tay and Strath Earn." That is the way for to admire, for to see; all, or nothing was Ruskin's way.

Ruskin married in Perth, one of its fairest maids, who lived on the slope of Kinnoul Hill; and then, unmarrying, the fair lady, looking very fair in the painted pictures, married a painter who once was very much about Perth.

Perth is also the "Muirton" of "The Bonnie

Brier Bush.'' So some have found these environs bonny.

In truth it is a lovely surrounding country. And have you not from childhood, if you read ''Macbeth'' as early as did Justice Charles E. Hughes, thought Birnam and Dunsinane the loveliest names in the world? Six miles up the Tay through bonny country, stands Dunsinnan Hill; not so lovely as our Dunsinane; once it was Dunscenanyse! But Shakespeare always gave words their magic retouching. And once there stood here the castle of Dunsinane where a certain Lady walked in her sleep, and then slept. And below, you see Birnam wood—

> "Till great Birnam wood
> Do come to Dunsinane."

To see that wood wave in the wind is fairly eerie!

Dunkeld is less of a city, more of a memory, exquisite in its beauty, lodged in a close fold of the Highlands. And you reach it through the station, cis-Tay, called Birnam!

It is a quiet peaceful place, more like a now quiet Border town. Hither to this cathedral, the precious remains of Saint Columba were brought by the MacAlpine. So I suppose they still rest here, that wandering dust, that missionary zeal. Also, inharmony, here rest (?) the remains of the Wolf of Badenoch, wicked son of Robert II, and—I am certain the pun has been ventured before—bad enough. Gavin Douglass of the Vergilian measure was bishop here, and Mrs. Oliphant has written stories round about.

"Cam ye by Athole, lad wi' the philabeg?"

We are getting into the Highlands, we are at them, from now on nothing but philabegs, pibrochs, pipes, tartans and heather, nothing but the distilled essence of heather—heather ale? the secret was lost when the Picts were conquered.

CHAPTER VII

HIGHLAND AND LOWLAND

MANY ways lead out of Perth, but best of these is the foot-path way, picked up anywhere in the Highlands. By rail the road leads down to the sea, past Glamis Castle, built in 1500, where the room is shown in which Duncan was murdered in 1000, although Shakespeare says it was at Inverness; and to Kirriemuir, if one would match the "Bonnie Brier Bush" with "The Window in Thrums." Or by rail the road leads to the lakes of the West, and to the Highlands of the North.

For one short space I took it northward to the Pass of Killiecrankie, almost in fear, as a regiment of English mercenaries is said to have been a-feared in the Forty Five, three-quarters of a century after Killiecrankie. For here in a last splendid moment, Graham of Claverhouse, Viscount of Dundee, and sometime Bonnie Dundee, was killed, the battle having gone gloriously his way, for the glorious cause of Stewart and *mon droit*—some say by a silver

GLAMIS CASTLE.

bullet, the devil having charmed the leaden bullets that were showered against his magic life; those who say it are Whigs.

Always called Bonnie Dundee by those of us who care for romance. To quote from Samuel Crothers, "And you say they are the same? I cannot make them seem the same. To me there are two of them: Graham of Claverhouse, whom I hate, and the Bonnie Dundee, whom I love. If it's all the same to you, I think I shall keep them separate, and go on loving and hating as aforetime."

The Pass is lovely enough, on a summer morning, with the sun shining fair on the Highlands, the blue hills misty in the distance, the trees thick green on both sides the bending Garry, and not a living thing in view, nothing which belongs to the Duke of Atholl who owns everything hereabout, except the air and the beauty and the memory, which I packed in my Pilgrim's Wallet.

Because the Duke owns the cathedral I did not claim any memory beside the dust of Bonnie Dundee—

"Fling open the Westport and let me gae free."

And now, to a certain defeat which I suffered near the Pass of Killiecrankie, when I "cam by

Athole." I was without a philabeg. If I had had it—it sounds so enhearteningly like usquebaugh—I think my courage would have been great enough to do the thing I had crossed over seas to do—to walk from Blair Athole through Glen Tilt and between the great lift of the Cairngorms, to Braemar. I had felt that I owed it to Scottish ancestors and to those who had lost in the Risings.

I remembered that Queen Mary had longed to be a man. When she had come into this North to punish Huntley, so the Scottish calendar states, "She repenteth of nothing, but when the lords and others came in the morning from the watch, that she was not a man to know what life it was to lie all night in the fields, or to walk upon the causeway with a jack and a knapschall (helmet), a Glasgow buckler, and a broadsword." Her father's errant soul was hers. And once she ventured it, but in fear of her life, when she fled from the wraith of Darnley, to the scandalizing of the mongers, "Her Majestic, in mennis claithes, buttit and spurrit, departed that samin nicht of Borthwick to Dunbar, quhairof no man knew saif my Lord Duke and sum of his servants, wha met Her Majestic a myll off Borthwick and conveyed her hieness to Dunbar."

GLEN TILT.

I added another Scottish defeat. For it was excessively warm that summer, and Scotland can be as warm and as dry as Kansas. It is thirty miles, the mountain way. There is no inn. There is possibility—there is danger—of losing the way. There are no wolves, I suppose, and certainly no Wolf of Badenoch. But there were the unknown terrors.

So we walked a certain stent into Glen Tilt, enough to know that it is wild, gloomy, one of the strangest wildest places, Ben-y-Gloe, the "Mountain of the Mist," rising out of the early morning mist, yet not so mysteriously or majestically as the Mountain Going to the Sun. But no valley in our Mountain West has ever seemed more empty. And I suppose since Pictish time this glen has been deserted. There were deer, red deer, that thought they were free, and who looked out of their coverts indifferently. We had not the heart to tell them that they belonged, body and soul, to the Duke of Atholl. After the Porteous riots, Queen Caroline, presiding in the place of George who was absent in his favourite Hanover, threatened "to turn Scotland into a hunting field." The Duke of Argyle thereupon hinted that he would have to "return to look after my hounds." Queen Caroline seems sovereign to-day. And especially on August eleventh, the day before St. Grouse Day, there is an ominous quiet.

So we returned by way of Coupar Angus—meekly remembering the proverb, "he that maun to Coupar, maun to Coupar." Here we changed cars, nearly losing the train, because we were so engrossed in watching the loading of the luggage, the Scotch porter cheering on his assistant, "we're twa strong men, haud awa, let's be canny." And in the great gold sunset that was like the glory of God upon the beavenly Highlands.

We came to Blairgowrie, where we heard in the twilight on the hills above the town a bird of magic such as I have never heard elsewhere. Was it a nightingale, or a night lark? It sang like these.

Next morning we took coach across these great hills, by way of Glenshee, a very lovely way of going, and not to be regretted, in its dashing splendour of a coach and six—except that it was not a thirty-mile walk. But it is to be historically remembered, because it is the way Mar's men came down to the Strath of Tay, and brought the Rising into the Lowlands. We would go to meet them.

It was a memorable day. Not even the Simplon pass taken on a June day when the road ran between fresh coach-out-topping walls of glittering snow can make one forget the road over the Spittal of Glenshee. There were impossibly purple mountains, indigo-deep, deeper purple than any hills I have ever seen, so does the ripened heather dye the distances more deeply. There were rocky glens, great loneliness, a mansion here and there only just on leaving Blairgowrie, Tullyveolan, of course; scarce a cottage even on the roadside; once a flock of sheep, near the Spittal, being worked by Scotch collies, with an uncanny, or, canny, second sense to get the master's direction. There was lunch at the Spittal, a one-time Hospice, like that on the Simplon. And I wondered if the song ran of this lovely little glen set in the midst of so much primeval world—

"O wharawa got ye that auld crookit penny,
For ane o' bright gowd wad ye niffer wi' me?
Richt fou are baith ends o' my green silken wallet,
And braw will your hame be in bonnie Glenshee.

"For a' the bricht gowd in your green silken wallet
I never wad niffer my crookit bawbee."

The road at the top of the world runs smoothly enough. But when the Devil's elbow is reached, a tremendous and dangerous turn in the road, every one dismounts from the coach, and the sight of an adventurous motor car coming down the turn does not decrease one's sense of peril.

Braemar

And then the sight of Braemar, and a consciousness that if you are about to spend more money at the Fife Arms or the Invercauld than any but royalty has a right to spend—royalty not having earned it—the adventure has been worth it.

And to have forgotten but as the coach flashes by to read the tablet—

> "Here Robert Louis Stevenson lived in the summer of 1881, and wrote 'Treasure Island.'"

this is to be home again.

Of course our first pilgrimage was to the Invercauld Arms, where we again set up the standard on the braes of Mar. It was here that Malcolm Canmore instituted the Highland Gathering which persists to this day. And here, under cover of the hunt, so did the loyal Jacobites conceal their intention, the Rising of the Fifteen was planned—and the hunters became the hunted.

It was evening, it was the Highlands, the

INVERCAULD HOUSE.

great circle of mountains lay round about. And if King James VIII and III had been defeated these two hundred years, and dead a lesser time, and our loyalty had always been to the Prince who came rather to establish his father than himself, the Fifteen seemed like yesterday. In this remote high corner of the world anything is possible, even the oblivion of time. It seemed very vital, that faraway moment, which in truth few persons to-day take into reckoning; even history recks little of it. But very near in this illusory twilight—was that the Fiery Cross that glimmered in the darkness?

"The standard on the braes o' Mar
Is up and streaming rarely;
The gathering pipe on Lochnagar
Is sounding loud and clearly.
The Highlandmen frae hill and glen,
In martial hue, wi' bonnets blue,
Wi' belted plaids and burnished blades,
Are coming late and early.

"Wha' wadna join our noble chief,
The Drummond and Glengarry?
Macgregor, Murray, Rollo, Keith,
Panmure and gallant Harry,
Macdonald's men, Clanranald's men,
Mackenzie's men, Macgilvrary's men,
Strathallan's men, the Lowland men
Of Callander and Airlie."

Next day we met a gentleman we forever call "The Advocate of Aberdeen." In any event the lawyers of Aberdeen have styled themselves "Advocates" since so addressed by King James. We did not know that when we named him, but we preferred it to any Sandy or "Mac" he might legally carry. Having been informed by him that our name was Lowland and we were entitled to none of the thrills of the Highlands, we failed to mount farther than the third stage of the Morrone Hill. The wind blew a gale from the nor'nor'west, like those better known to us from the sou'sou'west. It was humiliating to have the Advocate of Aberdeen instruct us when we returned that if we had gone on we might have proved our Highland blood.

We did not attempt Ben MacDui, although it may be approached by the ever-easy way of pony-back, even the queen—not Mary—having mounted it in this fashion. We were content to master, almost master, its pronunciation according to the pure Gaelic—Muich Dhui. And then we learned that by more accurate and later scientific measurement, MacDui is not the tallest mountain in the kingdom, but Ben Nevis out-tops it.

To make our peace with an almost forfeited

fate, we took a dander, that is, we walked back toward Glen Tilt by the way we had not come. There is a happy little falls a couple of miles from the town, Corrimulzie, plunging down a long fall through a deep narrow gorge, but very pleasantly. We passed white milestone after white milestone, measured in particular Scottish accuracy—we timed ourselves to a second and found we could measure the miles by the numbers of our breaths. The forest is thick and bosky, not an original forest, doubtless. But I was reminded that Taylor, on his Pennyless Pilgrimage came to Braemar three hundred years ago, and wrote "as many fir trees growing there as would serve for masts (from this time to the end of the worlde) for all the shippes, caracks, hoyes, galleyes, boates, drumiers, barkes, and water-crafte, that are now, or can be in the worlde these fourty yeeres." He lamented the impossibility of sending them down to tide water where they might meet their proper fate.

Only once did we meet a carriage in which we suspected that royalty, or at least ladies-in-waiting—if Duke's wives who are royal have such appendages—might be sitting.

And on to the Linn of Dee, which is truly a marvelous place. The Advocate of Aberdeen when we had asked him why so many of his townfolk came this way, explained with a sense of possession of the greater Dee, "we like to see what the Dee can do." Surely it can do it. In these rock walls it has spent centuries carving for itself fantastic ways, until not the Dalles of the St. Croix can excel its rock-bound fantasy. Given time, the Dee can "do" pretty much as it pleases in granite.

The few miles we ventured beyond the Linn were enough to prove that the way was long, the wind was cold, the minstrel was infirm and old. Had we walked all the mountain way we should have been much in need of a "plaidie to the angry airts." This air is very bracing.

But we sang many Jacobite songs in memory of the Risings. "Wha'll be King but Charlie?" and "Charlie is my Darling," and "Over the sea Charlie is coming to me," and "Will ye no come back again." And we sang with particular satisfaction that we were not, after all, to suffer royal wrongs—surely there is a falling away in the far generations in the far places, since a King's son could so adventure—

"Dark night cam' on, the tempest roar'd,
Loud o'er the hills and valleys,
An' where was't that your Prince lay down
Who's hame should been a palace?

BALMORAL CASTLE.

He row'd him in a Highland plaid,
Which cover'd him but sparely,
An' slept beneath a bush o' broom,
Oh, wae's me for Prince Charlie."

On these braes of Mar, and in these hills and beside these very streams, the Prince made his adventure—yes, and simply because of that adventure will be forever remembered by those who believe in the heroic mood.

To leave Braemar the road leads down to Ballater, with motor cars to take it swiftly; past the castles of Mar old and new, where betimes sits the present Earl of Mar, not conning Risings but writing to the magazines his idea of a free Scotland, which shall have its Home Rule like Ireland—which was once Scotland—and which may have it at the great peace; down through an increasingly pleasant country. Balmoral Castle looks deserted now of its queen—and when queens desert, places are much emptier than when kings leave. But "queen's weather" is still possible here, even though the castle and our way are overshadowed by Lochnagar, on which we bestow more than passing glance in memory of that Gordon who was Lord Byron.

"Ah! there my young footsteps in infancy wander'd;
My cap was the bonnet, my cloak was the plaid;

On chieftains long perished my memory ponder'd,
 As daily I strove through the pine-cover'd glade;
I sought not my home till the day's dying glory
 Gave place to the rays of the bright polar star;
For fancy was cheer'd by traditional story,
 Disclosed by the natives of dark Loch na Garr."

And one glance at Lumphanan— "This Macbeth then slew they there in the wood of Lumphanan," so runs the old chronicle.

Aberdeen

There is no city in Scotland which seems to me to have more personality, a more distinct personality, than Aberdeen. It is plainly a self-sufficient city, and both in politics and in religion it thinks for itself, mindless if its thinking is not that of the rest of the kingdom.

Its provost cannot leave its borders; once he attended a battle, many and many a year ago, nineteen miles from the city at Harlow, and sad to say, he was killed. So now the provost remains in the city, he cannot leave it more than President can leave Republic, or Pope the Vatican.

In religion, Aberdeen is strongly Episcopalian, where it is not Catholic. In truth there

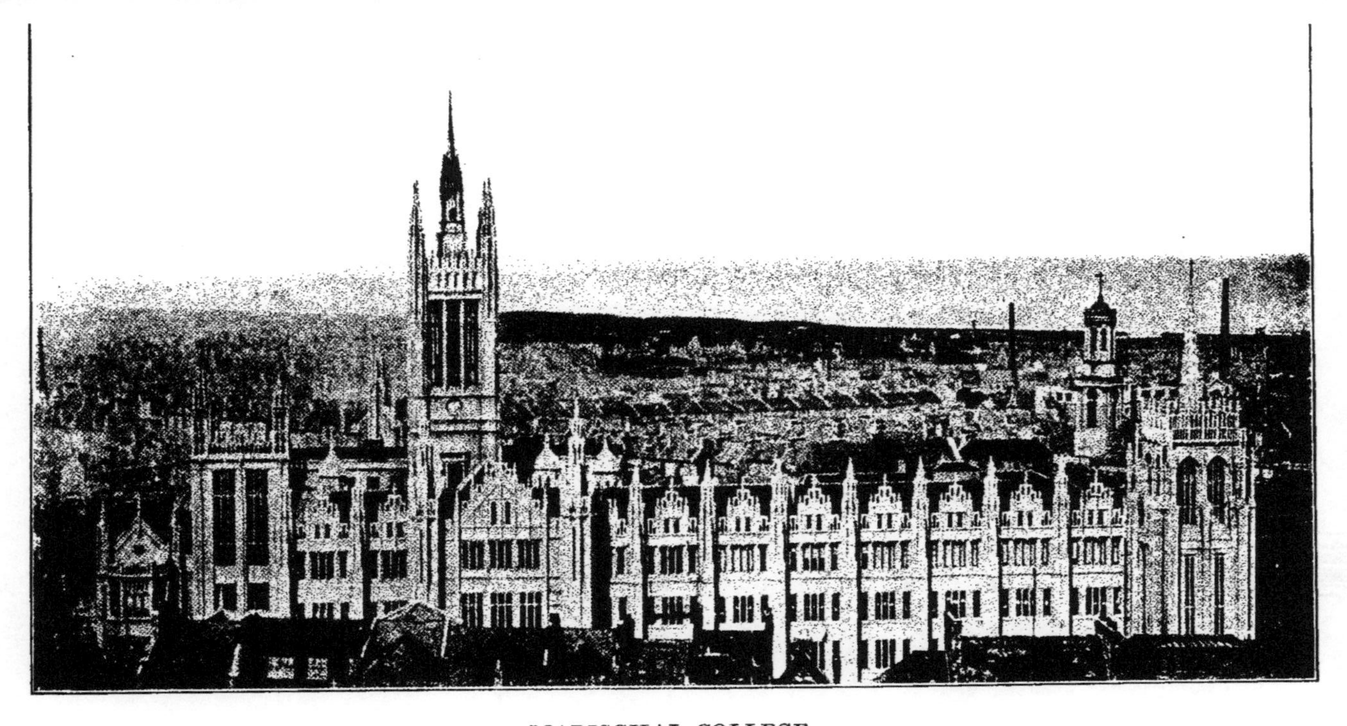

MARISCHAL COLLEGE.

is a band of Catholicism running across the country, from Aberdeen to Skye, through the heart of the Highlands. As might be expected, the Highlands never yielded to the reformatory methods of John Knox, but remained of the faith.

There is no city that looks so Scottish, and yet so different, as Aberdeen. It is a dignified and an extraordinarily clean city. After a rain its granite glitters as though it had been newly cut, and to one accustomed to smoke-grimed American cities Aberdeen looks as though it were built this morning, when no doubt much of this granite has a right to the hoar of antiquity.

Marischal College, founded by the Keiths, who were Earl Marischals, boasts of being the greatest granite pile in the world, after the Escorial. Having walked a day through a circumscribed portion of that Spanish granite, I chose to limit my footsteps in Marischal college. Only to verify the stone did I enter. And there it stood, over the doorway of the inner entrance hall, that stone which gives me a certain ancestral right of hauteur—

> Thay half said.
> Quhat say thay?
> Lat thame say.

Scots are astonishingly fond of mottoes. They carve them, like Orlando's verse, if not on every tree, on every lintel and over every fireplace; from *Nemo me impune lacessit* of the royal thistle race, to every clan and every cottage.

King's College (1495) is an older foundation than Marischal (1593), and where once they were rivals, since the Eighteen Sixties they have been harmonized, and since Mr. Carnegie gave them his benefaction, education is free in this University of Aberdeen. King's College, if not the next greatest granite pile, has a stone cross, which is the typical capping of noble edifice in Scotland; in truth it begins at Newcastle on Tyne when one enters the English beginning of the Border.

The cathedral of St. Machar's, first founded by the saint who was a disciple of Columba, was refounded by the saint who was David I—of course; what a busy saint this was—and looks the part of age, but of strength rather than arrogance, with its low lying towers.

There is an old town even in the new town, and the contrast is sharp. If one gets lost, turns suddenly into this old part, it is a curious experience. The buildings look medieval,

French provincial, and the people look strange and foreign; also they treat you, a foreigner, with all that curiosity, and something of that disrespect which you, of course, deserve, having interloped into their sanctuary. The Duke of Cumberland lived here for six weeks before advancing on Culloden, and while he did not "butcher" here to deserve his name, his soldiers left as ugly a fame behind them as Montrose's men, what time he made bloody assault on the city.

And in Broad Street may be found the house in which George Gordon, Lord Byron, lived in his school days. In Don Juan, he autobiographically remembers—

"As 'Auld Lang Syne' brings Scotland one and all,
Scotch plaids, Scotch snoods, the blue hills, and clear streams
The Dee, the Don, Balgownie's Brig's black wall,
All my boy feelings, all my gentle dreams
Of what I then dreamt, clothed in their own pall
Like Banquo's offspring;—floating past me seems
My childhood in this childishness of mine:
I care not—'tis a glimpse of 'Auld Lang Syne.'"

Aberdeen is a sea city, lying between the mouths of the Dee and the Don. A bridge, dating from 1320, crosses the Don, and Byron steadfastly avoided it, lest he, a single son, might be found thereon on the single foal of a mare, and the prophecy be filled, the brig fall down.

One day in a small booth off Union Street I stopped to buy strawberries—if you pick up southern England in early May and make Inverness in late August, you can follow red strawberries and red poppies in the wheat all the way from Land's End to John o' Groat's. I asked the price of the berries and was told. I asked again, and again. Finally, not ears but intuition told me. It was a Scandinavian-Gaelic-English. I remembered that in Edinburgh I had once asked a policeman the way, and hearing his reply I turned to my friend—"Wouldn't you think you were in Minneapolis?" For especially in Aberdeen you are looking to that Norway with which Scotland was so closely linked, as with all the Scandinavian countries, in the early centuries, till the Maid of Norway, granddaughter to Alexander III died on her way to take the crown, and till after Margaret of Denmark brought the Orkneys and the Hebrides to James III as her dowery.

"To Norroway, to Norroway,
To Norroway o'er the faem;
The King's daughter of Norroway,
'Tis thou maun bring her hame."

And I remember the tragedy of that frustrated journey—

> "O forty miles off Aberdeen,
> 'Tis fifty fathoms deep,
> And there lies gude Sir Patrick Spens,
> Wi' the Scots lords at his feet."

Remembering the sea, which I had not yet seen, I tried to make my way down to the shore, but Aberdeen is a sea-port, and docks instead of shore line its sea edge. What I was seeking was rather rocks—

> "On the rocks by Aberdeen,
> Where the whistlin' wave had been
> As I wandered and at e'en
> Was eerie—"

And after a visit to the fishmarket, which is a truly marvelous monstrous place, I set out to find the rocks, toward the south.

There is never a place more rock-bound, more broken into fantastic shapes, and worn daily and increasingly by the waves, than this east coast. Neither Biarritz nor Brittany nor Nova Scotia is more broken or more thunderous in resentment. I have not seen the Magellan straits.

One is constantly conscious of fish on this east coast. The railroads form the Great East

Fish route. I have been coming up in the night from London and had to hold my breath until we passed these swift fish trains which have the right of way to the metropolitan market. A little south of Aberdeen is the village of Findon; whence finnan haddie.

Dunnottar

The rocks which were my goal were those just below Stonehaven. At Stonehaven the French had landed supplies for the Forty Five —as from Montrose, a few miles farther down the coast, King James had sailed after the failure of the Fifteen. Fishing vessels lay idly in the narrow harbour, their tall masts no doubt come "frae Norroway o'er the faem," since the trees on the east coast have not increased from that day when Dr. Johnson found the sight of a tree here equal to that of a horse in Venice.

Dunnottar stands on a great crag of this coast, against which the sea has beaten angrily since time and the coast began, against which it moans and whines at low tide, and then, come high tide, rushes thunderously in to see what havoc it can work once more.

DUNNOTTAR CASTLE.

Dunnottar is impregnable. I cannot believe that sixteen inch guns—is it seventeen, now?—would make impression on this great red crag. I know they would; after Liege and Namur one knows that modern guns can outlaw any impregnability of the past. But I do not believe.

The road from Stonehaven runs for two miles over level country, and then, suddenly, the edge breaks in a sheer cliff.

Across a natural moat of great depth, on a cliff crag, stands the castle. The road picks its way down perilously; only a mule path, and that precipitous. Then it crosses the dry bed where once may have hung a draw bridge, and, entering through a portcullis, it climbs to the castle, through a winding, tortuous way, sometimes a climb, sometimes a flight of steps, sometimes open to the sky but ramped sternly on either side, sometimes through stone canyons; a place impossible to surprise. Finally you reach the top, the sky.

The top is three acres large.

Far back, no doubt in Culdee times, a church stood there. Because churches must be sanctuary they took the high places; otherwise why should one lift prayer to God when the mad sea was continually contradicting the faith?

Sir William Keith, being a warrior with a warrior's eye, looked on the place, found it strategically good, and built a tower thereon. He was excommunicated by the Bishop of St. Andrew's—who did not anticipate the Lords of the Congregation and the Covenanters. Sir William appealed to Rome. Rome ordered the ban removed. And ordered Sir William to build a church on the mainland, beyond the protestantism of the waves.

It began its war history early. In 1297 four thousand English took refuge here to escape Wallace. Nothing daunted, Wallace scaled the cliff, entered a window—the proof is there in the window—opened the gate, let in his men, and slaughtered the four thousand.

Edward III took it, and Montrose besieged it.

Then it swung back into loyal legal possession, and experienced a bit of history worth the telling. In 1652—Montrose had been dead two years—the Countess Dowager had taken into safe keeping the regalia of Scotland. The castle was besieged by those who had killed their king and would destroy the king's insignia. If the castle should fall the very symbol of the king's royalty would be melted, as Cromwell melted the regalia of England. The defense was not strong. At any moment it might be forced to surrender. But the regalia must be saved.

So the Lady Keith plotted. It was a woman's plot—always there is the woman in Jacobitism. The wife of the minister at Kinneff paid a visit to the wife of the governor of Dunnottar; Mrs. Grainger called on Mrs. Ogilvie. She had been "shopping" in Stonehaven, and was returning to Kinneff five miles down the sea. When Mrs. Grainger left the castle she carried with her the crown of Scotland. Sitting on her horse she made her way through the besieging lines, and her maid followed with the scepter of Scotland and the sword in a bag on her back. The English besiegers showed every courtesy to the harmless woman—and to the Honours of Scotland. Mrs. Grainger carefully buried the treasure beneath the paving of Kinneff church, and not until her death did she betray their hiding place to her husband.

Meanwhile Lady Keith sent her son Sir John to France. A little boat escaping in the night carried him to the French vessel lying off shore, and the Lady sent forth the rumour that Sir John had carried the regalia to the King o'er the water, to Charles II at Paris. It was after the Restoration that the aureate earth at Kinneff was dug up. The women had saved the Scottish crown for the rightful lawful king.

A dark chapter runs a quarter of a century later. The castle was still loyal. In truth it was always loyal except in brief usurpations, as all this corner of Scotland was loyal and royal and Jacobite. In 1675 in "Whig's Vault" there lodged one hundred and sixty-seven Covenanters as prisoners, and they lodged badly. Many died, a few escaped, the rest were sold as slaves. Coming on ship to New Jersey as the property of Scott of Pitlochry, Scott and his wife died and almost all the covenanting slaves. Only a few saw the plantations of the New World, and could resume the worship of their God. The story of Dunnottar is dark. The castle looks the dark part it played.

In Dunnottar churchyard on the mainland there is a Covenanter's stone, where "Old Mortality" was working when Scott came upon him. The stone carries a simple stern legend of heroism—and almost wins one to the cause.

And yet, there is evidence that in stern Dunnottar life had its moments other than war and siege. The remnants of the castle are of great extent; bowling gallery, ballroom, state dining-room, a library, a large chapel, speak a varied existence. There is a watch tower, a keep, rising forty sheer feet above the high rock, with ascent by a winding stair, somewhat perilous after the centuries; but from the Watchman's seat what a prospect, landward and seaward! What a sense of security in the midst of peril! And on the farther corner of the giddy height, above the rock and above the waves dashing far below, I found growing blue bells of Scotland.

There is one corner of the castle where I fain would inhabit, the northwest corner that looks down on the sea raging cruelly upon the rocks that are the first line of defense against the onslaught of the sea, and that looks far over the North Sea; that sea which is more mysterious to me and more lovely than the Mediterranean; I have seen it a beautiful intense Italian blue, with an Italian sky above it. I have never seen it still, always surging, raging, always cruel. Yet I should be willing to look out on it for many unbroken days. And to hear the somber movement of the "Keltic" sonata played upon the rocks.

The Earl Marischal liked the view, whatever his generation. The North was in his blood, and the sea, even though he was a landsman, spoke adventure. The Earl's bedroom is almost habitable to-day. Once it was a place of luxury. The plaster still clings to the walls in places, and there is a fireplace where still one could light a fire against the chill of the North. The date above is 1645, when Charles was still king, and there was no threat of disloyalty. The tablet unites the arms of the Keiths and the Seatons, the stone divided by a pillar surmounted by two hearts joined. The Keith motto, *Veritas vincit,* underlines the Keith shield; but I like better the Seaton motto —*Hazard yit forvard.*

The Earl's library opens out of this. And I doubt not it was richly stored in the days when the last Lord Marischal won here that mental habitude which made him equal in wit and wisdom to Voltaire. And no doubt here sat his mother, loyal Jacobite, steadfast Catholic, sending her two sons forth to battle for the lost cause of the Stewarts—never lost while women remember—while she looked forth on these waters and watched for the return. The story runs in the Jacobite ballad of "Lady Keith's Lament"—

"I may sit in my wee croo house,
At the rock and the reel fu' dreary,
I may think on the day that is gane,
And sigh and sab till I grow weary. . . .

"My father was a good lord's son,
  My mother was an earl's daughter,
An' I'll be Lady Keith again,
  That day our king comes o'er the water."

CHAPTER VIII

THE CIRCLE ROUND

THE iron road from Aberdeen to Inverness must follow somewhat the road which gallant Mary took on her way to punish Huntley. There is a bleak stern look about this country as a whole, but here and there stand castles, or lie low the ruins of castles, in many a chosen place of beauty; for harsh as were these lords, and devastating as were their deeds, life must have had its moments of wonder and of delight. If Malcolm Canmore destroyed Inverness before the Twelve Hundreds, and the fat Georges destroyed Inverugie late in the Seventeen Hundreds, and all through the centuries that stretched between strong men built strongholds and stronger men took them and made mock of them, still there must have been gentleness and beauty. There were women, other than Lady Macbeth; there were young men and maidens noble or common; and I suppose the glamour of romance, the reality or the illusion of love, was invented before peace and commerce became the occupations of men.

Peterhead

One brief journey I made along the bleak coast up to the town of Peterhead, which looks nearest to Norroway across the foam, and has a most uncompromising aspect. Peterhead is a penal town to-day; and it is one of a string of fishing villages, picturesque as fishing villages are, except to the nose, "that despised poet of the senses"; and not picturesque to the people, who lack the colour of fisherfolk in Brittany. But I wished to see with mine own eyes the ruins of Inverugie.

It is one of the castles belonging to the Lords Marischal. It came to them in a curious way of forfeiture, an abbot dispossessed or some such thing, like Dunnottar, but without the appeal to Rome. And one of the stones of the castle carried the promise, and the threat—

"As lang's this stane stands on this croft
The name o' Keith shall be abaft,
But when this stane begins to fa'
The name o' Keith shall wear awa'."

The last Lord Marischal came hither, late, late, in the Seventeen Hundreds. He had seen a century move through strife to peace. In person he had taken part in the Rising of the Fifteen, a young man, but still hereditary Lord Marischal, and loyal to the Stewart cause. He had taken no part in the Rising of the Forty Five; he was not "out" on that dark night. But the sweeping revenge of those English times made the Keiths attaint and—the stone dropped from its croft. The Lord Marischal and his brother made the continent their refuge, Paris in particular, although the activities of the proposed restoration took their Lordships to Madrid and Rome and Berlin and St. Petersburg.

The younger brother, James, was made a Field Marshal by Catherine of Russia, and that amorous termagant making love to him in the natural course of proximity, he discreetly fled, became Field Marshal for Frederick the Great, and not marrying—whatever the romance of the Swedish lady—he fell at the battle of Hochkirch in 1758, and lies buried in the *Garison Kirche* of Berlin. A statue stands in the Hochkirch kirche, and in 1868 the King of Prussia presented a replica to Peterhead. And even so late as 1889, the Kaiser, remembering the Great King's Field Marshal, named one of the Silesian war units, the Keith regiment.

There is no statue to the Lord Marischal—*Maréschal d'Ecosse,* always he signed himself. He was the friend of the wittiest and wisest and wickedest men of his time, of David Hume, and Voltaire, and Rousseau, and Frederick the Great. Neither did he marry. Dying at the age of ninety-two, he was buried in Potsdam. There is no statue to him, there or here. And Inverugie lies in low ruins.

Hither he came, when attaint was lifted, late in those tottering years. He drove out to the castle, remembering all it had meant, the long splendid records of the Earls Marischal, and how the King, James III and VIII—Banquo saw him also—

> "And yet the eighth appears, who bears a glass
> Which shows me many more."

James, not pretending but claiming, landed at Peterhead, lodged at Inverugie, summoned the loyal and they came. The Standard was lifted for a moment, and then fell.

Breaking into tears the old Lord Marischal realized all, an epoch closed, a Scotland no longer requiring a Marischal. He left Inverugie, even this ruin.

All this Northeast territory, no larger than a county in Dakota, bears these scars of the past.

At Elgin there are the ruins of a cathedral; ruined, not by the English but by the Wolf of Badenoch, because my Lord Bishop had given a judgment which did not please my Lord of Badenoch. And the Wolf, his fangs drawn, was compelled to stand barefooted three days before the great west gate.

At Canossa! Lands and seas and centuries divide—but there is slight difference.

A scant mile or two to the north of Elgin lies the ruined Spynie Castle of the Lord Bishop, a great place for strength, with massive keep—and fallen. "A mighty fortress is our God." Cathedrals, castles, bishops and lords, all pass away.

Cawdor

As we neared one of the last of the Northern stations, we turned to each other and asked, "How far is 't called to Forres?" And suddenly all was night and witch dance and omen and foretelling. For it is here in the palace that Banquo's ghost appeared and foretold all that history we have been meeting as we came north-

SPYNIE CASTLE.

ward. And next is the town of Nairn, which has become something of a city since Boswell found it "a miserable place"; it is still long and narrow, stretching to the sea with its fisher-folk cottages and bonneted women like the fisher wives of Brittany; and stretching to the Highlands at the other end, as King James said.

It was here that Wordsworth heard

> "Yon solitary Highland lass,
> Reaping and singing by herself; . . .
> Perhaps the plaintive numbers flow
> For old unhappy far-off things,
> And battles long ago. . . .
> The music in my heart I bore
> Long after it was heard no more."

But one leaves the train with a curious feeling. Of course one may be a little tired. Arm chair travel and arm chair tragedy have their advantages. But—Nairn is the nearest point to the blasted heath.

> "Where's the place?
> Upon the heath,
> There to meet Macbeth."

It is not entirely necessary that one should make Nairn and walk out to The Heath. Any of these northern silent Scottish blasted heaths will serve. It is as though the witches had made their mysterious incantations anywhere, everywhere. And if Shakespeare was in Scotland in 1589—as I like to think he was—it is doubtful if he saw The Heath. Johnson told Hannah More, so she reports, that when he and Boswell stopped for a night at a spot where the Weird Sisters appeared to Macbeth, they could not sleep the night for thinking of it. Next day they found it was not The Heath. This one is, in all faith, apocryphal. Still, if you come hither toward evening, when

> "Good things of day begin to droop and drowse"

it is fearsome enough. Such heaths demand their legend.

> "The thane of Cawdor lives
> A prosperous gentleman."

Not so prosperous now as when he lived in the life. Shakespeare took liberties with the Thane. He immortalized him into Macbeth! And Cawdor Castle, out from Nairn a few paces on the burn of Cawdor, might have been the very home of Macbeth. It is pleasant, flowery, lovely. But also, it is stern and looks like a castle for tragedy. But not for mystery. I did not hear a bird of prey, as some travelers report—

their mysterio
where. And
in 1589—as I
ful if he saw
nah More, so

th Weird Si

Next
This one is
you come hith

it is fearw

Not so pros

Thane. He i
And Cawdor

"The raven himself is hoarse
That croaks the fatal entrance of Duncan
Under my battlements."

There are iron girded doors and secret apartments; not for Macbeth, but for Lovat. This Lord of the Last Rising lived secretly for many months in Cawdor while the Prince was moving restlessly to and fro in the Islands. But the Prince was only twenty-five, and Lord Lovat was over eighty. I like to think he was as young and keen to adventure as the Prince. And I do not like to think of that beheading in the Tower—

"I must become a borrower of the night."

Inverness

The four chief cities of Scotland are arranged like a diamond for excursion and for history. Always Scotland, unlike Gaul, has been divided into four parts. Places of pilgrimage were Scone, Dundee, Paisley, Melrose. Places for the quartering of Montrose were Glasgow, Perth, Aberdeen, Stirling. And now four places are rivals; in trade somewhat, but Glasgow leads in beauty, but Edinburgh, after all, is unique in dignity, but Aberdeen is unbending; in the picturesque there remains Inverness.

The city deserves its honours. (William Black has painted it in "Wild Eelin.") It has a life of its own. For when I first came to Inverness there was a cattle fair on, and sheep from all over the kingdom, from Shropshire and from the Cheviots, came to be judged in Inverness; and men came with them who looked very modern and capable and worldly and commercial. It was all like a county fair of Iowa, only more dignified, with no touch of sideshow. And, of course, there is the Highland gathering in September, which has become too much like the sideshow, too much a show, to attract the groundlings, and not a gathering of the clans. Still—if one must take Scotland in a gulp—this is a very good chance at Highland colour and sound and remnants of valour.

The town itself is full of pictures. It does not announce itself. There is a close-built part, looking like a French provincial town, with gabled houses, and down on the banks of the Ness the women spread their clothes to dry as they do on a French river bank. There is a new cathedral, very new, with an angel at the font we remembered William Winter had liked, so we paid it respectful attention. There is a park on the Ness to the west, where many islands and many bridges form a spot of beauty.

And there is Tomnahurich—The Hill of the Fairies—a sudden steep hill-mound, where Inverness carries its dead—like the Indians who carried them to Indian mounds high above the rivers of the American West. The dark yews make it even more solemn; one wonders if the fairies dare play in these shades. But it is a sweetly solemn place, and we decided to care not what Invernessians lay buried here if we might sit on its convenient park benches and look at far rolling Scotland and think of fairies and of Thomas the Rimer, who, it seems, came hither all the way from Ercildoune from Melrose to heap this mound for his burial! The errant Scots!

There remains no stone of Macbeth's Castle to which the gentle Duncan came—"And when goes hence?" The county buildings—and a jail!—stand on its site, a most modern pile. Malcolm razed that castle after he had returned from England, and after Birnam wood had come to Dunsinane. It was builded again; Inverness was a vantage point. Perhaps that one was burned by the Lord of the Isles who afterward came to repentance and to Holyrood. And builded again so that Huntley could defy

Mary, and she could take the castle and order it razed. And builded again so that Cromwell could destroy it. And builded again as one of the five fortresses whereby he sought to hold Scotland "Protected." And destroyed at the Restoration which sought to destroy all the Protectorate had built. But builded again so it might be destroyed by Prince Charles Edward. No, I scarce think there is even the dust of the castle of Macbeth left in Inverness, or incorporated into modern Fort George. The "knock, knock, knock," which the porter heard at the gate, has battered down a score of ominous strongholds.

But still

> "The castle hath a pleasant seat; the air
> Nimbly and sweetly recommends itself
> Unto our gentle senses."

For all the north of Scotland, away from the east winds, is pleasant and lovely, with the mean climate that of London, and possible in winter and summer.

In the grounds there stands a statue of Flora Macdonald looking out to the West, and carrying the legend—

> "On hills that are by right his ain
> He roams a lanely stranger."

Could legend be better chosen to compress and carry all that story of loyalty and courage and devotion?

And so we moved out to Culloden.

It was on a gray wind-swept afternoon that we made our pilgrimage. There was no sense of rain. It was a hard sky. It spread leaden to the world.

We chose to walk the six mile stretch. Not with comfort or any show of splendour, not even with a one-horse carriage, would we approach Culloden.

The road leads over lonely Drumossie moor through a plantation of firs, to a wild and naked spot—where all that was Scotland and nothing else was burned out of the world by the withering fire of Cumberland, and the remnant that would not save itself but fought to the last was cut to pieces by his order.

I do not suppose that even on a hot sweet afternoon could any one with a drop of Scotch blood come hither and not feel in his face the rain and sleet of that seventeenth of April day, 1746. If one comes on that day the cairn is hung with flowers, white roses of course, for there are still Jacobites left in the world who have given to no other king their allegiance. "Pretender!" cried Lady Strange to one who had mis-spoken in her presence, "Pretender and be dawmned to ye!"

No, it was not the Pass of Thermopylæ, nor a Pickett's charge. Nor was it even war.

Nevertheless it was one of the brave moments in human history. If hopeless and even meaningless, does not bravery give it meaning? The Highlanders—they were the last Jacobites left, as the army of the Butcher, Cumberland, George Second's fat son swept northward and stopped for their larder to be well-filled before they went on—had had only a biscuit, the day before! They were five thousand to the English ten thousand.

At eleven in the morning the Highlanders moved forward, the pipers playing brave music, and they recked not that the English had the chosen ground; theirs was not even a forlorn hope. Not if the Macdonalds, sulky because they were on the left when since Bannockburn they had been on the right, had fired a shot would the end have been different.

On the battlefield, looking at these mounds, the long trench of the dead, one realizes that Scotland lies buried here. M'Gillivray, M'Lean, M'Laughlin, Cameron, Mackintosh, Stuart of Appin—so many brave names.

BATTLEFIELD OF CULLODEN.

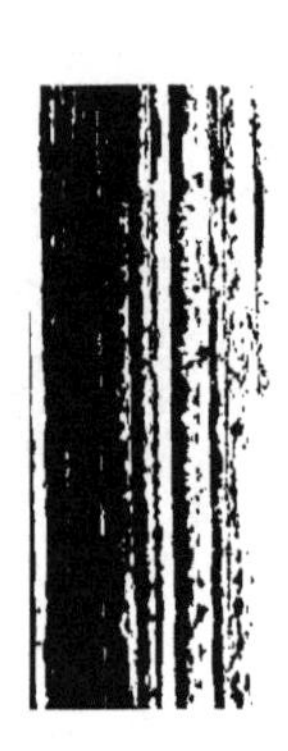

"The lovely lass of Inverness,
Nae joy nor pleasure can she see,
For e'en and morn she cries, alas!
And ay the saut tear blin's her e'e—

"Drumossie muir, Drumossie day!
A waefu' day it was to me!
For there I lost my father dear,
My father dear, and brothers three.

"Their winding sheet the bluidy clay—
Their graves are growing green to see;
And by them lies the dearest lad
That ever blest a woman's e'e.

"Now wae to thee, thou cruel lord!
A bluidy man I trow thou be;
For mony a heart thou hast made sair
That ne'er did wrong to them or thee."

The small remnant that was left, and was not butchered by Cumberland, fled to the West. Sometimes one could wish Prince Charles had died at Culloden! and yet one would not spare the wanderings, or Flora Macdonald. Thousands of the men fled to America; thousands of Scots in America to-day can say, "My great grandfather fought at Culloden." Hundreds of Scots to-day are sent "home" from America to be educated. I have met in the magnificent Highlands of Montana, Scotchmen, true Highlanders, who had been sent to Edinburgh university that they might be Scots, even though they carried "American" blood in their veins.

When Boswell and Johnson came here in 1773, twenty-seven years after the Forty Five, they found that many of the Highlanders were going to America, leaving the lairds and the land. One M'Queen of Glenmorison was about to go.

"Dr. Johnson said he wished M'Queen laird of Glenmorison, and the laird to go to America. M'Queen very generously answered he should be sorry for it; for the laird could not shift for himself in America as he could do."

Small wonder that Prince Charles, knowing of this exodus, and believing life still held for him its chances, its glories, away from Rome and even if he was fifty-five, looked longingly over the sea, in 1776, thinking that he might lead these rebellious colonists, so many of them of his rebellious people, and reëstablish the House of Stewart in the New World. Surely Burr, coming with Blennerhasset, thirty years after, had something of the Stewart in him.

The Orkneys

Scotland is divided by a deep geologic cleft. Glenmore, the Great Glen, runs southwesterly from Inverness to Fort William and Oban, cutting the country into two parts. One is Scotland; the other is the West, the Highlands and the Islands. One is known, the other unknown. One has been prosperous, royal, noble; the other has been wild, independent, chief and clans holding together. To-day, if the East is strangely quiet, the West is strangely silent.

In the East you know things have happened; remnants remain, ruined castles testify; in the West it is as though they had not happened, those far historic things; castles are heaps of blackened or crumbled stone; or, if they stand, they stand like prehistoric remnants, and the clachans are emptied; the Risings, the migrations, the evictions, the extensions of deer forests and sheep pastures and grouse preserves, the poverty, yes, and the wandering spirit of the people leading them ever afar—where always they are Scottish down to the last drop, always looking toward Home, but ever leaving it empty of their presence.

It is a stranger land, though so lovingly familiar, than any I have ever been in. I have been in valleys of the Rockies which were not so lonely as glens in Scotland. When Hood wrote his sonnet on "Silence," beginning

"There is a silence where hath been no sound,"

He went on to a correction—

> "But in the antique palaces where man hath been."

He missed the note of glens and valleys where man has been and is not.

From the Great Glen, a series of lochs lying in a geologic "fault," and connected more than a century ago by a series of locks, excursion may be had into remote places, so very remote even if they lie but a half dozen miles in the backward; the farther ones, to the Orkneys, to John o' Groat's, to Skye, the island of mist and of Prince Charlie and Dr. Johnson and Fiona McLeod, and vast numbers of places known to those who seek beauty only.

Three forts were built in the rebellious Seventeen Hundreds to hold this far country. The forts rather betray history. And they form convenient places of departure for those who would conquer the Highlands and the Islands for themselves.

Fort George, near Inverness, is still used as a depot for military stores and for soldiers. Fort Augustus has been surrendered to the Benedictines who are gradually developing here a great monastery which in these silences should rival the monasteries of old—if that may be. Fort William, most strategic of all, is also

THE OLD MAN OF HOY.

strategic for traveler's descent. Thus is the iron hand that succeeded the bloody hand at Culloden become rust.

To the men of old the Orkneys seemed at the back of beyond and a little farther. Yet, I cannot think how it has reduced the distance to a comprehensible length if farther ends of the world and endless waters have been reached; distance is three parts imagination in any event. As a man thinketh so is distance.

The run up the coast to Scrabster, the port of Thurso, is very much on the coast, with wild barren land on one side, and wild waste water on the other; with here and there a resting-place for the eye or mind, like Skibo Castle for our American Laird of Skibo, Dunrobin Castle for the magnificent Sutherlands, and on a branch line leading out to the sea the house of John o'Groat, perhaps the best known citizen above Land's End.

From Scrabster the Old Man of Hoy lifts his hoary head over the seas, and invites to Ultima Thule, if this be Ultima Thule. And I suppose that ever since Agricola came up this way the Old Man has sent forth his invitation. The Romans did not answer it, although Tacitus wrote about it; and it was left for much later folk to dispute the Picts and take the islands for themselves.

An archipelago of fifty-six islands lies scattered over the water, with only half of them inhabited, but not all the rest habitable; if, like Sancho Panza, you are looking for an island, you will not find the isle of heart's desire here. The scant inhabited twenty odd are not over filled with population; these islands are not hospitable to large numbers, not even of their own. They came to us through Margaret of Denmark, queen to James III, and were confirmed when Anne of Denmark came to be queen to James VI.

The sail over the Pentland Firth may be taken on a still day when the historic waters, as vexed as those of the Bermoothes, lie like glass. The rage of water, of any water, is not the frequent mood; but always it is the memorable. Blue above and blue below was the day of our going, twenty miles past high "continental" shores, like Dunnet's head, and between the outliers of the Orcadian group, at the end of a summer day that never ends in this North.

Yet I cannot think how I should ever again approach "Mainland" and the port of Kirkwall with such indifference to everything except the exquisite cool softness of this Northern air of mid-summer, with an indolent interest in the land ahead, hardly quickened into active interest which is the traveler's right, when we approached Scapa in the twilight.

I did remember that the Vikings were once here as kings. And when King Haakon of Norway was returning from the defeat at Largs in the west where his fleet suffered the blow repeated later against the Spanish armada, one ship was sucked down into a whirlpool near Stroma. And Haakon died here of a broken heart. All these seemed like old, far-off things that are not unhappy. Yet there was a suggestion of fate in the place; perhaps there always is in a Northern twilight. To approach Kirkwall after this, will always be to remember the Hampshire, going to its death in a water more dangerous than that of whirling Stroma, and Lord Kitchener going with it.

Kirkwall is a pleasant old town; or was, till war made it busy and new. It lies inland a mile or two across the isthmus, but no doubt stretching actively down to the south pier at Scapa during the years of the great war, when all the British fleet hovered about.

The town is gray, like all Scottish towns; nature does these things with perfect taste. And, in the midst, man has builded for his worship a church of red sandstone, the Cathedral of St. Magnus, older and in better condition than churches of Scotland more exposed to the change of faith; with a long dim interior that speaks the North, with massive Norman arches; one wonders how the reformed faith can conduct itself in this dim religious light.

But the Earl's Palace remains a thing of beauty. Earl Patrick builded it, the son of Robert who was half brother to Mary. If the palace had been built in Mary's day I should, in truth, have lamented that she did not come hither after the escape from Loch Leven, instead of going to defeat at Langside. Mary was valiant, and the stern North was, after all, in her blood.

But Patrick as "jarl" came a generation later, and he taxed the islands mercilessly to build this very beautiful palace. The roof is gone, but the beauty remains, oriel windows, fireplaces, and towers and turrets. No doubt when "the wind is blowing in turret and tree," Patrick's palace can be ruined enough. But on a day when the blue sky is sufficient vaulting, the palace is a place to dream in.

Over at Birsay, twenty miles across the Mainland—there are twenty mile stretches in this Mainland—there is another palace, built by

EARL'S PALACE, KIRKWALL.

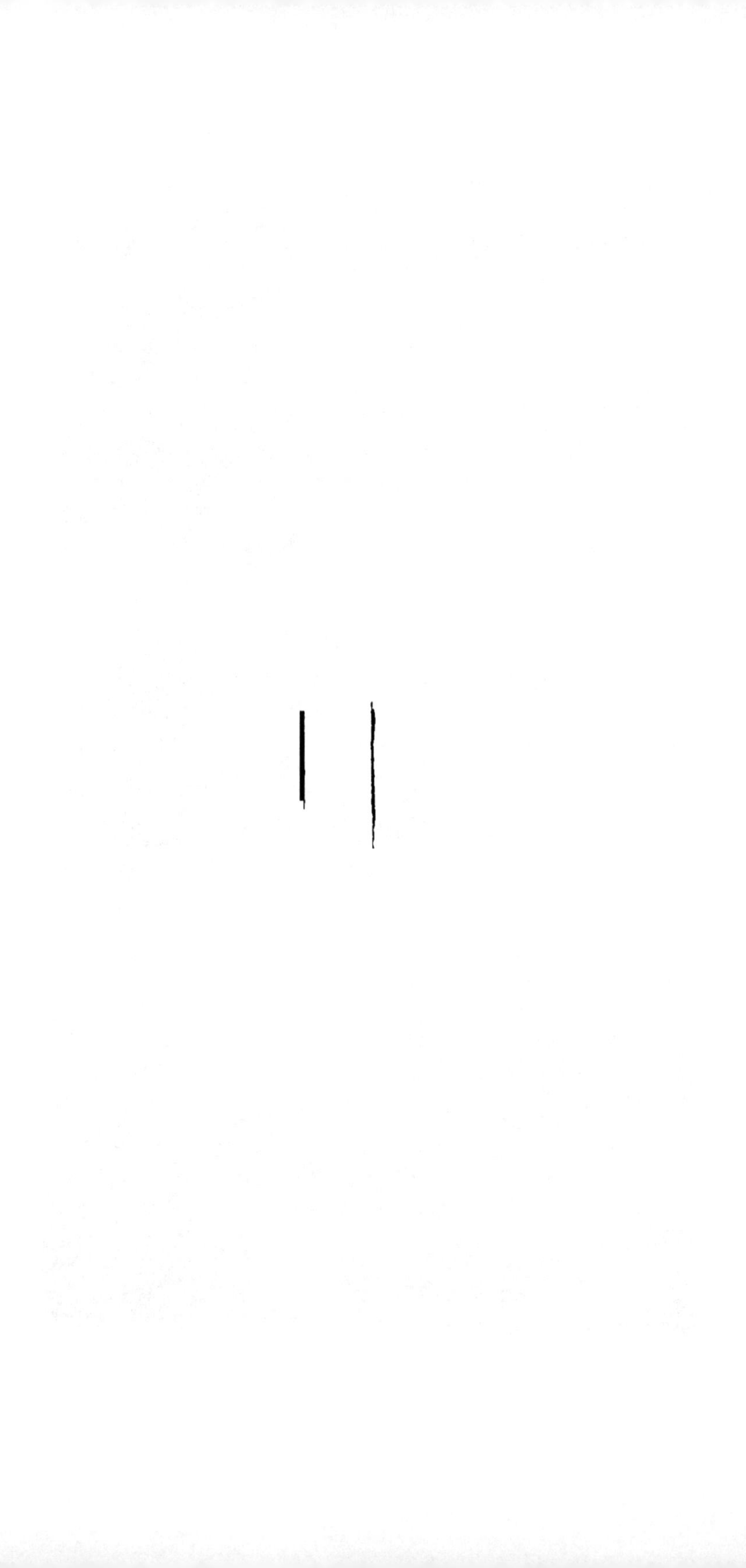

Robert, himself, who was, incidentally, Abbot of Holyrood as well as Earl of the Orkneys. The motto-stone declares—

> "Dominus Robertus Stuartus
> Filius Jacobi Quinti Rex Scotorum
> Hoc Opus Instruxit."

"Rex" said Robert, not "regis"; perhaps his Latin knew no better, but his spirit knew this was right. The nominative agreed with Robertus, not with Jacobi. Still, the ruler of the Orkneys was a supreme lord at this remove from king and counselors.

Here and there, but only here and there through the islands, lies traveler's lure. Motor boats make the run for tourist pleasure, and many of the "points of interest" can be seen from the waters; particularly the "brochs," the cairn-like towers of perhaps Pictish building; and the round tower of St. Magnus on Egilsay, which must date back very far, perhaps to the time when Columba came hither from Ireland and converted these people and gave them hints of Irish building.

There are remnants of life earlier than Columba, of faith earlier, though we know not the faith. The Circle of Bogar, old gray pillar-like stones, set in purple heather, are comparable with Stonehenge and Locmariaqueur.

Scott found them equal; Scott who had such an admirable way of finding in Scotland the equal of the world. In "The Pirate" he describes these stones, indeed he describes these Orkneys in this accurate guide book which is still "up to date."

To the blood shed and violence of old days has succeeded the quiet pursuit of agriculture; and instead of the boats that used to sail to the New World, H. B. C. boats and those to the Plantations, and to Russia for the Northwest Passage, and to the Arctic for the Pole, are the quiet boats of the fisherfolk. Except—when war fleets ride at anchor.

The Caledonian Canal

The Great Glen itself is a necessary journey, even though no side trips be made. I must believe that every one who has ever taken it and written account, journeyed down this waterway in a Scotch mist; which, of course, is not a mist at all, but something finite and tangible.

I, myself, went my ways that way. And, of course, those who had come north the day before me, and those who came south the day after, came through magnificent clearness, and marvels of marvels, Ben Nevis cleared of mists to his very crest and beyond, shining splendid and majestic and out-topping all Scotland, against the brilliant cloud-swept northern sky! Frankly, I am always tempted to be suspicious when any one tells me he has traveled the Great Glen and seen it all.

The scenery on both sides is wild, desolate, mountainous, a daring of nature. There are sheer hillsides where all is revealed; again, there are wooded hills where the men of the Forty Five might be still lurking.

Dochfour, Ness, Oich, Lochy, are the names of these "great lakes" that make the chain. There is quality to their names, like Superior, Huron, Erie, Ontario. But the Scottish chain is sixty miles long and can be made from morning to evening, with enough of the day left to go through Loch Linnhe and so to Oban; as one should add, through the St. Lawrence and so to Quebec. Yet when one has passed from Inverness to Oban the mind is as full, it has come through as much contact, nay, more, as in the journey from Duluth to Quebec.

There are ruined castles by the way. Urquhart, looking very picturesque, especially if the mist is but half come down over the world and the purple of the distances is of that deep royal purple so characteristic of the water and mountain distances of this wild west country. Yet the sunny distances are as much a marvel of colour in their pale blue that has so much intensity, so much real vivacity. Purple one has learned to associate with distance; or, since some painter has shown us the truthful trick. But blue, this particular Scottish blue, I have never seen elsewhere. It is woven of mists and sunlight in equal proportions.

And so, Urquhart in its ruin, standing romantically on a fir clad promontory, is most alluring as the boat rounds it on its early way. I do not know anything of Urquhart. The name rather suggests the middle name carried by a once famous actress. Somehow I half believe that in that castle Charlotte Corday may have stabbed Marat. But then, facetious and unromantic, I wonder at the baths in Urquhart in the old days when skene dhus served in the place of daggers.

There are other romantic lures in the names which seem to have dropped so carelessly anywhere. Inverarigaig—which sounds more musical than it looks on the page—stands at the head of the pass through which The Prince came after that day at Culloden on his way to the West as wanderer. Far down the stretch of water rises Mealfourvournie, a rounded naked hill overlooking the ravine where once the church of Cilles Christ stood; and once, full of Mackenzies, was set on fire by the Macdoualds, and all the Mackenzies burned. The act is not singular among the clans. McLeod of Dare gives it to the Macdonalds and McLeods. And so one comes to believe the story of a traveler coming on a Highland cottage and asking if there were any Christians within, got back the reply,—"no, we're all Macdonalds." Surely Saint Columba was needed in later centuries than the Sixth.

The Falls of Foyers are across the lake, surrendered now to aluminum works. And yet Burns wrote of them

> "Among the heathery hills and rugged woods
> The roaring Foyers pours his moving floods."

Christopher North wrote a better, a prose poem, which sounds somewhat curiously in American ears. "What a world of waters now comes tumbling into the abyss! Niagara! hast thou a fiercer roar? Listen—and you think there are momentary pauses of thunder, filled up with goblin groans! All the military music-bands of the army of Britain would here be dumb as mutes—Trumpet, Cymbal and the Great Drum!"

Fort Augustus closes the end of the loch, and here the Benedictines, black-robed, move in somber file where once the red-coated soldiers marched.

Five locks raise the steamer fifty feet, into the Highlands. And while the boat is waiting the rise, here, as at any of the locks, there is entertainment. Fellow travelers get out to stretch their legs, and that is amusing enough, tolerantly considered. There are tea houses at every lock, many of them, sometimes charmingly rose-embowered like the houses along the Thames. There are pipers who march majestically up and down, swinging their sporrans, swaying their kilts; one is almost afraid to give a penny.

And I remember at one of these pausing places where the passengers remained on the boat, that a very pleasing gentleman who looked as George Washington may have looked on gala occasions did sing for my entertainment and that of my fellow passengers; except one fellow American who expressed her disapproval. Perhaps George Washington did not dress so gaily; it was just the hat. There was a black coat, white breeches, crimson waistcoat, blue stockings, silver buckled shoes, and a cocked hat. And this pleasing gentleman sang to a tune that was no tune but very cheering, about "the hat me faither wore." And he was so doing his best, which was very good indeed, that I was forced to get change for a sixpence—it cannot be ethical, and certainly is not fun to throw a little silver disk when six large coppers may be thrown. And the American female fellow passenger said, "Doesn't it seem as though he could get something nearer a man's job?" Yet he was such a pleasant person. And they're not common to be met on the highway.

From Fort Augustus on there are memories of the Risings, chiefly of Prince Charlie, in the glorious before, in the tragic aftermath. He came hither as conqueror, that mere stripling, belted and plaided as a Royal Stewart, and retook his kingdom. The coat skirts of Johnny Cope you can still see in retreat to Inverness, if you look well. From Gairlochy the way leads to Glenfinnan where he raised his Standard, and the Castle of Lochiel, ruined because of him. And hither he came, after Culloden. At Fort Augustus the head of Roderick Mackenzie was presented to the Butcher as that of Prince Charles, and near Gairlochy, and near Lochiel —"beware of the day"—is the "cage" of Cluny

MacPherson where he harboured during those days of red pursuit. And the thirty thousand pounds are yet to be paid for betrayal.

Loch Oich, littlest and highest, with wooded islands and heavily wooded shores, larches and delicate silver birches, is the exquisite bit of the way. And here stands Invergarry Castle, which saw Prince Charles when first he came gallant from the West and Moidart, and saw him when last he came defeated to the West.

Laggan Avenue runs between Loch Oich and Loch Lochy, a narrow waterway with soft fir-trees lining the way in a most formal fashion; it has a peculiar magic when the mist has shut out the rounded hills of the higher background.

Banavie—to move according to the schedule—is at the top of the locks, three miles of them, Neptune's staircase, leading down to Fort William and to the sea. The railroad is the swifter way and breaks the journey, and passes the ruins of Inverlochy. It is a place to which French and Spanish merchants came in far days of the Seven Hundreds. But better, a place where Montrose won a victory.

Here took place (1645) the battle between the Marquis of Montrose and the Marquis of Argyle, and so splendidly that Montrose and Charles thought the kingdom was coming back

INVERGARRY CASTLE.

to its own. Montrose had started through the Great Glen for Inverness, but hearing that the Campbells were massing at Inverlochy, he turned back, and gave battle. The victory was so tremendously with the royal Montrose that he wrote a letter to Charles, then negotiating with the parliamentarians, and Charles believed so that he broke off the parleying—

"Give me leave, after I have reduced this country, and conquered from Dan to Beersheba, to say to Your Majesty, as David's general to his master, 'Come thou thyself, lest this country be called by my name.' "

In five years, the two were both beheaded, one at Whitehall in London, the other at the Tolbooth in Edinburgh, the Marquis sixteen months later than the King. "To carry honour and fidelity to the grave."

At Inverlochy looks down the mountain of them all, Ben Nevis, taller than Ben Muich Dhui, taller than Snowdon or Helvellyn. And from its vantage point, the Observatory Tower, one may look over all the territory in many directions whither one proposes to go; the routes can be planned from this top of Scotland. As Sir Archibald Geikie mapped it in his glorified geography—

"While no sound falls upon his ears, save

now and then a fitful moaning of the wind among the snow-rifts of the dark precipice below, let him try to analyze some of the chief elements of the landscape. It is easy to recognize the more marked heights and hollows. To the south, away down Loch Linnhe, he can see the hills of Mull and the Paps of Jura closing the horizon. Westward, Loch Eil seems to lie at his feet, winding up into the lonely mountains, yet filled twice a day with the tides of the salt sea. Far over the hills, beyond the head of the loch, he looks across Arisaig, and can see the cliffs of the Isle of Eigg and the dark peaks of Rum, with the Atlantic gleaming below them. Farther to the northwest the blue range of the Coolin Hills rises along the skyline, and then, sweeping over all the intermediate ground, through Arisaig and Knoydart and the Clanranald country mountain rises after mountain, ridge beyond ridge, cut through by dark glens, and varied here and there with the sheen of lake and tarn. Northward runs the mysterious straight line of the Great Glen, with its chain of locks. Then to east and south the same billowy sea of mountain tops stretches out as far as eye can follow it—the hills and glens of Lochaber, the wide green strath of Spean, the gray corries of Glen Treig and Glen Nevis, the distant sweep of the moors and mountains of Brae Lyon and the Perthshire Highlands, the spires of Glencoe, and thence again to the blue waters of Loch Linnhe."

This may not be "the roof of the world," but it is a very high gable.

CHAPTER IX

THE WESTERN ISLES

Oban

THERE is something theatrical about Oban, artificial, and therefore among Scottish towns Oban is a contrast. It is as uncovenanted as—joy! And it is very beautiful, "the gay and generous port of Oban," as William Winter calls it, set in its amphitheater of high hills, and stretching about its harbour, between confining water and hill. An embankment holds it in, and at twilight the scimeter drawn from the scabbard of night flashes with light, artificial, but as wonderful at Oban as at Monte Carlo. One is content to be, at Oban. Quite certainly Oban has centered its share of Scottish history and romance, history from the time of the Northmen, romance from the time resurrected by Scott and continued indigenously by William Black. But in Oban and round about Oban, one is quite content to take that past as casually as one takes yesterday.

It is very interesting, very fascinating; one wakes now and then, here and there, to keen remembrance, to a sensitiveness that so much beauty could not be only for to-day and of to-day, that men must have come hither to claim it or dispute possession of it in the beginning of time. Of course the Stewarts came out of this Island West! But, either because one has made a round circle of Scotland from out of romantic Edinburgh, or because one has come from practical Glasgow and is about to make a round circle of Scotland, Oban has a peculiarly satisfying and yet undemanding beauty.

It is set for pageantry; life is always, has been always, a procession at Oban. If ever the history of Scotland is set forth as pageant—I do not know that this has ever been done, but it should be—it should be staged at Oban, on the esplanade.

Life moves swiftly through the streets and across the waters. For it is a place that all the world comes to, in its search for the next beautiful place. Steamers from the Caledonian Canal and Inverness, steamers from the Crinan Canal and Glasgow, coaches from the near country, railroads from the east and north, bring the world to Oban. And from Oban boats move out on the Firth of Lorne and the Sound of

Mull and through the broken waters of the Hebrides, out into the unbroken waters of the Atlantic. People come and go, come and go. It is not that Oban is filled with people. Very often the inns are filled and the careless traveler may seek eagerly if not vainly for a lodging for the night, to find his landlady a Campbell of the Campbells.

But there is seldom a feeling of too many people in Oban. They come and go, night and morning. They do not stay. In the evening the esplanade may be filled and the crowd very gala; the circle of lights marking the embankments, steamers lying at their ease after the day's work, looking, yes, like pirates, retired pirates, rakish, with tapering spars and brave red funnels, the soft plash of oars out on the bay and the moving lights of the rowboats, with perhaps—no quite certainly—a piper, or two or three, dressed in tartan, more like the red and black of the Campbells in this historic region of Argyle, piping up bravely "The Campbells are Coming, yoho, yoho."

It is lively in the evening, there is always a touch of pageantry. Yet Oban is a very good place in which to stay and make the little foot excursions that penetrate only a few miles into the circumurban territory. The most constrained walker may find rich foot-interest out of Oban; nowhere do comfort and beauty and story combine in more continuous lure. Easy and attainable is Dunolly Castle, much more attainable than it was in the old days when the Lord of the Isles made his permanent seat here, and defied the world and the king; more attainable now than when Scott came this way seeking "copy" and "colour" and declaring "nothing can be more beautifully wild than Dunolly." To-day Dunolly is beautiful, but scarcely wildly beautiful; that is, in comparison with other wild castles of this wild West; and very attainable, the walk being provided with seats all the way, casual "rest and be thankfuls," of the municipal corporation.

But beyond Dunolly, four miles of good highway, with Loch Linnhe breaking magnificently on the eye, and Loch Etive reaching off endlessly into the deep purple, is Dunstaffnage, which, before Stirling, or Perth, or Edinburgh, was capital of Scotland and the place of destiny. Very redoutable it sits on its high crag, as picturesque a castle as there is in the world —and we are in a land of castles picturesquely set. The walls above the waters lift themselves in lofty height, and promise to remain, with their great thickness presented to the consuming world. It is still towered for strength and scope, and looks its part of royal residence. Here was found the Stone of Destiny—after Jacob or another had carried this Jacobite sleeping pillow hither from Palestine. Kenneth McAlpine, somewhat sacrilegiously, carried the Stone away to Perth. And Edward sacrilegiously carried it down to Westminster, where George V sat on it, in 1911, or nearly on it, so as to prove his destined right.

Bruce took the castle from the Lord of Lorne, at what time he was taking all the castles of Scotland. And even The Bruce in his busy days of castle-storming, must have paused in this height, at these bastions, to look over this western world and decide that it was good and should be added to his Scottish world. Across Loch Linnhe he could see the bens of Morven and of Appin, and up Loch Etive, Ben Cruachan—even as you and I. The Highlands and the Islands are still primitive, man dwindles here, and the world becomes what it was before the Sixth Day.

But The Bruce did not see these brass cannon from a wreck of the Armada, The Bruce lived too far before that great day to see the coast "strewn with the ruined dream of Spain." And he was too early for the ancient ruined

Gothic chapel of much austere beauty which stands near.

It is from Pulpit Hill that Oban gives the best view of all the lyric lay of this water and land world; on a clear day when the wind is from the west, when sunshine has been drenching the world, and when the sun is about to sink behind Ben More. Pulpit Hill is a wooded steep bluff to the east of Oban, at its foot parklike drives and forest-embowered cottages with their windows open to the sea, with rich roses filling the air and flaunting fuchias filling the eye. It is an easy climb, even after a day of Scotch-seeing in the backward of the land.

Here one may sit and meditate on the life and character of David McCrae, to whom the pulpit is dedicated. Or one may look over the land and "soothly swear was never yet a scene so fair." Or, to borrow again from that same Scottish scene painter, and another scene—"One burnished sheet of living gold."

The eye runs far out over the world, across the Bay of Oban, across the Island of Kerrera, across the Island of Mull set against the late sky, and over to Lismore which lies shining and tender against the deepening purple background of Morven. The sun casts slant rays across the land and across the bay, bathing the far land in tender lilac, the sea in steely blue, while Kerrera lies in patches of dark and light, a farmhouse sharp against a rose mist that rises in shallow places and quickly fades, leaving all the world purple in hue. Shepherd lads and shepherd dogs may be seen at this last moment preparing to watch the flocks by night, and long horned shaggy cattle browse at peace in the fading light. Flocks of birds fly over, starlings in scattered black patches, sea swallows poising for prey, and sea gulls resting on the wave after a weary day. Everything is at peace.

Two longer excursions one must make from Oban; to Loch Awe, to Glencoe. Each is possible in a day, and yet a night in Glencoe is almost imperative if one would be played upon by its full tragic compass; and a lifetime of summers would not exhaust Loch Awe.

The Loch I would visit; because of its beauty; and because of Kilchurn Castle, which is picturesque in fact as well as in picture, on its densely wooded island with its broken outline lying against the farther mountain; because of Ardchonnel Castle, ivy covered, and "it's a far cry to Loch Awe"; because of Fraoch-Eilean (isle of heather) which is the island of Ossian's Hesperides; and because,

KILCHURN CASTLE.

capitally because, Innishail is the island where Philip Gilbert Hamerton established his camp through so many summers and through a number of Scottish winters.

One must belong, oh, quite to "another generation," to admit any debt of instruction or pleasure to Philip Gilbert Hamerton. I do not think that this generation knows him, hardly as a name. But when I was young, collegiately young, Hamerton was an authority on life and art, and a preceptor of beauty. And, if one read "The Intellectual Life," then, of course, one read the rest of him. And so, one came to Loch Awe before one came to Loch Awe.

To the lake I went quite shamelessly on train. But repenting half way, over-awed by Ben Cruachan, as who should not be, I left the train at the "platform" and won the memory on foot. The mountain looks as high and as mighty as a Rocky, and the white foaming threads of falls, hundreds of feet high, dashed down the sides in a true "Rocky" splendour; like those on the Cut bank or the Piegan trails in Glacier Park, yet not quite so high. I did not climb Ben Cruachan to look on the Atlantic—but I have not made my last journey to Scotland. On foot and alone, I threaded "the dark pass of Brandir," and felt in my blood and bone that something in me ancestral had been there before. Perhaps we inherit where we hero-worship. In any event, Sir William Wallace went through this defile in 1300, and King Robert Bruce in 1310, with his faithful friend Sir James Douglass, fighting John of Lorn (the dead are still heaped beneath these gray cairns), and going on to take Dunstaffnage. Sir Walter Scott came here when he sought environ for "The Highland Widow."

On one side is the sheer cliff which guards the foot of Ben Cruachan. On the other the rapid awesome dash of the River Awe. "You will not find a scene more impressive than the Brandir Pass, where the black narrowing water moves noiselessly at midnight between its barren precipices, or ripples against them when the wind wails through its gates of war."

In the Loch lies the island of Innishail, still green, and not less solitary than when Hamerton entertained travelers, unaware of his identity. It still carries old gravestones, for islands in the far days were the only safe places, safe for the dead as for the living; war and ravage would pass them by. Throughout this western land you will find island graveyards, and the procession of quiet boats carrying the dead to their rest must have been a better expression than can be had by land.

From here one sees Ben Cruachan to advantage, even as one saw it in 1859 with Hamerton.

"At this moment the picture is perfect. The sky has become an exquisite pearly green, full of gradations. There is only one lonely cloud, and that has come exactly where it ought. It has risen just beyond the summit of Cruachan and pauses there like a golden disk behind a saint's white head. But this cloud is rose-colour, with a swift gradation to dark purple-gray. Its under edge is sharply smoothed into a clearly-cut curve by the wind; the upper edge floats and melts away gradually in the pale green air. The cloud is shaped rather like a dolphin with its tail hidden behind the hill. The sunlight on all the hill, but especially towards the summit, has turned from mere warm light to a delicate, definite rose-colour; the shadows are more intensely azure, the sky of a deeper green. The lake, which is perfectly calm, reflects and reverberates all this magnificence. The islands, however, are below the level of the sunshine, and lie dark and cold, the deep green Scotch firs on the Black Isles telling strongly against the snows of Cruachan."

It was even as Hamerton had told me so long

ago, a trifle different in July from what he saw it in December, but equal in magnificence, and the outlines had not changed in a half-century.

And so I did not hesitate to go with Hamerton to Glencoe, lovely and lonely and most terrible glen. There is such a thing as being haunted, the dead do cry for revenge, the evil that men do does live after them.

It is a wide valley, yet closed in by great granite precipices, for safe guarding against betrayal. The first section of the strath is calm enough, human, green, habitable, with Loch Leven, a branch of Loch Etive, sparkling in the sun. The second wide opening is terrible as massacre, not green, very stern, and wild as Scottish nature, human or not, can become. Even the little clachan of the Macdonalds seems not to welcome the world except on suspicion. And that murder, that assassination (February 14, 1692) when William was king—William who might have been "great" except for Boyne and Glencoe—still fills the memory.

Hamerton painted the picture—"In the vastness of the valley, over the dim, silver stream that flowed away into its infinite distance, brooded a heavy cloud, stained with a crimson hue, as if the innocent blood shed there rose from the earth even yet, to bear witness against the assassins who gave the name of Glen Coe such power over the hearts of men. For so long as history shall be read, and treachery hated, that name, Glen Coe, shall thrill mankind with undiminished horror! The story is a century old now (1859). The human race has heard it talked of for over a hundred years. But the tale is as fresh in its fearful interest as the latest murder in the newspapers."

Yet, a half century still later, I have heard those who declared Glencoe lovely and not terrible. No doubt the generation does not read history and does not feel story.

We did not go on to the King's House, built in the days of King William, when roads were being driven through the Highlands in order that they might be held to a doubtful Stewart sovereignty. For we had read how Hamerton thought it more than enough to drink a glass here, and we doubted not he had read of the trials of Dorothy Wordsworth, sheets that must be dried for hours before the beds could be made, the one egg for breakfast, and—could we have found that china cup that Dorothy forgot? Rather, we chose to return down the lake side for another look at the red roofs of the home of Lord Strathcona, that wizard of the nineteenth century, who had left Scotland with only his wits and returned from America with his millions and a title.

Iona

There is no pilgrimage which can be taken to any shrine excelling pilgrimage to Iona. And all the pilgrim way is lined with memory and paved with beauty.

On almost every promontory stand ruined castles, not so frequent as the watch towers on the Mediterranean heights, and therefore not so monotonous. One knows that each of these, as of those, has had its history, and here one ponders that history, perhaps tries to remember it, or, tries to evoke it. Dunolly which we visited in the day's drift from Oban stood up on the right with the city still in view. But it is when the Firth opens into the Sound that the glory of the water-world of the West comes on you.

The Sound of Mull is, so Sir Walter has said, "the most striking water of the Hebrides." It is very lovely in this shell-pink light of early morning, it could not have looked lovelier when Sir Walter estimated it. The hills begin to stand boldly forth, for the gray mists of the morning are rising. It is to be a fine day,

AROS CASTLE.

which here because of its exception means a brilliant sun-stricken day, and all things clear as geography. But, at least once, one should see things one wishes always to keep as material for remembrance and for imagination, not in the mist dimly, but face to face like this. Or, as the Maid of Lorn in Ardtornish, when she was led

> "To where a turret's airy head
> Slender and steep and battled round,
> O'erlooked, dark Mull! thy mighty Sound.
> Where thwarting tides, with mingled roar
> Part thy swarth hills from Morven's shore."

On the left of Mull stands the grim Castle of Duart on its high rock, on the right on Morven the Castle of Ardtornish, and Aros a little farther on, and Kinlochalive at the top of the bay of the Loch—mighty were these lords of the islands, and most mighty the Lord of the Isles.

Perhaps—it has been suggested—Sir Walter overstated the might of the Lord, the grandeur of the islands, the splendour of those thirteenth century days. It depends on what light one views them in.

Tobermory is the capital of Mull, and is a place of some resort. Like all these little capitals it is set in the wilderness world, and what one would like best to do instead of sailing past them is to stay with them and go far into the backward. Perhaps traversing Mull as did McLeod of Dare when he hunted so royally—and in such a moonstruck way; or David Balfour when he was shipwrecked and walked through Mull; or the Pennells when they sought to walk through and did not take pleasure in it. It is the pilgrims who won their goal one chooses to remember—not the defeated Pennells. And here—I am leaving Mull and Tobermory behind me, perhaps for always.

Suddenly one sweeps out into the Atlantic! The stretch is wide, oceanic, although far and away there are islands, black lines thickening here and there the horizon edge. The sea is exquisitely, deeply blue, like the Mediterranean at its best.

One passes Ardnamurchan point, the most westerly point of the mainland of Great Britain, "Cape of the Great Seas"; how one loves the poetic grandeur, the sufficing bigness of these names, and the faith, and the limitations back of them; as though there should never be a greater world with greater seas and mountains in the greater West. To the south the boat passes Trehinish isles, black gems lying on the sea.

ENTRANCE TO FINGAL'S CAVE.

Far out on the horizon lie Col and Tiree, low clouds in the line. "Col," I heard the professorial people—from Oberlin—speak the name. "Col! So that is Col!" they said to each other, "so that is Col off there!" "Col," I said to myself, "so that is Col." And we all became related through the great Doctor.

One is bound to Staffa, incidentally, on the way to Iona, and for the sake of Mendelssohn. Always afterward one is bound to Staffa because of itself. If only one could have Staffa for one's self. But there are always fellow travelers, there is no inn, no habitation here, not even a shepherd's shieling, visible from the water. There are a few sheep, a shepherd, and so there must be a shieling. To be marooned here—was it here Stevenson understudied for Bill Gunn, and "cheese, toasted mostly"?

The cave is truly wonderful, a superb cathedral nave, with dark basaltic columns lifted in marvelous regularity, and arches lifting over with groining the hand of God.

> "Nature herself it seemed would raise
> A minster to her Maker's praise."

The broken surfaces of the walls are in mosaic with green sea grasses and gleaming limpets, and the floor is a shifting thing of surging waves. The ocean thunders through the narrow gate as it has done since the time Staffa began, and since Mendelssohn, a mighty organ surge, like the "Overture to Fingal's Cave," and yet, more than that. To be here alone, to be the shepherd of Staffa, and come to this cathedral, with the might and mystery of the night about, and the winds and the sea making symphony—life will always hold many things in possibility, which cannot die!

From the top of Staffa, if one flees the passengers a moment, may be seen the islands lying about whose names are romance, Trehinish, and Inchkenneth on Mull and Skerryvore, "the noblest of all deep sea light," a mere speck on the far Atlantic—what vigils the man must have in the house of light built by Stevenson's father; and on to the far north and Skye; and to the near south and Iona.

> "Where is Duncan's body?
> Carried to Colme-kill,
> The sacred storehouse of his predecessors,
> And guardian of their bones."

Very definite was Shakespeare about these things. A more modern antiquarian would have doubted, and sent us wandering from pillar to post of royal burial places. But not the man who created what he declared. Icolmkill —Iona—certainly.

That such a little island could have had such a large history. It is so small a place, yet a beautiful island withal, and with its cathedral, now alas, "restored" and "reformed," and all its far sounding memories of Columba.

He came up from the South as we came down from the North, but his voyage was across the wide seas to unknown goals; while we have the advantage of having come after him to Iona. And yet, to Columba, valiant adventuring saint, Iona nor any other place was unknown goal. There was to him but one purpose in life, one goal. And he found it everywhere.

It was a large life and simple, austere but with unlimited horizon, that Columba lived here. It is a small exquisite life that is lived here to-day. Or, perhaps my belief in its proportion and perfection came because of contact with a certain two persons, man and woman, who had taken this life to themselves. While being practical in that they sold exquisite wares, in silver and gold and brass and bronze, each article, large or little, carrying some Ionian insignia, still they must have a very beautiful life, ever making things of beauty out of the historic heritage of this island. It was a large accumulation of jeweled hints they discovered here, in the ornamentations of the stones of Iona. They have used them to very lovely ends. And they have lived the life of memories and of the keen sea air.

One may have forty minutes, or day after day in Iona. And, of course, the reward and the intimacy is in proportion. It is a quiet fragment of land, the little village with its white-washed cottages in prim lines, and its simple cotters, perhaps a little more sophisticated than those of other western islands because of their continuing contact with a curious world; and yet these men and women and serious children live here the year round, and in winter there is no world, and the Atlantic thunders on the little land as though one beat of the wave would carry all into the abyss, or smashes on the rough granite coast of Mull across the strait.

The western shore of the island is cruel, even on a summer day. And if the "merry men" ran their violent ways on the shore of Mull, there are other Merry Men just as merry, just as lurking. As McLeod of Dare saw it—

"Could anything have been more beautiful than this magnificent scene . . . the wildly rushing seas, coming thunderingly on the rocks, or springing so high in the air that the snow-white foam showed black against the glare of the sky; the near islands gleaming with a touch of brown on their sunward side; the Dutchman's Cap with its long brim and conical center, and Lunga also like a cap with a shorter brim and a higher peak in front, becoming a trifle blue. And then Col and Tiree lying like a pale strip on the far horizon; while far away in the north the mountains of Rum and Skye were faint and spectral in the haze of sunlight. Then the wild coast around, with its splendid masses of granite; and its spare grass a brown-green in the warm sun, and its bays of silver sand; and its sea birds whiter than the clouds that came sailing over the blue.''

On many of these western islands, and the northern, and it is said particularly on the far northern Shetlands, there are some dark somber faces remaining over from the Armada. The sea has never been kind; it breaks the rocks, it breaks men.

There are low-lying hills, the chief is Dun I, there are pasture lands, and still there are fields of wheat and clover. Just before he died, Columba was carried out to see the men at work in the fields. No doubt he lifted his eyes and looked around, on his little island, and the great sea, and the great world beyond. No doubt he wished he might live longer and labour farther. St. Columba who carried the Gospel and his gentle Irish gospel from the sixth century of Ireland into the far North until it swung round and met in Durham and York the Gospel and the culture coming up from Rome; and that neither so polished nor so Christian. Yes, even Columba regretted leaving the world behind him, though he was going to the other world.

Yes, I am certain he regretted leaving the island world behind him. Did he not sing of his longing—

"Delightful would it be to me to be in *Uchd Ailiun*
On the pinnacle of a rock,
That I might often see
The face of the ocean;
That I might hear the song of the wonderful birds,
Source of happiness;
That I might hear the thunder of the crowding waves
Upon the rocks;
At times at work without compulsion—
That would be delightful;
At times plucking dulse from the rocks;
At times fishing."

Thirteen hundred years ago; and the song is undimmed, and the world has not faded. The Port of the Coracle on the far side is still open to boats adventuring across pleasant or perilous

CATHEDRAL OF IONA AND ST. MARTIN'S CROSS.

seas. The very rock on which Columba landed, the traveler seeking the subtle transubstantiation from the past may stand on. And there is the White Beach of the Monks, where the companions of Columba paced to and fro in those days and in this lovely land that seems too far away to be believed in.

The entire island is the shrine of the Saint, and not only the cathedral of Iona. In truth this particular church dates from six hundred years later than Columba, six hundred years backward from us. The crosses that stand in the cemetery of St. Oran, St. Martin's and the Maclean, the only two left out of nearly four hundred, cannot date much farther back than this, or than "gentle Duncan." There is a long line of graves, each with its aged granite slab, of the kings, Norwegian and Irish and Scottish, of those early centuries. I do not remember that I saw the one that speaks of Duncan. But I do remember that the carvings were very curious and often very fascinating, the "pattern" intricate and intriguing.

Once the cathedral was a place of magic, an unroofed broken shrine, where the winds might wander in search of the past, and where the moonlight might shine through as lovely a casement, tracery as exquisite, as at fair Melrose.

If the generations coming six hundred years after us are to know of St. Columba, and not to reproach us for our coöperation with time the vandal, these roofs, this protection, must be afforded. Still, the gate is so close locked to-day that even Joseph Pennell could not steal in, and so closely watched that no black lamb or ram or other hobgoblin could affright Miss Gertrude White or cause her to cease loving the daring McLeod of Dare.

Yet, if one resolves as did Boswell, to leave the close inspection to Dr. Johnson, and "to stroll among them at my ease, to take no trouble to investigate minutely, and only receive the general impression of solemn antiquity," one will come upon much that is of particular impression, like the carvings about and on the capitals, with the early grace of the later Italians; quite worth careful preserving. And here is the altar, and I doubt not at this very spot—church shrines continue in this steadfast Scotland—Columba knelt before the God whose worship he had brought over the seas, and was to carry still farther over land and seas. There may be one shrine in the Christian world more sacred. But not more than one. Dr. Johnson is still quite right— "The man is little to be envied whose patriotism would not gain force upon the plains of Marathon, or whose piety would not grow warmer among the ruins of Iona."

The storm did not come, although we waited three days for it. Nothing but calm in the island of Iona, and peace on the deep of the Atlantic; tender dawns, still high noons, twilights of soft visible gray that lasted over to the next morning; a land of hushed winds and audible sounds, the seas lying like glass.

Not even on a Sunday morning when in a coracle, or some such smaller boat than one usually cares to venture, perhaps a lug, whatever that may be, we accompanied the clergyman to the mainland of Mull, and watched the stern sad faces of these far away folk as they listened to a very simple sermon of an old simple story. I remembered that at Earraid, Robert Louis Stevenson had been interested in the religious services held for the workmen who were cutting stone for a lighthouse building by Thomas Stevenson. From these people religion will go very late, if at all. Surely men and women need what Columba brought hither, now as ever.

And because of David Balfour I walked a little way into Mull, which still must look as he saw it, for except for the roadway it looked as though I were the first who had ever ventured that way since time and these rough granite heaps began.

"Sing me a song of a lad that is gone,
Say, could that lad be I?
Merry of soul he sailed on a day
Over the sea to Skye.

"Mull was astern, Rum on the port,
Egg on the starboard bow;
Glory of youth glowed in his soul:
Where is that glory now?

"Give me again all that was there,
Give me the sun that shone!
Give me the eyes, give me the soul,
Give me the lad that's gone!"

CHAPTER X

THE LAKES

ALL the world goes to the Trossachs. Yet there are only two kinds of people who should go, and they are as widely separated as the poles; those who are content and able to take the Trossachs as a beautiful bit of the world, like any lake or mountain country which is unsung, and then they will not take it but merely look at it; and those who know the Trossachs as theirs, The Trossachs, who can repeat it all from—

> "The stag at eve had drunk his fill
> Where danced the moon on Monan's rill,
> And deep his midnight lair had made
> In lone Glenartney's hazel shade.

On to

> "The chain of gold the king unstrung
> The links o'er Malcolm's neck he flung
> Then gently drew the golden band
> And laid the clasp in Ellen's hand."

Half knowledge is exasperating to those who have whole knowledge; and half love—half love is maddening, should lead to massacre by those whose love is all in all.

I cannot remember when I did not know "The Lady of the Lake"—which, of course, is the Trossachs. It is as though I knew it when I first knew speech, lisped in numbers and the numbers came. It was the first grown-up book I ever owned, and I own the copy yet. It is not a first edition, this my first and only edition. I presume that in those far away days when it was given to me, "a Christmas gift"—I always chose to receive it from my Scottish grandmother, though she had been dead thirty years before I came—I might have had a first edition for a song; but the preciousness of first editions had not yet become a fetich. Since then I have looked with respect and affection on that impress of "1810." I have never looked on it with longing. So much better, that first edition of mine, an ordinary sage-green cloth-bound book, with ornamental black and gold title, such as the inartistic Eighties sent forth; I do like to note that the year of its imprint is the year of my possession. It has not even a gilt edge, I am pleased to state. The paper is creamy, the ink is not always clear. And because it went through one fire and flood, the pages have little brown ripples, magic marginal notes. There is not a penciled margin in the whole volume. That, in a book owned by one who always reads with a pencil in hand, is beyond understanding! And yet it was many and many a year ago, in a kingdom by the sea. Memory was tremeudously active then, not quite the memory of a Macaulay, but still one reading, or at least one and a half, was sufficient to thrust the rimes of these two-edged couplets into unsurrendering possession. Criticism was in abeyance; there is not even a mark among the notes. I cannot be certain that I read them. Who reads notes at the age of eight?

I remember how my acquaintance began with "The Lady of the Lake," even before I read it. In those days there was little literature for children, and there was prejudice against that which was provided. There was especial prejudiec in my own household. I think my teacher in school may have shared it. If he were an adult he would read, ostensibly to us, but for himself, something he could tolerate. Yes, it was he; an exception in those days, for in the public schools men seldom taught in "the grades."

He must have been a young man, not more than nineteen or twenty, waiting to mature in his profession. And Scotch, as I think it now;

not only because his name was Kennedy, but because of his Highland dark eyes and hair, and because of certain uncanny skill in mathematics —as I thought who had not even a moiety— and because, oh, very much because, of the splendid tussle he had—tulzie! that's the word —a very battle royal to my small terrified fascinated vision, there on the school-room floor, with the two Dempsey boys, who were much older than the rest of us; they must have been as old as fourteen! One merited the punishment and was getting it. The other, with clan loyalty, came to his rescue. And the Highlander, white to the lips, and eyes black-and-fire, handled them both.

Oh, it was royal understudy to the combat at Coilantogle ford—

> "Ill fared it then with Roderick Dhu
> When on the field his targe he threw."

The Trossachs

To write a guide to the Trossachs—that has been done and done more than once; done with much minutiæ, with mathematics, with measurement; to-day it is possible to follow the stag at eve, and all the rest of it, in all its footsteps;

to follow much more accurately than did even Sir Walter; to follow vastly more accurately than did James Fitz James.

For, in the first place, the world is not so stupendous a place as it was in the days of Fitz James, or of Sir Walter. The Rockies and the Andes have been sighted, if not charted, and beside them the Grampians look low enough. Yet, fortunately, the situation can never be "beside them." The most remembering traveler has crossed the seas and buried his megalomanian American memories, let it be hoped, in the depths of the Atlantic. Neither Rockies nor Andes carry so far or so rich memories. Sir Walter has never projected an imaginary Roderick Dhu or a King errant into any of the majesty or loveliness of those empty lakes and mountains. I can imagine in what spirit the Pennells came to Loch Lomond and declared that it "looked like any other lake." Dr. Johnson was quite right, sir. "Water is the same everywhere," to those who think water is water.

Of course the traveler should not come upon the land by way of Lomond. Fitz James came from Stirling. He came to subdue the Highlands. They were seething in revolt—for no other reason than that Highlanders so long as they were Highlanders had to seethe and revolt.

And if we would subdue the Highlands or have them subdue us, we must follow the silver horn of the Knight of Snowdoun when he rode out of Stirling; to subdue, yes, and to adventure.

Yet perhaps it is better to have possessed Scotland, en tour, and to go back to Stirling with Fitz James, as a captive, but bearing the golden ring—

> "Ellen, thy hand—the ring is thine,
> Each guard and usher knows the sign."

So one leaves Glasgow, the unromantic, threading through its miles of prosperity and unbeauty, passing Dumbarton where Wallace was prisoner, passing the river Leven, which ought to interest us, for once its "pure stream" on his own confession laved the "youthful limbs" of Tobias Smollett, until the open country is reached and Loch Lomond swims into sight.

> "By yon bonnie banks, and by yon bonnie braes
> Where the sun shines bright on Loch Lomond,
> There me and my true love spent mony happy days,
> On the bonnie bonnie banks of Loch Lomond."

No, the Pennells might criticize "me and my true love." As for us, we mean to be romantic and sentimental and unashamed and ungrammatical. And spend mony days; Harry Lauder would spell and spend it, "money."

DUMBARTON CASTLE.

The lake opens wide and free in the lowland country of Balloch. At the left lies Glenfruin, the Glen of Wailing, where took place the terrible clan battle between the MacGregors and Colquhouns, where the MacGregors were victorious. But as Scott wrote, "the consequences of the battle of Glenfruin were very calamitous to the family of MacGregor." Sixty widows of the Colquhouns rode to Stirling each on a white palfrey, a "choir of mourning dames." James VI, that most moral monarch, let loose his judicious wrath, the very name of the clan was proscribed, fire and sword pursued the MacGregors. The Highlanders are dauntless. There still exist MacGregors and with the MacGregor spirit. And who that heard the Glasgow choir sing the superb "MacGregors Gathering"—Thain' a Grigalach—but will gather at the cry, "The MacGregor is come!"

"The moon's on the lake, and the mist's on the brae,
And the Clan has a name that is nameless by day;
Then gather, gather, gather, Grigalach!
Gather, gather, gather.

"If they rob us of name and pursue us with beagles,
Give their roofs to the flame, and their flesh to the eagles,
Then vengeance, vengeance, vengeance, Grigalach!
Vengeance, vengeance, vengeance.

"Through the depths of Loch Katrine the steed shall career,
O'er the peak of Ben Lomond the galley shall steer,
Then gather, gather, gather, Grigalach!
Gather, gather, gather."

There are twenty-four islands marooned in this part of the lake; for according to the old legend, one of these was a floating island and so to chain one they chained all. The first island is Inch Murrin, at which I looked with due respect, for it is a deer park of the present Duke of Montrose. I know not if he is descended from The Montrose, or from Malcolm Graeme and Fair Ellen, but let us believe it; it does not do to smile at the claims of long descent in this persisting Scotland. The Duke lives in Buchanan Castle, near the lake. Also he owns Ben Lomond. Also—I read it in "More Leaves" of Queen Victoria's Journal—"Duke of Montrose to whom half of Loch Lomond belongs."

It was here that Dorothy Wordsworth looked and recorded, "It is an outlandish scene; we might have believed ourselves in North America." And so, I knew the Lomond country for my own.

The steep, steep sides of Ben Lomond are in view at the top of the Loch, but the ballad may well have contented itself with the sides. For

I know one traveler who wished to be loyal to the Ben, and having seen it in 1889, and not seen it for the thick Scotch mist, returned again in 1911, and had her only day of rain in sailing across Loch Lomond. The ballad turned into a coronach—

"But the broken heart kens nae second spring
Though resigned we may be while we're greetin'.
Ye'll tak the highway and I'll tak the low way."

It is all MacGregor country, that is to say Rob Roy country. We are bound for Inversnaid, so was he. All about Lomond he had his ways, Rob Roy's prison, Rob Roy's cave, Rob Roy's grave, and all. And though there are other claims hereabout, and although Robert Bruce himself preceded Robert Roy in the cave, such is the power of the Wizard that it is the later Robert one permits to inhabit these places.

We remembered that Queen Victoria had preferred the roads to the steamer. So we left the boat at Rowardennan pier. Not to walk the pleasant ambling highways, that by some good public fortune run near the "bonny bonny banks," and, in spite of the Duke of Montrose, make the lake belong to us, to whom, of course, it does belong, but to walk to the top of the Ben.

The path, if one keeps the path, and he

should, is safe, the gradation easy; an American is like to smile at the claims of long ascent of a mountain which is but 3192 feet from the sea to top. But let one wander ever little from the path, attempt to make a new and direct descent, and let one of those mists which hang so near a Scotch day actually descend upon the top of the Ben—it is not the mildest sensation to find one's foot poised just at the edge of a precipice. It is not well to defy these three thousand feet because one has climbed higher heights. Ben Lomond can do its bit. And it can furnish a panorama which the taller Ben Nevis cannot rival, cannot equal. The Castle Rocks of Stirling and of Edinburgh, on a clean clear day; nearer, Ben Ledi and Ben Venue, names to thrill a far remembrance; Ben Cruachan, bringing the Mull country from near remembrance. And farther across, pale but apparent, the mountains of Ireland. A marvel of vision.

At Inversnaid one is again with Dorothy Wordsworth. It was here or hereabouts that William dropped the package of lunch in the water. So like William! I wonder Dorothy let him carry it. It was here William saw the Highland Girl, and wrote those lovely lines of her—

"Now thanks to Heaven! that of its grace
Hath led me to this lonely place.
Joy have I had; and going hence
I bear away my recompense.
In spots like these it is we prize
Our memory; feel that she hath eyes. . . .
For I, methinks, till I grow old,
As fair before me shall behold,
As I do now, the cabin small,
The lake, the bay, the waterfall;
And thee, the spirit of them all!"

And now one really begins to thrill. One is really going to Loch Katrine, to the Trossachs. The road is preferable, five miles of foot-pleasure, as against the filled coaches with perhaps "gallant grays," and certainly fellow travelers who quote and misquote the lines. No, it shall be on foot, up through the steep glen of Arklet water, out on the high open moor where the Highland cattle browse, with Ben Voirlich constantly in view, and Ben Venue coming even to meet us; with William and Dorothy Wordsworth and Coleridge walking beside us all the way. (Dorothy always called it "Ketterine," but then, she came hither seven years before "The Lady" was published.)

The old Highland fort was a perplexity to the Wordsworths. William thought it a hospice like those he had seen in Switzerland, and even later when told it was a fort Dorothy did not quite believe. It was built at the time of the Fifteen to keep caterans—of which Rob Roy was one—in subjection. And the American looks with interest because here, in his youth—which was all he ever had in truth—General Wolfe, who fell on the Heights of Abraham but won Quebec, commanded the fort of this Highland height. I could but wonder how the French travelers who throng these Scotch highways feel when they remember this victor over Montcalm. Now that they have fought together "somewhere in France," no doubt they feel no more keenly than an Englishman at Bannockburn.

There is not too much lure to keep one's mind and one's feet from Loch Katrine. There was a piper on the way, tall and kilted in the tartan of the MacGregor. (Helen MacGregor, wife of Rob Roy, was born at Loch Arklet, and across the hill in Glengyle Rob Roy was born, conveniently.) The piper piped most valiantly. I should like to have set him a "blawin' " o' the pipes with our piper on the Caledonian loch, something like the tilt which Alan Breck had with Robinoig, son of Rob Roy.

The road drops down to Stronachlachar. Through the hill defile one catches the gleam, and quickly "the sheet of burnished gold" rolls

LOCH KATRINE.

before the eye. It is more splendid than when Dorothy Wordsworth viewed it, "the whole lake appeared a solitude, neither boat, islands, nor houses, no grandeur in the hills, nor any loveliness on the shores." Poor Dorothy! She was hungry and tired, and did not know where she should lay her head. Later, next day, at the farther end, she loved it, "the perfection of loveliness and beauty."

As for us, it was early morning, we had breakfasted, fate could not harm us, and we knew our way. We were approaching it from the direction opposite to Majesty, the soft gray clouded stillness, early out of the morning world. But Scott had seen this picture also—

"The summer's dawn reflected hue
To purple changed Loch Katrine blue;
Mildly and soft the western breeze
Just kissed the lake, just stirr'd the trees,
And the pleased lake, like maiden coy
Trembled but dimpled not for joy;
The mountain shadows on her breast
Were neither broken nor at rest;
In bright uncertainty they lie,
Like future joys to Fancy's eye.
The water-lily to the light
Her chalice rear'd of silver bright;
The doe awoke and to the lawn
Begemm'd with dewdrops, led her fawn.
The gray mist left the mountain side,
The torrent show'd its glistening pride,

Invisible in flecked sky,
The lark sent down her revelry;
The black-bird and the speckled thrush
Good morrow gave from brake and bush;
In answer coo'd the cushat dove,
Her notes of peace, and rest, and love."

Here we hit upon a device to possess Loch Katrine, both "going and coming," to see the lake at dawn, simply as beauty, and then to come upon it as came Fitz James. With a glass of milk for fast-breaking—we had had a substantial breakfast at Inversnaid, and this glass was but for auld lang syne, a pledge of my companion to her early memories—we set out for "far Loch Ard or Aberfoyle."

I think had we known how very modern is this way which curves about the west side of Katrine we might have shunned it. Certain the stag would have done it. He did, you remember; refusing to charge upon Ben Venue, and thus avoiding the future site of the Water Works of the Corporation of the City of Glasgow. Perhaps Glasgow is the best equipped municipality in the world. Yet, what city but Glasgow would have tapped Loch Katrine to furnish water for Glaswegians!

Our road ran in the deep defile that lies between the two great bens, Lomond (3192) and Venue (2393). The top of Lomond was clear in the increasing sunlight, but mists still skirted his feet; while Venue was mist-clad from base to summit, the thin white veils tearing every now and then, as they swayed against the pine trees jagged tops, and lifting and then settling again.

And soon, we were at "far Loch Ard." It is a lovely little bit of water; we wondered why the stag was not tempted to turn aside hither —but then, we remembered, the stag did know, did save himself. Fishermen were out in their boats, and altogether we decided that if the stag did not come here we should, in the distant time when we should spend a summer in this Highland peace.

Ard is little, but a large-in-little, a one-act play to Lomond's big drama. We chose our "seat," and we hoped that the owner of The Glashart would be gracious when we sent him word of his eviction. Glashart is a short way above the pass of Aberfoyle where, to our pleasure, the troops of Cromwell were defeated by Graham of Duchray.

But this time, after twelve miles of walk, come noontide and a keen appetite, like the stag who

"pondered refuge from his toil"

we were content to house ourselves in the hotel

at Aberfoyle. We chose the one called "Baillie Nicol Jarvie," because this is all Rob Roy country. In truth we felt at home with the Baillie, and with the Forth flowing in front of the town, and the old clachan of Aberfoyle marked by a few stones.

In the late afternoon of this already full day we found there was a coach leaving for Lake Menteith which would return in the late twilight, too late for dinner, but Baillie Nicol was kind and we could have supper on our return. So we were off to Menteith, and to an old memory, reaching back to the daughter of James Fitz James. But at this far distance she seemed to belong to an older day.

Menteith is a little lake, a fragment of the abundant blue of Scotland's waters, and it is surrounded by hills that are heather clad; only the southern shore is wooded. Near the southern shore lies anchored the Island of Inchmahone—isle of rest—where once stood a priory, and now only a few arches keep the shadowy memory in their green covert. The stones of the dead lie about, for the Isle of Rest was an island of burial.

Hither came Mary Queen of Scots, when she was five years old, here for an island of refuge, since the defeat at Pinkie meant that Henry

VIII was nearer and nearer the little life that stood between him and Scotland's throne—

> "O ye mariners, mariners, mariners,
> That sail upon the sea,
> Let not my father nor mother to wit,
> The death that I maun die!"

She came with her four Maries, and together they went to France, together they made merry and made love at the French court, and, all unscathed, they returned fifteen years later—

> "Yestreen the queen had four Maries,
> To-night she'll hae but three;
> There was Marie Seton, and Marie Beatoun,
> And Marie Carmichael and me—"

It was as though she were lost from the world, as we went back in the dimming day; almost the only time I have ever lost her since historic memories came to be my own personal memories. And yet, I knew I should find her again. Mary is one of the women who do not go into exile once they have made harbour in the affections.

Next day, half by a hill-road and half by a foot-path, with mountains whose names were poems evoking the one poem of the region, with the far view, and with birches closing in the highway now and then, and now and then opening into a near-far view of glen and stream and strath and path, we came to—The Trossachs.

It is a walk of perhaps eight miles through a charming memory-haunted land, lovely certainly, lonely; there were few people to be met with, but there was no sense of desertion. It was a day of quick clouds, rushing across a deep blue, compact white clouds which say nothing of rain, and very vivid air, the surfaces and the shadows being closely defined. The birch leaves played gleefully over the path as we left the highway, and that sweet shrewd scent of the birch leaf, as I "pu'd a birk" now and then, completed the thrill, the ecstasy—if one may be permitted the extravagance.

"But ere the Brig o' Turk was won
The headmost horseman rode alone,
Alone, but with unbated zeal—"

Here I should take up the thread of the old poem and weave it entire. But first because I had come adventuring, even like the Gudeman o' Ballengeich, and taking my chances as they came along, and meeting no Highland girl and no Fair Ellen, I did seek out lodgings in one of the cottages which cluster about the foot of Glen Finglas, typical Highland cottages. Not the kind, I regret and do not regret, which Dorothy Wordsworth describes with such triumph, where William and Dorothy and Cole-

THE BRIG O' TURK.

ridge put up—"we caroused our cups of coffee, laughing like children," over the adventure; but still a cottage, with a single bed room. These cottages, no doubt because artists now and then inhabit them and because all the world passes by and because they are on Montrose property, are what the artist and the poet mean by a cottage, low-browed, of field stone, and rose-entwined.

The hurried traveler with no time to spare and no comforts, lodges at the Trossachs hotel, which aspires to look like a Lady-of-the-Lake Abbotsford, and is, in truth, of an awesome splendour like some Del Monte or Ponce de Leon.

There is a parish church—I heard the bell far off in the woods—near the hotel, but standing mid

"the copsewood gray
That waved and wept on Loch Achray."

It waved gently, and wept not at all that peaceful Sunday morning when we made our way by path and strath into the dell of peace. The people coming from the countryside repossess their own, and of course the tourists are not in the church, or if there, with a subdued quality. The coaches do not run, and there fell a peace over all the too well known, too much trodden land, which restored it to the century in which it truly belongs.

In the late afternoon, under that matchless sky which the wind had swept clear of even rapid clouds—we were glad we could match it by no other Scottish sky, and only by the sky which shone down when we first came to the Lake, that æon ago—and by the scant two miles that lie between the Brig and the Lake, "stepping westward," we followed the far memory till it was present.

The road leads through the forest beautifully, peacefully. If on that early September day no birds sang, still one missed nothing, not even the horn of the Knight of Snowdoun. The paths twine and retwine, through this bosky birchen wood, with heather purple, and knee deep on either side, and through the trees swift glimpses of the storied mountains.

Suddenly the way changes, the ground breaks, rocks heap themselves, a gorge appears, —it is the very place!

> "Dashing down a darksome glen,
> Soon lost to hound and hunter's ken,
> In the deep Trossachs' wildest nook
> His solitary refuge took."

I can never forget the thrill I had in the old schoolroom when Mr. Kennedy first read the

trodden land, which restored it to the century in which it truly belongs.

In the late afternoon, under that matchless sky which the wind had swept clear of even rapid clouds—we were glad we could match it other Scottish sky, and only by the sky shone down when we first came to the that æon ago—and by the scant two that lie between the Brig and the Lake, "stepping westward," we followed the far memory till it was present.

[illegible] through the forest beautifully, if on that early September day [illegible] [illegible] and even

The Trossachs

the horn of [illegible] Snowdoun. The paths twine and [illegible], through this bosky birchen wood, with heather purple, and knee deep on either side, and through the trees swift mountains.

changes, the ground rocks heap themselves, a gorge appears, the very place!

> "Dashing down a darksome glen,
> Soon lost to hound and hunter's ken,
> In the deep Trossachs' wildest nook
> His solitary refuge took."

I can never forget the thrill I had in the old schoolroom when Mr. Kennedy first read the

story and I knew that the stag had escaped. I felt even more certain of it in this wild glen. Surely he must be in there still. And so I refused to go and find him.

I could not discover where fell the gallant gray. I mean I was without guide and could map my own geography out of my own more certain knowledge. So I chose a lovely green spot—notwithstanding my remembrance of "stumbling in the rugged dell"—encircled with oak and birch, the shadows lying athwart it as they would write the legend.

> "Woe worth the chase, woe worth the day,
> That costs thy life, my gallant gray."

And then, by a very pleasant path, instead of the tortuous ladderlike way which James Fitz James was forced to take, I came again to The Lake, splendid in the evening as it had been mysterious in the morning.

> "The western waves of ebbing day
> Roll'd o'er the glen their level way;
> Each purple peak, each flinty spire,
> Was bathed in floods of living fire.
> But not a setting beam could glow
> Within the dark ravine below,
> Where twined the path in shadow hid,
> Round many a rocky pyramid,
> Shooting abruptly from the dell
> Its thunder-splintered pinnacle."

No shallop set out when I raised my imaginary horn and blew my imaginary salute to the lovely isle. There were no boats to hire, on this Sunday, and I was not Malcolm Græme to swim the space. But there it lay, bosky and beautiful, a green bit of peace in a blue world. Nothing could rob me of my memory of Loch Katrine, not even the very lake itself.

Stirling

Stirling stands up boldly—in the midst of Scotland.

That is the feeling I had in coming on it by train from the West. Highlanders coming on it from the North, English coming on it from the South, must have seen even more conclusively that Stirling rises out of the midst of Scotland.

I should have preferred to approach it on foot. But then, this is the only conquering way in which to make one's descent on any corner of the world one seeks to possess; either on one's own valiant two feet or on the resounding four feet of a battle charger. Alas, to-day one does neither. But—there lies Stirling rising from the water-swept plain, through the gray of a Scotch morning, entirely worthy of being "taken," and looking completely the part it has played in Scottish history.

Scotland is curiously provided with these natural forts, the Rocks of Edinburgh and Dumbarton and Stirling. They have risen out of the plain, for the defense and the contention of man. And because Stirling lies, between East and West, between North and South, it has looked down on more history, seen more armies advance and retreat than—any other one place in the world?

Standing upon its wind-swept battlements—I can never think that the wind dies down on the heights of Stirling—one looks upon the panorama of Scottish history. The Lomonds lie blue and far to the east, the Grampians gray and stalwart to the north, and on the west the peaks of the Highlands, Ben Lomond and all the hills that rampart "The Lady of the Lake." All around the sky were ramparts of low-lying clouds, lifting themselves here and there at the corners of the world into splendid impregnable bastions. Stirling looks a part of this ground plan, of this sky battlement.

Soldiers, from yonder heights!—and you know the rest. From this height you who are far removed from those our wars, a mere human speck in the twentieth century look down on seven battlefields. Did Pharaoh see more, or as much, from Cheops? The long list runs through a thousand years and is witness to the significance of Stirling.

Here, in 843, was fought the battle of Cambuskenneth, and the Painted People fell back, and Kenneth, who did not paint, made himself king of an increasing Scotland.

Here, in 1297, was fought the battle of Stirling Bridge, and William Wallace with a thousand men—but Scotsmen—defeated the Earl of Surrey and the Abbot Cressingham with five thousand Englishmen.

Here, in 1298, was fought the battle of Falkirk, and Wallace was defeated. But not for long. Dead, he continued to speak.

Here, in 1313, was fought the battle of Bannockburn, forty thousand Scots against a hundred thousand English, Irish and Gascons. And The Bruce established Scotland Forever.

Here, in 1488, was fought the battle of Sauchieburn, the nobles against James III, and James flying from the field was treacherously slain.

Here, in 1715, was fought the battle of Sheriffmuir, when Mar and Albany with all their men marched up the hill of Muir and then marched down again.

Here, in 1745, Prince Charles experienced one of his great moments; how his great moments stand forth in the pathos, yes, and the bathos, of his swift career.

It is a tremendous panorama.

> "Scots, wha ha'e wi' Wallace bled!
> Scots, wham Bruce has aften led!"

I listened while the guide went through with the battle, which, of course, is the Battle of Bannockburn. How The Bruce disposed his army to meet the English host he knew was coming up from the south to relieve the castle garrison; how they appeared at St. Ninians suddenly, and the ever-seeing Bruce remarked to Moray, who had been placed in charge of that defense —"there falls a rose from your chaplet"—it is almost too romantic not to be apocryphal; and how Moray (who was the Randolph Moray who scaled the crags at Edinburgh that March night) countered the English dash for the castle and won out; how in the evening of the day as King Robert was inspecting his lines for the battle of the to-morrow, a to-morrow which had been scheduled the year before—"unless by

St. John's day''; they had then a sense of leisure—the English knight Sir Henry de Bohun spurred upon him to single combat; it is worth while listening to the broad Scots of the guide as he repeats his well-conned, his well-worn, but his immortal story—

> "High in his stirrups stood the King
> And gave his battle-ax the swing,
> Right on de Boune, the whiles he passed,
> Fell that stern dint—the first, the last,
> Such strength upon the blow was put,
> The helmet crashed like hazel nut."

And all the battle the next day, until King Edward rides hot-trod to Berwick, leaving half his host dead upon this pleasant green field that lies so unremembering to the south of the castle. There is no more splendid moment in human history, unless all battles seem to you too barbaric to be splendid. But it made possible a nation—and, I take it, Scotland has been necessary to the world.

If this is too overwhelming a remembrance, there is an opposite to this, looking across the level lands of the Carse. The view leads past the Bridge of Allan, on to Dunblane, near which is the hill of Sheriffmuir. You can see the two armies in the distance of time and of the plain, creeping on each other unwittingly—and the guide, too, is glad to turn to a later and less revered moment—

"Some say that we wan,
Some say that they wan,
And some say that nane wan at a', man;
But o' ae thing I'm sure,
That at Sheriffmuir
A battle there was that I saw, man;
And we ran, and they ran,
And they ran, and we ran,
And they ran and we ran awa', man."

To-day the wind has swept all these murmurs of old wars into the infinite forgotten. The world is as though MacAlpine and Wallace and The Bruce and Prince Charles had not been. Or, is it? It looks that way, at this quiet moment, in this quiet century, and in this country where there is such quiet; a country with such a long tumult, a country with such a strange silence. But the rest of the world would never have been as it is but for the events that lie thick about here, but for the race which was bred in such events.

"And the castle stood up black
With the red sun at its back."

There is something more dour about Stirling than Edinburgh. It is, in the first place, too useful. One never thinks of the castle at Edinburgh as anything but romantic, of the troops as anything but decorative. Stirling is still used, much of it closed, and it has the bare, uninviting look of a historic place maintained by a modern up-keep.

Evidently when Burns visited it he found a ruin, and was moved to express his Jacobitism —would a poet be anything but a Jacobite?—

"Here Stuarts once in glory reign'd,
And laws for Scotland's weal ordain'd;
But now unroof'd their palace stands,
Their scepter's sway'd by other hands;
The injured Stuart line is gone,
A race outlandish fills their throne—"

Soon after you enter the gate you come upon the dungeon of Roderick Dhu, and here you get the beginnings of that long song of the Lake, which lies to the west, when Allan Bane tunes his harp for Roderick—

"Fling me the picture of the fight,
When my clan met the Saxon's might,
I'll listen, till my fancy hears
The clang of swords, the crash of spears!"

You may look into the Douglass room, where James II stabbed the Earl of Douglass (1452). It is a dark room for a dark deed. And the guide repeats Douglass's refusal to the king:

burgh as anything but ornamental, of the troops
as anything but decorative. Stirling is still
closed, and it has the bare, uninviting look of historic place maintained by
a modern up-keep.

visited it he found a
express his Jacobitism
but a Jacobite?—

Stirling Castle

after you enter the gate you come upon
the dungeon of Roderick Dhu, and here you get
the beginning of that long song of the Lake,

"No, by the cross it may not be!
I've pledged my kingly word.
And like a thunder cloud he scowled,
And half unsheathed his sword.
Then drew the king that jewel'd glaive
Which gore so oft had spilt,
And in the haughty Douglass heart
He sheathed it to the hilt."

The Douglasses, we see, still thought themselves "peer to any lord in Scotland here," and the provocation to the Stewart, merely a second Stewart, must have been great—"my kingly word"! and a "half sheathed" sword! Perhaps we shall have to forgive this second James about whom we know little but this affair, who seems as ineffective a monarch as James the Second of two centuries later.

It is rather with Mary, and with her father and her son, that we associate Stirling. James V took his commoner title of "the Gudeman of Ballengeich" from here, when he went abroad on those errantries which all the Stewarts have dearly loved. At Stirling it seems more possible that James V did write those poems which, yesterday in Edinburgh I felt like attributing to James IV. North of the bridge there is a hill, Moat Hill, called familiarly Hurley Haaky, because the Fifth James enjoyed here the rare sport of coasting down hill on a cow's skull.

The Scot can derive coasting from "Hurley" and skull from "Haaky"—a clever people!

Queen Mary was brought to Stirling when a wee infant and crowned in the old High church, September 9, 1543—and cried all the time they were making her queen. Surely "it came with ane lass and it will pass with ane lass." It was from Stirling that she was taken to France, and when she returned she included Stirling in her royal progress. I cannot think she was much here. Mary was not dour. Still, historic rumour has her married here, secretly to Darnley, and, in the rooms of Rizzio! And she came here once to see her princely son, hurriedly, almost stealthily, as if she felt impending fate.

That son was much here. Stirling was considered a safer place for James VI than Edinburgh, and then, of course, it was such a covenanted place. James was baptized here also, and his Royal Mother was present, but not Darnley. He refused to come, but sat carousing—as usual—in Willie Bell's Lodging, still standing in Broad Street, if you care to look on it. Young James merely looked at the ceiling of the High church, and pointing his innocent finger at it, gravely criticized, "there is a hole." James was crowned in the High church, Mary being at Loch Leven, and the coronation sermon was preached by Knox, who "enjoyed the proudest triumph of his life." Then, I know, baby James had to sit through a two or three hour sermon. For once I am sorry for him.

From the courtyard one sees the iron bars in the palace windows placed there to keep James from falling out—and others from stealing in? And here in the royal apartments, King James was taught his Latin and Greek like any other Scots boy, and by that same George Buchanan who was his mother's instructor—and her defamer. Perhaps he was the author of the betraying Casket letter; in spite of Fronde's criticism based on internal evidence, that only Shakespeare or Mary could have written it. I can almost forgive Buchanan, for at one time when James was making more noise than beseemed a pupil of Buchanan, this schoolmaster birched him then and there, whereupon the royal tear fell, and the royal yowl was lifted—and Lady Mar rushed in to quiet this uproarious division in the kingdom.

The archives of Stirling were once rich in Scottish records. But General Monk removed them to London when he moved on that capital with the king also in his keeping. Years and years after, when Scotland demanded back her records, they were sent by sea, the ship foundered, and sunk—and we have a right to accept legend as history in this land of lost records.

One may use Stirling Castle for lovelier ends than history or battle, for temporal ends of beauty—which is not temporal. Else would the prospect from these ramparts not linger immortally in the memory and flash upon the inward eye as one of the most wonderful views in all the world.

From Queen Mary's Lookout there is the King's Park, with the King's Knot, the mysterious octagonal mound; it may have looked lovelier when Mary looked down on its flower gardens and its orchards, but this green world is sightly.

From the battlements above the Douglass garden there is a magnificent survey; the rich Carse of broad alluvial land with the Links of the Firth winding in and out among the fields, shining, and steely, reluctant to widen out into the sea. The Ochils from the far background, and nearer is the Abbey Craig, thickly wooded and crowned by the Wallace monument, which while it adds nothing to the beauty of the scene, would have made such a commanding watch tower for Wallace. Just below is the old Bridge which—not this bridge, but it looks old enough with its venerable five hundred years—divided the English forces. Near by, on one of the Links, stands the tower of Cambuskenneth Abbey, a pleasant walk through fields and a ferry ride across the Forth, to this memoried place, which once was a great abbey among abbeys; I doubt not David founded it. Bruce once held a parliament in it. Now it is tenanted chiefly by the mortal remains of that Third James who took flight from Sauchieburn, and whose ghost so haunted his nobles for years after. Queen Margaret also lies here, she who sat stitching, stitching, stitching, while those same nobles raged through Linlithgow and sought their king. Cambuskenneth—the name is splendid—is but a remnant of grandeur. But there are a few charming cottages nearby, rose-embowered, perhaps with roses that descend from those in Mary's garden.

Across to the north is the Bridge of Allan, come to be a celebrated watering place—

> "On the banks of Allan Water
> None so fair as she."

Far across to the north is Dunblane, with a restored-ruined cathedral—

> "The sun has gone down o'er the lofty Ben Lomond
> And left the red clouds to preside o'er the scene,

While lanely I stray in the calm simmer gloamin'
To muse on sweet Jessie the flower o' Dunblane."

In the green nestle of the woods, away to the right, are the battlements of Donne—

"Oh, lang will his lady
Look frae the Castle Doune,
Ere she see the Earl o' Moray
Come sounding through the toun."

The Bonnie Earl was murdered at Donibristle Castle, on Inverkeithing Bay across the Forth from Edinburgh, where the King sent his lordship—"oh, woe betide ye, Huntly"—to do the deed. It was our same kingly James VI, and I like to think that his life had its entertaining moments, even if Anne of Denmark did have to look long and longingly down from the battlements of Doune.

The lookout to the north is called the Victoria—as if to link Victoria with Mary! But the old queen was proudest of her blood from the eternally young queen. An inscription on the wall registers the fact that Queen Victoria and the Prince Consort visited the castle in 1842.

And not any sovereign since until 1914.

I had reached the city in the mid-afternoon, unconscious of royalty, that is, of living royalty, as one is in Scotland. It seems that the

DOUNE CASTLE.

king and queen, George and Mary, were making a visit to Stirling. Consequently there were no carriages at the station—and one must be very careful how one walked on the royal crimson carpet. Two small boys who scorned royalty, were impressed into service, to carry bags to the hotel. But the press of the people was too great. The king and queen had issued from the castle, were coming back through the town

> "The castle gates were open flung,
> The quivering drawbridge rock'd and rung,
> And echo'd loud the flinty street
> Beneath the coursers' clattering feet,
> As slowly down the steep descent
> Fair Scotland's King and nobles went."

I took refuge in a bank building, and even secured a place at the windows. For some reason the thrifty people had not rented these advantageous casements. The king and queen passed. I saw them plainly—yes, plainly. And the people were curiously quiet. They did not mutter, they were decorous, there was no repudiation, but—what's a king or queen of diluted Stewart blood to Scotsmen of this undiluted town?

That afternoon in the castle I understood. An elderly Scotsman—I know of no people whom age so becomes, who wear it with such grace and dignity and retained power—looking with me at the memorial tablet to Queen Victoria and Prince Albert, in the west lookout, explained—"It's seventy years since royalty has been here. Not from that day to this."

It seems that on the old day, the day of 1842, when royalty rode in procession through the streets of Stirling, the commoners pressed too close about. It offended the queen; she liked a little space. (I remembered the old pun perpetrated by Lord Palmerston, when he was with Queen Victoria at the reviewing of the troops returned from the Crimea, and at the queen's complaining that she smelled spirits, "Pam" explained—"Yes, esprit de corps.") So she returned not at all to Stirling. I could wish King Edward had, the one Hanoverian who has succeeded in being a Stewart.

The view is almost as commanding from Ladies Rock in the old cemetery, whither I went, because in the very old days I had known intimately, as a child reader, the "Maiden Martyr," and here was to find her monument.

There are other monuments, none so historic, so grandiose, so solemn. The friends of a gentleman who had died about mid-century record that he died "at Plean Junction." Somehow it seemed very uncertain, ambiguous, capable of mistake, to die at a Junction out of which must run different ways.

And one man, buried here, was brought all the way, as the tombstone publishes, from "St. Peter, Minnesota." It's a historic town, to its own people. But what a curious linking with this very old town. I thought of a man who had hurried away from Montana the winter before, because he wanted to "smell the heather once more before I die." And he had died in St. Paul, Minnesota, only a thousand miles on his way back to the heather.

Viewed from below, the castle is splendid. The road crosses the bridge, skirts the north side of the Rock, toward the King's Knot; a view-full walk, almost as good, almost, as Edinburgh from Princes Gardens; this green and pastoral, that multicoloured and urban. The whole situation is very similar, the long ridge of the town, the heaven-topping castle hill. Stirling is the Old Town of Edinburgh minus the New Town. And so we confess ourselves modern. Stirling is not so lovely; yet it is more truly, more purely Scottish. Edinburgh is a city of the world. Stirling is a town of Scotland.

CHAPTER XI

THE WEST COUNTRY

Glasgow

I CANNOT think why, in a book to be called deliberately "The Spell of Scotland," there should be a chapter on Glasgow.

I remember that in his "Picturesque Notes," to the second edition Robert Louis Stevenson added a foot-note in rebuke to the Glaswegians who had taken to themselves much pleasure at the reservations of Stevenson's praise of Edinburgh—"But remember I have not yet written a book on Glasgow." He never did. And did any one ever write "Picturesque Notes on Glasgow"?

I remember that thirty years ago when a college professor was making the "grand tour"—thirty years ago seems as far back as three hundred years when James Howell was making his "grand tour"—he asked a casually met Glaswegian what there was to be seen, and this honest Scot, pointing to the cathedral declared, "that's the only aydifyce ye'll care to look at."

I should like to be singular, to write of picturesque points in Glasgow. But how can it be done? Glasgow does not aspire to picturesqueness or to historicalness. Glasgow is content, more than content, in having her commerce and her industry always "in spate."

Glasgow is the second city of size in the United Kingdom, and the first city in being itself. London is too varied and divided in interests; it never forgets that it is the capital of the world, and a royal capital. Glasgow never forgets that it is itself, very honestly and very democratically, a city of Scots. Not of royal Stewarts, and no castle dominates it. But a city made out of the most inveterate Scottish characteristics. Or I think I would better say Scotch. That is a practical adjective, and somewhat despised of culture; therefore applicable to Glasgow. While Scottish is romantic and somewhat pretending.

Glasgow is the capital of the Whig country, of the democratic Scotland of covenanting ancestry. Glasgow is precisely what one would expect to issue out of the energy and honesty and canniness and uncompromise of that corner of the world. Historically it belongs to Wallace, the commoner-liberator. And if

Burns is the genius of this southwestern Scotland, as Scott is of the southeastern, it is precisely the difference between the regions; as Edinburgh and Glasgow differ.

The towns are less than an hour apart by express train. They are all of Scotch history and characteristics apart in quality and in genius. Edinburgh is still royal, and sits supreme upon its hill, its past so present one forgets it is the past. Glasgow never could have been royal; and so it never was significant until royal Scotland ceased to be, and democratic Scotland, where a man's a man for a' that, came to take the place of the old, to take it completely, utterly. So long as the world was old, was the Old World, and looked toward the East, Edinburgh would be the chief city. When the world began to be new, and to look toward the New World, Glasgow came swiftly into being, and the race is to the swift.

There is history to Glasgow, when it was a green pleasant village, and there was romance. It is but a short way, a foot-path journey if the pleasant green fields still invited, out to Bothwell Castle; splendid ruin, and, therefore, recalling Mary and Darnley and the Lennoxes, but not Bothwell. But Landside, where Mary was defeated, is a Glaswegian suburb, Kelvin-

PORTRAIT OF THOMAS CARLYLE, BY WHISTLER.

grove—"let us haste"—is a prosperous residence district. The Broomielaw, lovely word, means simply and largely the harbour of Glasgow, made deliberately out of Clyde water in order that Glasgow's prosperity might flow out of the very heart of the city. "Lord, let Glasgow flourish according to the preaching of Thy word," ran the old motto. It has been shortened of late.

The heart of the city is dreary miles of long monotonous streets, where beauty is never wasted in grass blade or architecture. George's Square may be noble, it has some good monuments, but it is veiled in commercial grime, like all the town. What could be expected of a city that would name its principal business street, "Sauchieburn," memorializing and defying that petty tragedy?

There is an art gallery with Whistler's "Carlyle," and a few other notable pictures (John Lavery's I looked at with joy) to redeem miles of mediocrity. (Here I should like to be original and not condemn, but there are the miles.)

There is a cathedral, that "aydifyce" of note, touched almost nothing by the spirit of "reform"; for the burghers of Glasgow, then as now, believing that their cathedral belonged to them, rose in their might and cast out the despoilers before they had done more than smash a few "idols." Therefore this shrine of St. Kentigern's is more pleasing than the reformed and restored shrine of St. Giles. The crypt is particularly impressive. And the very pillar behind which Rob Roy hid is all but labeled. Of course it is "authentic," for Scott chose it. What unrivaled literary sport had Scott in fitting history to geography!

There is a University, one of the first in the Kingdom; the city universities are gaining on the classic Oxford and St. Andrews.

But chiefly there are miles of houses of working men, more humble than they ought to be. If Glasgow is one of the best governed cities in the world, and has the best water supply in the world—except that of St. Paul—would that the Corporation of the City of Glasgow would scatter a little loveliness before the eyes of these patient and devoted workingmen.

But what a chorus their work raises. In shipyards what mighty work is wrought, even such tragically destined work, and manufactured beauty, as the *Lusitania!*

From Glasgow it is that the Scot has gone out to all the ends of the earth. If the "Darien scheme" of wresting commerce from England failed utterly, and Glasgow failed most of all, that undoing was the making of the town. It is not possible to down the Scot. The smallest drop of blood tells, and it never fails to be Scottish. Most romantic, most poetic, most reckless, most canny of people. The Highlander and the Lowlander that Mr. Morley found mixed in the character of Gladstone, and the explanation of his character, is the explanation of any Scot, and of Scotland.

Ayr

Always the West is the democratic corner of a country; or, let me say almost always, if you have data wherewith to dispute a wholesale assertion. Sparta was west of Athens, La Rochelle was west of Paris, Switzerland was west of Gesler; Norway is west of Sweden, the American West is west of the American East. And Galloway and Ayrshire are the west Lowlands of Scotland.

The West is newer always, freer, more open, more space and more lure for independence. The West is never feudal, until the West moves on and the East takes its place. Here men develop, not into lords and chiefs, but into men. Wallace may come out of the West, but it is after he has come out that he leads men, in the establishment of a kingdom, but more in a wider fight for freedom; while he is in the West he adventures as a man among men, on the Waters of Irvine, in Laglyne Wood, at Cumnock. And a Bruce, struggling with himself, and setting himself against a Comyn, may stagger out of a Greyfriars at Dumfries, and, bewildered, exclaim, "I doubt I have slain the Comyn!" When a follower makes "siccar," and all the religious and human affronts mass to sober The Bruce, a king may come out of Galloway, out of a brawl, if a church brawl, and establish the kingdom and the royal line forever.

If a Wallace, if a Bruce, can proceed out of these Lowlands—and a Paul Jones!—a poet must come also. And a poet who is as much the essence of that west country as chieftain or king. Everything was ready to produce Burns in 1759. William Burns had come from Dunnottar, a silent, hard-working, God-fearing Covenanter, into this covenanting corner of Scotland. It was filled with men and women who had grown accustomed to worshiping God according to their independent consciences, and in the shelter of these dales and hills, sometimes harried by that covenanter-hunting fox, Claverhouse—to his defeat; finally winning the right to unconcealed worship. Seven years gone, and William Burns having built the "auld clay biggan" at Alloway, he married a Carrick maid, Agnes Broun, a maid who had much of the Celt in her. And Robert Burns was born.

It is of course only after the event that we know how fortunate were the leading circumstances, how inevitable the advent of Robert Burns. Father and mother, time and place, conspired to him. And all Scotland, all that has been Scotland since, results from him. It is Scott who reconstructed Scotland, made the historic past live. But it is Burns who is Scotland, Scotland remains of his temper; homely, human, intense, impassioned; with a dash and more of the practical and frugal necessary for the making of a nation, but worse than superfluous for the making of a Burns.

Three towns of this Scottish corner contend not for the birth but for the honours of Burns. If Dumfries is the capital of Burnsland and the place of his burial, Ayr is gateway to the land and the place of his birth; while Kilmarnock, weaver's town and most unpoetic, but productive of poets and poetesses, claims for itself the high and distinct literary honours, having published the first edition in an attic, and having loaned its name as title for the most imposing edition, and having in its museum possession all the published Burns editions.

To follow his footsteps through Burnsland were impossible to the most ardent. For Burns was a plowman who trod many fields, and turned up many daisies, and disturbed many a wee mousie, a poet who dreamed beside many a stream, and if he spent but a brief lifetime in all, it would take a lifetime, and that active, to overtake him.

"I have no dearer aim than to make leisurely pilgrimages through Caledonia; to sit on the fields of her battles, to wander on the romantic banks of her rivers, and to muse on the stately towers or venerable ruins, once the honoured abodes of her heroes."

He did this abundantly. We have followed him in many a place. But in Burnsland it were all too intimate, if not impossible. He knew all the rivers of this west country, Nith, Doon, Ayr, Afton.

> "The streams he wandered near;
> The maids whom he loved, the songs he sung,
> All, all are dear."

He did not apparently know the sea, or love it, although he was born almost within sound of it; and he sings of it not at all. He knew

Ayr River

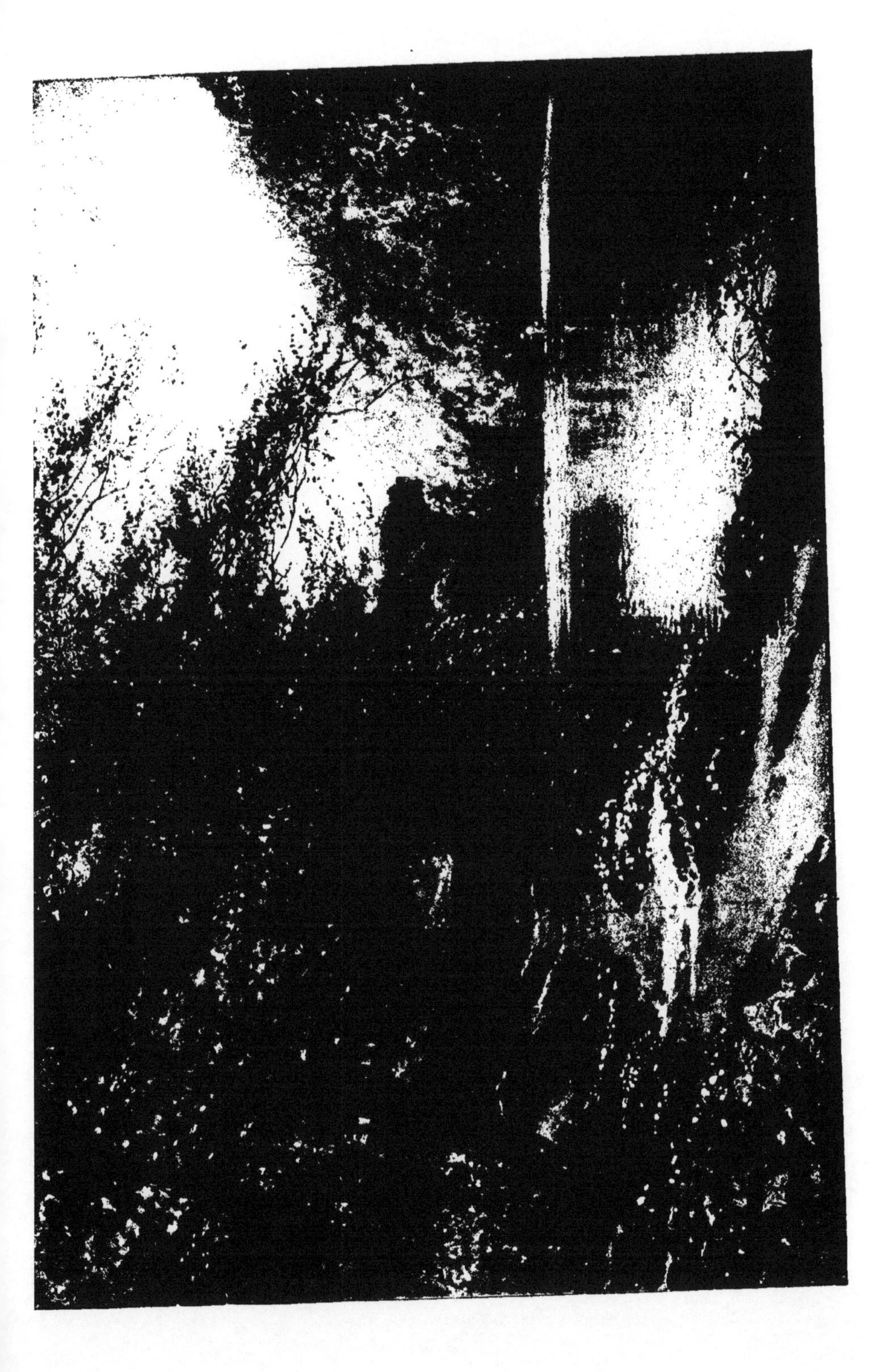

the legends of the land. "The story of Wallace poured a Scottish prejudice into my veins," and he deliberately followed the Bruce legend, hoping it would enter into his blood and spirit, and something large and worthy would result. It did, not an epic, but the strong song of a nation, "Scots wha hae."

His land was the home of Lollards and Covenanters. Independence was in the blood. It was the land of the "fighting Kennedys," who disputed with each other, what time they were not furnishing an Abbot of Crossraguel to dispute with John Knox, or a Gude Maister Walter Kennedy to have a "flytting" with the Kynge's Makar, William Dunbar. Where Burns secured his Jacobitism I do not know, but, of course, a poet is by nature a Jacobite; as he himself said, "the Muses were all Jacobite."

Burnsland is rich in other literary associations. Johannes Scotus is reckoned to have been born also at Ayr; and there are John Galt, James Boswell, James Montgomery, Alexander Smith, Ainslie, Cunningham, and the Carlyles, and Scott in some of his most lively romances. The Book of Taliessin is written in part of this land, the Admirable Crichton was born here. It is a close-packed little portmanteau of land. There is pursuit enough for at least a summer's travel. And, without doubt, there are as many pilgrims who explore Ayrshire as Warwickshire, and much more lovingly.

The entrance is by Ayr. And this I think can be made most claimingly, most fitly, by steamer from Belfast. For one thing, it avoids entrance at Glasgow. Ayr is still a sea port of some importance; and Ireland, democratic, romantic, intimate, is a preparation for this similar country of Galloway and about; both lands are still Celtic.

Ayr looks well from the sea as one comes in, although in the day of Burns the Rattonkey was a more casual place, and harbour works to retain the traffic were not yet built. But the town sits down well into the waterside of its Doon and Ayr rivers, much like a continental town where fresh waters are precious. There is long suburban dwelling, not as it was a hundred and fifty years ago.

And Ayr looks out on the sea with a magnificent prospect from any of her neighbouring segments of coast, with ruined castles set properly, with the dark mass of romantic Arran purple across the waters, with Ailsa Rock evident, and to a far-seeing eye the blue line of Ireland whence we have come.

There is small reason for staying in Ayr, unless for a wee bit nappie in Tam o' Shanter's inn, which still boasts itself the original and only Tam and hangs a painting above the door to prove itself the starting point, this last "ca' hoose," for Alloway.

To Alloway one may go by tram! It sounds flat and unprofitable. But the gray mare Meg is gone, has followed her tail into the witches night. And if it were not the tram it would be a taxi. And what have witches and warlocks to do with electricity, in truth how can they compete with electricity?

> "Nae man can tether time or tide;
> The hour approaches Tam maun ride;
> That hour, o' night's black arch the keystane,
> That dreary hour he mounts his beast in;
> An' sic a night he taks the road in
> As ne'er poor sinner was abroad in."

To follow, in a tram, in broad daylight, oh, certainly the world has changed, and the Deil too since "the Deil had business on his hand." The occupations that are gone! It is a highway one follows to-day, suburban villas and well-kept fields line the way; no need to "skelpit on thro' dub and mire." Tam would be quite without adventure. And to-day one wonders if even the lightning can play about this commonplace way. There is however the Race-course—some reminder of Meg!

Yet, it is possible to forget this pleasant day, and to slip back into old night as

> "Before him Doon pours a' his floods;
> The doubling storm roars through the woods;
> The lightnings flash frae pole to pole;
> Near and more near the thunders roll;
> When, glimmering through the groaning trees,
> Kirk Alloway seem'd in a bleeze."

The walls of the Auld Kirk lie before us—and "Auld Nick in shape o' beast" is sitting under "the winnock bunker i' the east." Who would deny that he also like Tammie "glower'd amazed and curious"?

> "The piper loud and louder blew,
> The dancers quick, and quicker flew;
> They reel'd, they set, they cross'd, they cleekit,
> Till ilka carlin swat and reekit,
> And coost her duddies to the wark,
> And linket at it in her sark."

The ride on this tram has developed a dizziness.

> "Wi' tippenny we fear nae evil;
> Wi' usquebae we'll face the devil!"

Did we cry "weel done, cutty sark!" Then

we, too, must descend and hurry on foot to the old Brig o' Doon. Not pausing long for The Monument, even to look at the wedding ring of Jean Armour, or the Bible Burns gave to Highland Mary; but on to the Auld Kirk which stands opposite.

To Burns we owe this church in more ways than one. When a certain book of "Antiquities" was being planned, Burns asked that the Auld Kirk of Alloway be included. If Burns would make it immortal? yes. So the story of Tam o' Shanter came to make Kirk Alloway forever to be remembered. What would William Burns, covenanter, have thought? For I cannot but think that William looked often askance at the acts of his genius-son. But William was safely buried within the kirk, and if the epitaph written by the son reads true, William was excellently covenanted.

"O ye whose cheek the tear of pity stains,
Draw near with pious rev'rence and attend.
Here lies the loving husband's dear remains,
The tender father, and the gen'rous friend.
The pitying heart that felt for human woe,
The dauntless heart that fear'd no human pride,
The friend of man, to vice alone a foe,
For 'ev'n his failings leau'd to virtue's side.'"

The auld clay biggan still stands in Alloway,

and "the banks and braes o' bonnie Doon" bloom as "fresh and fair" to-day as they did a century and a half ago. It is a simpler place than the birth house on High Street in Stratford, and a simpler environment than College Wynd in Edinburgh. This is a true cotter's home, and Saturday nights within must have been of the description.

Somehow it is less of a tourist's way of forced entry, this through the barn, than the basement door at Abbotsford; and so one passes through the byre and into the kitchen, where stands the bed in which Robert Burns was born. It is all beautifully homely, as lowly as a manger; and, how the world has been filled by what was once small frail life herein!

It is difficult to divide the poet's relics among so many claimant places, but here and in the museum are many mementoes of the poet. For this as well as Kirk Alloway is a national monument, or something like.

There was a century during which this was merely a clay biggan, and a public house, and that offended no one, least of all the friends of the poet. Except Keats. He came hither in 1818. The host was drunk most of the time, and garrulous. Keats complained that it affected his "sublimity." And, for once, Keats

BURNS' COTTAGE, BIRTH-PLACE OF ROBERT BURNS, AYR.

turned severe self-critic. "The flat dog made me write a flat sonnet."

It was while living at Mount Oliphant, two miles east of Ayr, when Burns was fifteen, that he began that long, long list of lasses whom he loved and whom he made immortal with a verse. He might have said with James V,—and much he resembled that Gudeman o' Ballangeich—"it came wi' ane lass and it will gae wi' ane lass." The first was Nelly Kilpatrick, daughter of the miller of Perclewan—

"O, ance I lov'd a bonnie lass,
Ay, and I love her still."

The last was Jessie Lewars, who ministered to him in those last days in the Millhole brae in Dumfries—

"O wert thou in the cauld blast
On yonder lea, on yonder lea,
My plaidie to the angry airt,
I'd shelter thee, I'd shelter thee."

To Kilmarnock one goes for its name. But "the streets and neuks o' Killie" are changed since that Burns' day. It is a sprawling, thriving factory town, a town of weavers—and a town of poets. There is something in the whirr of wheels, to those who are within it, which establishes rhythm in the ear, and often leads to well-measured poetry! Surely a weaver is equal to a plowman, and I fancy that many a workingman and working lass with lines running through the head walk this Waterloo street, pass Tam o' Shanter's arms, and looks above the Loan Office at the attic where that precious first edition was printed in 1786. Poems and pawn broking—Waterloo Street is a suggestive Grub street.

From Kilmarnock to Dumfries by train is a Burns pilgrimage, even though it be taken without break, and in seventy-seven minutes! And interspersed are other memories. It is entirely what Burnsland should be, nothing set down in high tragedy, but all lyrical, with gentle hills, whispering rivers, and meadows and woodlands all the way.

Mauchline, where the burst of song was like that of a skylark, the very outpouring of the man's soul; here lies the field where he turned up the daisy and found an immortal lyric.

Auchinleck, where Boswell and Dr. Johnson paused on their journey and where to the hot-flung query of the Doctor, "Pray, what good did Cromwell ever do the country?" the judicial and wrathful father of our Boswell flung the hotter retort—"He gart kings ken they had a lith in their necks." The Scottish tongue is the tongue of rebellions. Should we stay in this corner of the world longer we might turn covenanting and Cromwellian!

Cumnock, which William Wallace made his headquarters between the battle of Stirling bridge and that of Falkirk.

New Cumnock, whence the Afton so sweetly falls into the Nith—

"Flow gently, sweet Afton, amang thy green braes,
Flow gently, I'll sing thee a song in thy praise."

Kirkconnel, which is said not to be the Kirkconnel where Fair Helen lies—but like the blasted heath, will it not serve?

"I wish I were where Helen lies,
Baith night and day on me she cries."

And in any event "The Bairnies cuddle doon at Nicht" were "waukrife rogues" in Kirkconnel.

Sanquhar to Thornhill, with rounding green hills along the Nith, with memories of Old Queensberry and Defoe and Wordsworth and Coleridge and Allan Ramsay and Dr. John Brown, and Carlyle. Thornhill is Dalgarnock, where fairs were held—

"But a' the niest week, as I petted wi' care,
I gaed to the tryste o' Dalgarnock,
And wha but my fine, fickle lover was there?

I glowr'd as I'd seen a warlock, a warlock,
I glowr'd as I'd seen a warlock."

Dunscore lies to the right with "Redgauntlet" memories, and a few miles farther on is Craigenputtock.

Ellisland a brief moment, where immortal "Tam" was written as under the spell of a warlock.

Dumfries

It is a proud little city, more than a bit self-satisfied. It realizes that its possession of the mortal remains of Burns gives it large claim in his immortality, and the Burns monument is quite the center of the town.

Yet Dumfries is well satisfied from other argument. Historically, it goes back to Bruce and Comyn, and even to a Roman beyond. But there is nothing left of old Greyfriars where the killing of Comyn took place. Dumfries had its moment in the Forty Five, for the Bonnie Prince was here as he went down to the invasion of England, and his room in what is now the Commercial Hotel may be looked into but not lodged in; Dumfries, in spite of Covenant, has its modicum of Jacobitism.

It is in "Humphrey Clinker" that Smollett

CAÉRLAVEROCK CASTLE.

compels some one to say "If I was confined to Scotland I would choose Dumfries as my place of residence." Confined to Scotland, forsooth!

Dumfries is larger than it was in the days of Burns, and very busy withal, in factories and railroads. But it is still a country town, still hints at something of dales and woods and streams, even on High Street. The land about is true Burnsland; low, gentle hills closing in the horizon in a golden sea of warmth and sunlight, and the Nith a pleasant stream. It makes a great bend about Dumfries, with Maxwelltown across the water, and still

"Maxwellton's braes are bonny
Where early fa's the dew."

Farther a-field there lies Sweetheart Abbey, built by the Lady Devorgilla, widow of John Balliol, and founder of Balliol at Oxford; one of the most beautiful ruins not only in Scotland but in the Kingdom. Caerlaverock castle, the Ellangowan of "Guy Mannering," stands on the Solway, which still, like love, ebbs and flows. Ecclefechan lies east. "O, wat ye wha's in yon toun," Burns sang from here, but later it was made a place of pilgrimage, with its immortal dust come back from London for Scottish rest.

And in St. Michael's Burns was laid to rest in 1796, and twenty years later was placed in this mausoleum in the corner of the churchyard. A sumptuous monument for so simple a man.

"He came when poets had forgot
How rich and strange the human lot;
How warm the tints of Life; how hot
Are Love and Hate;
And what makes Truth divine, and what
Makes Manhood great.

"A dreamer of the common dreams,
A fisher in familiar streams,
He chased the transitory gleams
That all pursue;
But on his lips the eternal themes
Again were new."

The road leads southward, the Via Dolorosa Mary took after Langside, the Via Victoriosa which Prince Charles took—

"Wi' a hundred pipers an' a', an' a',
Wi' a hundred pipers an' a', an' a',
We'll up and gie them a blaw, a blaw,
Wi' a hundred pipers an' a', an' a'.
Oh, it's ower the Border awa', awa',
It's ower the Border awa', awa',
We'll on an' we'll march tae Carlisle Ha'
Wi' its yetts and castles an' a', an' a'.
Wi' a hundred pipers an' a', an' a'."

BIBLIOGRAPHY

ALLARDYCE, A.: Balmoral. F. (For Deeside and Dunnottar.)
ANDERSON: Guide to the Highlands, 3 vols.
ARMSTRONG, SIR WALTER: Raeburn.
BARR, ROBERT: A Prince of Good Fellows. F. (James V.)
BARRIE, JAMES: Auld Licht Idylls. F.
— Little Minister. F.
BARRINGTON, MICHAEL: The Knight of the Golden Sword. F. (Claverhouse.)
BAXTER, J. DOWLING: The Meeting of the Ways. F. (The Roman Wall.)
BELL, J. J.: Wee Macgreegor. F.
BLACK, WILLIAM: Wild Eelin. F. (Inverness.)
— MacLeod of Dare. F. Mull.
— Strange Adventures of a Phaëton. F. (Moffat.)
BORLAND, ROBERT: Border Raids and Reivers.
BUCHAN, JOHN: The Marquis of Montrose.
CARLYLE, THOMAS: Burns, in The Hero as Man of Letters.
— Knox, in The Hero as Priest.
CHAMBERS, ROBERT: Traditions of Edinburgh.
COWAN, SAMUEL: Mary Queen of Scots, and who wrote the Casket Letters?
CROCKETT, W. S.: Footsteps of Scott.
— The Scott Country.
CROCKETT, S. R.: Raiderland. (Galloway.)
— The Men of the Moss Hags. F. (1679) F.
— The Standard Bearer of Galloway. F.
CUNNINGHAM, ALLAN: Life and Land of Burns.
— Sir Michael Scot. F.

DEBENHAM, MARY H.: An Island of the Blest. F. (Iona.)
DICK, STEWART: The Pageant of the Forth.
DOUGALL, CHARLES S.: The Burns Country.
DOUGLASS, SIR GEORGE: Ed. The Book of Scottish Poetry.
— The New Border Tales. F.
FLEMING, GUY: The Play Acting Woman. F. (Contemp.)
FRAPRIE, FRANK S.: Castles and Keeps of Scotland.
GALT, JOHN: The Ayrshire Legatees. F.
— Annals of the Parish. F.
— The Provost. F.
— Lawrie Todd. F.
— Ringan Gilhaize, or The Covenanters. F.
GEIKIE, SIR ARCHIBALD: The Scenery of Scotland, viewed in connection with its physical geography.
GIBBON, JOHN MURRAY: Hearts and Faces. F. (Contemp.)
HAMERTON, PHILIP GILBERT: A Painter's Camp. (Awe.)
HAMILTON, LORD E.: Mary Hamilton. F.
HAWTHORNE, NATHANIEL: Our Old Home.
HENDERSON and WATT: Scotland of To-day.
HEWLETT, MAURICE: The Queen's Quair. F.
HILL, G. BIRKBECK: Footsteps of Dr. Johnson.
HUME-BROWN: Scotland in the Time of Queen Mary.
— Early Travellers in Scotland.
HUME, MARTIN: Love Affairs of Mary Queen of Scots.
JACKSON, H. H.: Glimpses of Three Coasts.
JAMES, G. P. R.: Gowrie, the King's Plot. F.
JOHNSON, SAMUEL: Boswell's Journal of a Tour to the Hebrides.
JUSSERAND, J. J.: A Journey to Scotland in the year 1435. (In English essays.)
KIPLING, RUDYARD: Puck of Pook's Hill. F.
— A Centurion of the 13th.
— On the Great Wall.
— The Winged Hats.
LANG, ANDREW: Short History of Scotland.
— The Mystery of Mary Stuart.
— St. Andrews.
LANG, JEAN: A Land of Romance. (The Border.)
LAUDER, SIR THOMAS DICK: The Wolf of Badenoch. F.

LESLIE, AMY: Bawbee Jack. (Contemp.)
LINDSAY, ROBERT, of Pitscottie: History of Scotland. (Sixteenth Cent.)
LOCKHART, JOHN: Life of Scott.
M'AULAY, ALLAN: The Safety of the Honours. F.
MACLAREN, IAN (John Hay): Graham of Claverhouse. F.
—The Bonnie Brier Bush. F.
MASON, A. E. W.: Clementina. F. (1715.)
MASSON, DAVID: Edinburgh Sketches and Memories.
MASSON, ROSALINE: Edinburgh.
MONCRIEFF, A. R. HOPE: Bonnie Scotland.
—The Heart of Scotland (Perthshire).
—The Highlands and the Islands.
MORLEY, JOHN: Burns.
MUNRO, NEIL: John Splendid. F. (For Montrose, royalist.)
—The New Road. F.
PENNELL, JOSEPH and ELIZABETH R.: Our Journey to the Hebrides.
PERCY: Reliques.
PORTER, JANE: Scottish Chiefs. F. (Wallace and Bruce.)
QUEEN VICTORIA'S Highland Journals.
SCOTT, SIR WALTER: The Abbot. F. (Mary Stuart.)
—The Antiquary. F. (East Fife.)
—Black Dwarf. F. (Lowlands and Border.)
—The Bride of Lammermuir. F. (East Lothian.)
—The Fair Maid of Perth. F.
—Guy Mannering. F. (Caerlaverock castle.)
—The Heart of Midlothian. F. (Edinburgh.)
—Lady of the Lake. Poetry. (Katrine and Stirling.)
—Lay of the Last Minstrel. Poetry. (Border.)
—The Legend of Montrose. F.
—The Lord of the Isles. Poetry. (Hebrides.)
—The Monastery. F. (Melrose.)
—Marmion. Poetry. (Flodden.)
—Old Mortality. F. (Covenanters.)
—The Pirate. F. (Orkneys.)
—Redgauntlet. F. (1745.)
—Roy Roy. F. (Trossachs Region and Glasgow.)
—St. Ronan's Well. F. (Tweedale.)

—Tales of a Grandfather.
—Waverley. F. (Prince Charles Edward.)
SHORT, JOSEPHINE H.: The Charm of Scotland.
STEVENSON, R. L.: David Balfour. F. (After 1715.)
—Kidnapped. F. (After 1715.)
—The Master of Ballantrae. F.
—Picturesque Notes of Edinburgh.
—St. Ives. F. (After 1815.)
SHAKESPEARE: Macbeth.
SHELLEY, MARY: The Fortunes of Perkin Warbeck. F.
SMOLLETT, TOBIAS: Humphrey Clinker. F.
STEUART, J. A.: The Red Reaper. (For Montrose, Covenanter.)
SWINBURNE, ALGERNON S.: Bothwell, a tragedy.
—Chastelard, a tragedy.
—Mary Stuart, a tragedy.
SUTCLIFFE, HALLIWELL: Willowdene Will. F. (1745.)
—The Lone Adventure. F.
TAYLOR, BAYARD: In Picturesque Europe.
TODD, G. EYRE: Cavalier and Covenanter. F. (Charles II.)
UPSON, ARTHUR: The Tides of Spring. (Poetic drama.)
WATKEYS, FREDERICK W.: Old Edinburgh.
WESLEY, JOHN: Journal. Vol. 3.
WARRENDER, MISS: Walks near Edinburgh.
WHYTE-MELVILLE, G. J.: The Queen's Maries. F.
WIGGIN, KATE DOUGLAS: Penelope in Scotland.
WILLIAMSON, M. G.: Edinburgh. (Ancient Cities series.)
WINTER, WILLIAM: Brown Heath and Blue Bells.
—In Gray Days and Gold.
WORDSWORTH, DOROTHY: Tour in Scotland.

INDEX

D

E

S

T

Dumbarto